Old Befana's Endless Tales:
The Journey Continues

Donna Kendall

Old Befana's Endless Tales
Primary category: Fiction – adult and young adult.

General

Country of Publication: United States

Publication date: October, 2015

Language: English

Italian legends, Christmas legends, Folk Tales, Faith, Friendship, Christian Cultural traditions

Library of Congress Number: applied for

Primary category: Fiction – adult and young adult. Copyright © 2015 Donna Kendall

ISBN: 13: 978-1517681838
ISBN-10: 1517681839

For my granddaughter,
With all the love in my heart

About the Author

Donna Kendall has written several novels of pure fiction, one memoir of her mother's immigration story, a work of non-fiction and some children's literature. She continues to teach and learn and lives in Williamsburg, Virginia.

Also by Donna Kendall

Travels with Old Befana: A Christmas Story
The Consistent Choice for Better Living in a Better World
Stitch-A-Story
Uncle Charlie's Soup
Dancing with Bianchina
In the Shadows of Sins
Sailing on an Ocean of Tears

A Heart in Bloom was published in an anthology: *The Tale that Must be Told: True Stories of Transformation*; it was autobiographical.

"The search is what anyone would undertake if he were not sunk in the everydayness of his own life. To become aware of the possibility of the search is to be onto something. Not to be onto something is to be in despair."

- *Walker Percy*

Prologue

"Then Herod called the Magi secretly and found out from them the exact time the star had appeared. He sent them to Bethlehem and said, 'Go and search carefully for the child. As soon as you find him, report to me, so that I too may go and worship him.'

After they had heard the king, they went on their way, and the star they had seen when it rose went ahead of them until it stopped over the place where the child was. When they saw the star, they were overjoyed. On coming to the house, they saw the child with his mother Mary, and they bowed down and worshiped him. Then they opened their treasures and presented him with gifts of gold, frankincense and myrrh. And having been warned in a dream not to go back to Herod, they returned to their country by another route.

When they had gone, an angel of the Lord appeared to Joseph in a dream. 'Get up,' he said, 'take the child and his mother and escape to Egypt. Stay there until I tell you, for Herod is going to search for the child to kill him.'

So he got up, took the child and his mother during the night and left for Egypt, where he stayed until the death of Herod. And so was fulfilled what the Lord had said through the prophet: 'Out of Egypt I called my son.'

When Herod realized that he had been outwitted by the Magi, he was furious, and he gave orders to kill all the boys in Bethlehem and its vicinity who were two years old and under, in accordance with the time he had learned from the Magi. Then what was said through the prophet Jeremiah was fulfilled:

*'A voice is heard in Ramah, weeping and great mourning,
Rachel weeping for her childrenand refusing to be comforted,
because they are no more.'"*

(Matthew 2: 7-18)

1

Befana

Sunshine seems to be in short supply in this part of the world. It peeked out just once this morning and then it disappeared behind some mean looking clouds for the rest of the day. If I didn't know any better I'd say that these clouds were acting like bullies, standing shoulder to shoulder all day long forcing their gloom on the nice folks below who are just aching for a bit of brightness and warmth. It's hard to tell whether the clouds have rain or snow on their minds but in my experience both forms have the same result: forcing people to stay inside, even children who should be playing outside in the sun. Sun or no sun this place has its charm and appeal, with meadows and streams maneuvering through a quaint little town. Isn't it wonderful when beauty can radiate through gloom? This lovely place called Pataskala. From what I've gathered, a very long time ago the natives of this region gave it this name because of the bright waters flowing from its nearby river. And it's true, the waters remain bright whether they reflect a bright sky or not! They seem to sparkle from something within, no matter what the weather. The cresting ripples look like dancing fairies, cheerful despite the menacing clouds above. It's a delightful place to begin my stories about the people of this region.

Not too far from the native burial ground there is an old wooden bridge that, in my opinion, is not safe to cross on foot much less for children to play on or to cross over on their bicycles. But children do these things, and I get that old familiar beat of trouble when I see them racing across it or casting their makeshift fishing poles into the deep waters below. I'm not a babysitter, for heaven's sake. I'm just an *Old Befana* and it's my job to be a positive presence to the children I come across in my journeys; I'm not equipped to save them from calamity. I do my best wherever I am to support the little ones. Parents can't be everywhere, grandparents get too weak, and children need all the love and support they can get from caring people who have their eyes wide open and some very strong arms to hold them. I'll get back to these children in just a bit; I seem to be getting ahead of myself.

I'm *Old Befana* and how I ended up in this place is a *very* long story. It all began one night long ago when I noticed a very bright star in the sky and decided to trail after a group of people who happened to be following that star to a place where a new king had been born to save humanity from evil. But, this is more than just an old tale; it's a continuing legend about our journeys through the twists and turns of life. I was a real person a long time ago and now my spirit travels the world sharing the gift I received on that special night. Now, listen to me, it wasn't a gift like gold jewelry or anything like that. I never had such things. It wasn't a nice bouquet of flowers – no one ever gave me those. And it certainly wasn't any of those fancy perfumes. I don't wear that stuff – I sneeze just thinking about them. So, what was my special gift? That's what I want to tell you about. It takes a long time to explain this gift because it unfolds each day like petals of a rose in the month of May. I'll give you some clues about my special gift: it's very high in value but you can't buy it. It is mysterious because no matter how much I use it, it never runs out, and the joy of my gift begins with a search! It always begins with some kind of a quest. My search began by following the path to this baby named Jesus and he alone knows where my story will end because my journey is far from over. As I search for this newborn king named Jesus I find glimmers of him in people, experiences, and inspirations wherever I go. Along the way I always leave a little treat or nugget of wisdom for the children I encounter. The little ones I meet live in different circumstances: some are born to wealth and good fortune, while others are born to poverty and sickness but they all have one thing in common – they want something they may not have or do not know they have. The rich children are never satisfied with all their *things*, and the poor youngsters just want what is basic to survival. When it comes right down to it, regardless of their circumstances, children want love and acceptance; they want happiness and freedom (sometimes they think these ideas are one and the same), and they want a feeling of security and respect. It's a tall order but every little one deserves to have all of these gifts. Do you have any idea what parents go through to provide their children with the whole package? Sometimes it's hard enough to provide for just some food and clothes.

What was interesting about this baby king named Jesus that I'd learned about on that starry night was that he was born in very humble circumstances (in a stable with animals, no less!) even though he was a king! He had no earthly wealth at all! That's what surprised me into following this new king. I thought all kings were fancy and rich and born on clouds of feathers and gold. It was the meager conditions of his entry into the world that showed me what we really need in life, not riches and treasures, but the love it takes to fill up the gaps in our souls and the souls of others!

There was a fella back then, a philosopher of sorts that everyone talked about; he said that people need to forget about the delusion that there is another life beyond this one and we should just go after happiness now because that's the only good thing there is. When the search for happiness is done, that's it, we're finished, there is nothing more to look forward to. But then when Jesus came he corrected what that *goosehead* and others like him were saying and showed us that love is the only good thing there is and it continues long after our bones are in the dirt because it can live on in our spirits. The kind of love Jesus talked about was the kind his Father showed us – to give happiness to others, not try to get it all for ourselves. This kind of life would lead to an everlasting life.

I took that message very seriously and now that's why I'm known as Old-Befana-on-a-Mission. (I call myself that name!) I want people to know about Jesus and his message. I want to help children and their families because our lives on earth are short and it's difficult to accomplish this tall order in the time we have. But, I can't do it alone; I'm in league with countless helpers and angels who stand close to each child each and every day. Don't misunderstand – everyone needs this kind of love and special guidance, not just little ones. I do what I can for all of them. I travel from one place to another and it is not always clear to me why I'm there but as long as I follow the way I've been shown I am in the place where I'm supposed to be and hopefully doing some good.

In this delightful little place called Pataskala I am meeting some new people, some are poor, some are rich, and some have no idea what they have going for them. I always have my work cut out for me. Yes, sometimes I feel weary; I have no idea where I get the energy to keep going but when something wonderful happens, I get zesty again. Sometimes I do fail. I can lead a lamb to the stack of hay but I can't make him munch it. Some people just don't want help. There is nothing you can do about that. Others think they can do everything all on their own, they don't need help from above. Some people think they know what they need but they're aiming rather low. While still others want more than is possible to fulfill in one lifetime. Forgive me if I've started to ramble. There is much for me to do and much for me to share with you. I like telling the stories of my adventures and encounters. I visit many places and meet many people. I'm never alone. That's the important message I carry with me. No one is ever alone. Children may feel isolated sometimes. I know, I've been there, but the moment you realize you have someone beside you at all times to guide you through this messy life, you know that everything will be all right.

An old African proverb suggests that it takes a village to raise a child but from where I see things, it takes a whole lot more than a village. Some villages have lost their way so you need the help of those who rely on wisdom, not trends.
It takes *heaven and earth* to help raise a child.

2

Salvatore

Mamma Mia, the rains have not let up for two weeks now. I suppose it's normal for this time of year to get a rain spell but with a break or two in between bouts. Before you know it winter will be here so I've made a decision to go outside and pick the last of the tomatoes off the vines before the frost hits but it's hard to get out there in this pouring rain. This year, we had a long and fruitful growing season and the plants grew tall and lush but the remaining tomatoes will never ripen a deep red color unless the sunshine returns; I'll have to pick them green and put them on the window sill. If walking through my muddy garden without an umbrella makes my neighbors think I'm a loon, fine, but it does my old heart good to be out here with things that are growing instead of staying in an empty house day after day, remembering a time when it was full of laughter and raucous children, tears and bickering, and plenty of bleating about what we didn't have. In my head, we had it all. I had my feisty bride, Annalisa, my three squirrely boys and my precious girl. I had enough work to keep this old roof over our heads and enough food on the table. There was plenty of love to go around and fair discipline to keep things from getting out of control. The kids tell me I wear rose-colored glasses now when I remember the past but it's better than wearing dark glasses so that everything looks bleak. Of course I remember the hard times, too, but why let those thoughts loiter around in my head? It was never my intention to live my golden years filled with regrets and I'm not about to start now. I'd hate to think that is what they think I should be doing.

Darn it! The sky started getting darker again and the thunder sounded like it was directly overhead; I probably should have headed back inside the house but I didn't think I was going to make it. The shed was closer and the old wooden door was hanging open almost inviting me to *get in there, old man*. A deafening crack of thunder pealed across the sky as a bolt of lightning struck my tulip poplar at the rear of the yard just as I reached the inside of the shed and pulled the door shut. Within seconds I heard an ear-splitting fracture and the sound of the poplar crashing down outside the shed door. It sounded like one of the larger branches hit the metal roof but the shed seemed to hold up against the weight. Well, isn't this a pickle, I thought to myself? I figured the tree was probably covering the door and when I went to look for a flashlight I had the feeling that I was in trouble. What a conundrum. I needed some light to find the darn flashlight. It wasn't the first time I've had to feel my way around the old shed to find something in there but, Lord, have mercy, it gets harder every time. Just as I'd fingered my way over to the shelf where I keep a bag of peat moss and rose powder I tripped over a bag of mulch and fell head first into the rakes and shovels. Blasted shed, I couldn't see a darned thing. My bad knee hit the ground hard enough to send a good bit of pain shooting up my spine, and I could feel a spoke from the garden rake on – no, *in* my head, and suddenly I couldn't move. At my age mysterious pain has become my natural companion but injuries are something I can do without. Once I caught my breath I thought I could wiggle out of my predicament and get up but I didn't seem to have the energy to budge. *Pain reminds us that we're alive* I used to tell my Annalisa before her pain became so bad she couldn't bear it anymore and she left me for heaven. She would smile and say *"pain is often what you feel just before you die, old man."* Tears started to form in the corners of my eyes as I felt the blood trickling down my forehead. *Lord, if you're still listening to this old man this is not how I envisioned I would make my passage to the other side, trapped in a garden shed with a rake stuck inside my head. I've always enjoyed your sense of humor, unless it was at my expense.*

My kids have been after me for quite a while to make some changes. I haven't been very receptive to their suggestions. *Dad, you really should think about selling the house and moving into one of those nice little condos with other people your age. You would enjoy it, I think. They have activities everyday and you could make some new friends.* My oldest son, Joe, had launched this pitch after Annalisa died ten years ago. *Nonsense,* I'd told him, *this is my "condo;" I don't need anything else; this is my home; I can't leave my garden, and I don't want any new friends. I'm happy here. I don't think I would be happy there with a bunch of strangers.*

Over the years Joe has been irritated by my reluctance to consider his suggestion. *You're just staying in this old house to keep yourself dependent on your family,* he'd said. *You could think of us, you know. We're not getting any younger, either. It's hard for us to take care of ourselves, our families and grandkids, and come over here to take care of you, too. You could do it for our sake.*

I'll admit I was a little irked by his comments. *Dependent? Dependent,* I repeated. *Are you out of your mind? When have I ever been able to depend on any of you kids? Get out of here; you don't have to help me. Go on; go help your family. I don't need your help. I'm fine, here. And I'm happy. I'm not dependent on anybody.*

The nice thing about my Joe is that he doesn't hold grudges. Dutifully, Joe still comes by once a month to check up on me even though he'd probably rather not. I know he has his own family to take care of and his grandkids. I never said I needed anything from him. I respect my eldest son, though, for thinking that he needed to take care of me regardless of my stubborn pride. He's a good man; he's been a good father to his son and an involved grandfather to his new grandkids. He does something I guess I never did – *he goes to them* to have a relationship. I suppose my generation always believed younger people needed to come to us. People don't think that way anymore but I don't brood over being alone so much. At least I don't think I do. I stay busy in the garden. If only this rain would stop, I could clean up the garden and get ready for winter but I think time is running out.

Joe was just here last week. I don't think he'll come by for a few weeks yet. Getting out of the shed on my own posed several difficulties, especially with the tree blocking my exit. *Here is a cell phone, Dad. Keep it with you in your pocket. Call me if you need me,* Joe had said when he gave me that little contraption. I told him, *I can't use this thing. It's too complicated.* I know it wasn't a very gracious reply but he told me to *just hit this little button and it will dial the emergency number if you need it.* I looked at that darn plastic toy. *That's not a button,* I said. *It's a picture of a button and my fingers aren't that skilled at using it.*

Joe had sighed. *Just keep the phone with you, Dad. I'll feel better if you have it with you in case of an emergency, okay?* Okay, so I should have listened. Today, I had one of those emergencies on my hands but, of course, I didn't have that contraption in my pocket. I never remember to carry it with me. Darn it, I didn't want anyone to find me in this situation. I know I looked and felt quite foolish finding myself in such a pickle. I grew very tired and fell asleep.

3

Sister Maria Nicola

There was a time when I went by the name of Elizabeth Parker and I knew without a doubt that this was where I wanted to be; I was called to a life of service and I could think of no better service than to teach children and give myself to God completely. For many years I could hear gentle whispers within my heart calling for me to put love into action. I desired, more than anything, to break through the din of worldly noises and focus on the delicate melodies of heaven. I wanted to wake up each morning with songs of praise on my lips and a resolution to surrender to God's will in my heart. *Be it done to me according to thy Word.* That was all I ever wanted. I believed that if I followed this prayer each morning my life would find meaning and fulfillment. As I've discovered along the way giving one's life to God does not resemble a fairy tale filled with singing characters and happy endings. It is very often quite lonely, painful, frightful, and appalling. Why does our perception of reality appear differently from the outside and seems to change once we enter into it? I envisioned my vocation as a Sister of Benevolence as strenuous yet rewarding work that would bring me closer to God and make me happy, but each morning I wake up anxious and scared that I am not up to the challenge. I am frightened right down to my black cotton underskirts because what I thought I was doing to comply with God's will seems to conflict with ideas that maybe I should be doing something different. Was it my will that led me to a religious life or was it God's? Is it my own self-doubts that are clouding my judgment or is it his soft voice telling me to move in a different direction? I feel that the worst of my misgivings are related to a weakness of not having enough faith and trust. I thought I had unshakable belief and commitment at one time but now fear and confusion lay a foundation for my prayers; all I can do is to ask God to stand by me, to answer my questions, and guide me to the place where I am needed. I could be wrong but I sense that if I were truly in the place where God wants me to be I would not be frightened at all. But then I am reminded that it is human to feel afraid even when we are doing God's will.

This morning was no different than any other morning. My lesson plans were ready for the day and I'd gone over them twenty times or more to make sure that I would glide through my day with ease and perfection, but since I was scheduled to be observed by Sister Maria Reyna, our provincial superior, I felt more anxious than usual. True, I have been teaching for ten years and I should not succumb to the insecurities of a novice but the woman really rattles me. She is determined to find the smallest errors, weaknesses, and miscalculations that one may fall into when trying to avoid the far greater danger of complete failure. It is usually in my desperation to achieve flawless success that I encounter my weakest blunders. *Dear God in Heaven please help me today. All I ever wanted was to serve you well but all I can see in my recent days are a succession of disappointments. I can live with my own mistakes but only if I haven't hurt you or these precious children who are in my care. Don't leave me alone in there with Sister Maria Reyna. She frightens me. I have no idea what her problem is, but she has one. She seems so convinced of my complete incompetence. If it is your will that I should be doing something other than teaching the children at St. Asterius then show me what you want me to do instead. I'm here, Lord. I'm listening. Don't let me do anything that is contrary to your will. And please, let Sister Maria Reyna find something good to say.*

Like an athlete before a major event I took a bunch of deep breaths and prepared to follow my lesson plans. She came in during my third period English class, and this is the class that does not care one iota for this subject but every now and then I am able to generate an ounce of enthusiasm; it's a matter of discovering a way to relate old literature to something contemporary in art, film, or especially *music*. The students, of course, always detect when I'm on edge and some have tried to take advantage of this situation. They seem to have their own ways of making things interesting. I kept hoping that Michael didn't try to get Carrie's attention with inappropriate gestures as he usually does. I prayed that Kelly didn't display her usual cries for attention by prompting other children into foolish debates. Last week, before our final test on Unit 3, she'd felt the need to argue that Francie (from *A Tree Grows in Brooklyn*) probably inherited ADD because her father was an alcoholic and that was why she didn't recognize when she was in danger, and why she couldn't remember her abduction afterwards. People with ADD, she'd remarked, didn't have a good grasp of reality in the present moment. Lord, didn't she stir up a hornet's nest with the students who'd taken this personally? My planned discussion points went right out the window from that moment forward. Her self-satisfied smile throughout the debate rankled my sensibilities. I had to work harder than usual to turn things around. What if, I suggested, Francie was no more ADD than the rest of us? What if there is more than one cause, more than one reason, why we can't always act in a way that people expect? Are there times when we feel so consumed by the problems we have that we can't behave as we should, I asked my class? Perhaps the conditions we live with make it impossible, not only physically, but emotionally, to follow what we should be doing all the time. The students began adding their own reasons why they believed Francie wasn't ADD and each one demanded to be heard. I suggested that there might be as many different reasons as there are students in this classroom for ADD-like behavior and I wanted to understand all of their points of view. The end result was an added homework assignment, an essay presenting various reasons why young people might not be able to conform on demand at all times, and to address the kinds of problems they might experience that prevent them from concentrating very well. Kelly frowned; though she'd earned her much-needed attention for a few moments she ended in losing more than she'd bargained for.

Everyone was irritated with her, first for being insensitive to students who are actually afflicted with ADD, also because of those students with alcoholic parents, and then for those who'd experienced trauma similar to Francie. She had also earned the class an extra homework assignment and that never fares well among one's peers. I feared that if this kind of scenario occurred in front of Sister Maria Reyna my place at St. Asterius School could be in jeopardy. Our Superior insists that we run a tight ship. Under her direction teachers who can no longer manage their classrooms are counseled into other possible careers. I've worked late into the night for the past week trying to find a lesson that will engage the students without inviting complete disaster. I do not wish any harm to Kelly McNally, but if she were absent today it wouldn't upset me one bit. I say this for her own good as well as mine. I don't think Sister Maria Reyna really likes children in general, but especially agitators. If Kelly should start something during my observation, it would mean both our necks in a proverbial noose.

4

Befana

As wonderful as it is to be the bearer of good things, such as: the occasional treats for children on the Feast of the Epiphany (the day Jesus received his gifts from the Magi), the unexpected chance to be there when someone needs comfort, performing as a small talisman that gives new courage or promise to someone who is struggling, or stepping into the role of messenger with a few crumbs of wisdom to offer; sometimes the need feels far greater than what one little old woman who carries a broom and a sack of cookies can provide. Many times life's forces are at work from so many different directions that it becomes impossible for me to untangle the mess and see the good. I get rattled a lot. I think that's what happens when people get too busy to be still and listen and I'm just as guilty of this as anyone else. I've never seen anything like the web we're in right now. Kids are too busy to play, to discover minnows in a pond, to blow dandelion seeds into the air, or to look through the grass for buttercups or four-leaf clovers. I'd shake my head if I could but my neck is stiff from years of strain. Parents are stressed not only because of their responsibilities at work but also because they try to keep their kids very busy in the hopes of keeping them out of trouble. Family time has become frenzied and often reduced to a picture of busyness that people put up on some social network to show that there is such a thing as family time. But most people are even too busy to look at the pictures.

I will be honest, the good things I bring don't always appeal to everyone. There are times when the truth isn't as sweet as my cookies, comfort may only come through sorrow, and hope may be on the other side of entanglement. What I represent isn't custom-fitted for every *self* out there; goodness and happiness are goals to strive for, not guarantees stamped on a birth certificate. I had no part in designing what is truly good nor did I create such a thing as happiness. It is incredible how many people think they can customize their own truth and joy out of a fantasy they have. I don't think they care much for the route to where true happiness lies so they try to take shortcuts; this usually gets messy and the result is that they forget their destination. More often than not what I see is more frustration and new shortcuts. And that is how life can become entangled. They try all sorts of new things to get to a happy place but they abandon the way before they reach it and once again try something new. It would be funny if it weren't so sad. Lady Goodness is sitting in the midst of a jungle with Happiness sitting on her lap as calm and content as you please while people are running circles around them, pointing in a hundred different directions and saying, *this is what's good and this is what makes me happy,* and feeling more stressed and worn out than ever because they can't find what is right in their midst. By the time I reach them with some comfort, courage, or wisdom, they are not able to recognize these gifts.

This kind of frenzied living reminds me of a young woman named Catalina who I met a very long, long time ago. I came to her as I do to most people - as a little statue gift from a loved one. I was wrapped in linen and stored in a velvet pouch and ignored on a shelf with other baubles and trinkets.

Catalina didn't really *need* much of anything, her family was comfortable enough, but she suffered from a terminal case of wanting. Desire was the ruling governor in her life. From the time she was a small child she would spend every waking moment trying to satisfy some wish or appetite. Her first thoughts of the day went to something *special* she wanted to eat or drink, or something new to entertain her, or even a different way to experience an excess of leisure (which she never truly understood because she was so busy trying to find it). Her parents did not mean to indulge her – no, not at all, they tried to tame her intemperance but it didn't work. Even when they gave in to some yearning, she wasn't satisfied or happy; she wanted more. *Wanting* made her feel alive; *having* numbed the wanting. Feeling benumbed was unacceptable so she had to want even more than she had. I'd never quite met anyone who was such a slave to self-indulgence. Honestly, it made me laugh at the time because her days were so busy and consumed with something quite unattainable. Sucking the life out of life did not satisfy her thirst for it. It just made her thirstier than ever.

I heard that a wise man once said that goodness is a balancing act between plenty and empty, between gain and loss, between everything and nothing. It is a rather tricky balance because no one alive has everything, and no one who has life has nothing. Happiness comes from finding that place where good things satisfy us. Catalina did not understand this concept. Happiness was always out of reach because it was something she *wanted*. By her twelfth birthday she had perfected the art of coveting. If dinner was laid out before her she'd quickly scope out the largest piece of meat or the choicest berries or the richest sweets and grab them before anyone could blink an eye. She'd search for the easiest way to win the largest prize at games. She would devise ways to take from others what she felt she did not have and if met with any resistance she would use emotional scheming to get it – crying large tears and reminding everyone around her that it wasn't fair that others had what she did not.

At seventeen, she met a young man named Guido and she decided that life with him would bring her happy days, plenty of sunshine, romance, and laughter – after all, he was kind and handsome, thoughtful and creative, and quite entertaining. She thought it would make her happy to fall in love, so she did, and quickly convinced Guido to marry her. She bore him two children, one right after another. She once thought that these were the things she wanted and they would bring her happiness. But happiness eluded her; Guido was only human. He had to work to support her appetites, and so he was not home enough to amuse her. The children were – well, children. They cried when they needed something, they had tantrums when they didn't get something they wanted, they played loudly and disturbed her, and they were the ones who now always *wanted* something from her. Catalina was not put on this earth to satisfy *their* wants, it was all she could do to satisfy her own. In just a few years' time she left Guido and the children and went after someone new she wanted – an older man named Antonio. However, Antonio was still married to Elisa. This fact did not stop Catalina from going after what she wanted. Wanting something or someone that is free is one thing; wanting what belongs to someone else isn't healthy. Taking what belongs to another person to add to your possessions messes up the balance of goodness in a big way! Her out-of-control passions created quite a web of unhappiness, for Guido and her children and now for Antonio's family. I couldn't seem to stop her. She ran away with Antonio and had him quite conveniently at her beck and call for about a year until Arturo came along and he wanted Catalina. She did not really want Arturo, but he was offensively rich and persisted in lavishing her with things she didn't even know she wanted so she left Antonio and ran off with Arturo. Within months Arturo was bored with Catalina and left her for someone new and more desirable. At that point Catalina was left with nothing – no husband, no children, and no lovers. She was outraged, scandalized and embittered. Her disposition turned an ugly shade of black, lacking in goodness and devoid of happiness. She had no idea what she wanted anymore and her lack of wanting destroyed her hope of having anything.

Catalina's only wish at that point was to escape a meaningless life so she purchased a vial of poison, laid down on the banks of the Arno River and prepared to make her final wish come true. All she wanted now was for her life to be over and done with. She was tired of wanting and never feeling fulfilled. Lord, this problem was bigger than me – I had no idea how to help this woman. She never listened to me anyway. I needed help to help her. I don't know why she'd started to carry me around in her pocket but somehow as she stretched out on the grass I rolled out of her pocket and down the embankment just shy of falling into the river.

Some might say Catalina was rotten because of her insatiable wants. Others, however, would say that her wanting wasn't bad – we all want happiness and we work hard each day to find it. Happiness is a good thing but sometimes we want more than we have; we want what's bigger than us, *infinite* you might say, and until we find it we aren't happy. I'd never encountered such an impossible task as trying to help Catalina so I as I rolled next to the flowing river I asked God, the one *who is infinite*, to help poor Catalina because I couldn't help her. As I began to sink into the mud I knew he'd heard me. A little girl named Diana, walking along the bank of the river spotted me in the slimy muck. She was enjoying the peacefulness of the afternoon and singing an enchanting tune:

> *Tiny angels-*
> *You comfort weary souls,*
> *You help to light our way,*
> *When we are wandering and lost…*

This young girl seemed filled with so much joy. When she picked me up she giggled sweetly and said, "Are you lost, too, little wanderer?" Little did she know! She turned to look for my owner. Climbing up the hill she saw that Catalina was in terrible distress and about to throw her life away by drinking a vial of poison. Diana quickly climbed the hill and sat down next to Catalina. She put her arm around her and Catalina wept inconsolably for over an hour into this little stranger's arms. She poured out her brokenness and emptiness and explained that nothing could fill her, nothing could make her happy.

Diana quietly listened. She was just a slip of a girl, no more than fifteen years old so she really shocked me when she spoke: "*Oh dear*, Diana told her, "*you are one of those wonderful people that have more to give than you're able to receive. You've just had your thinking on backwards.*"

Catalina stopped crying. She had no clue what this young girl had just said; it didn't make any sense. She asked Diana to repeat it.

"You have more to give than to receive. That's why receiving never makes you happy. It's backwards, you see. Giving is what will make you happy, silly woman."

Never in her life had Catalina considered the idea that happiness was to be found in *giving*, not receiving. She wiped her tears and listened as Diana told her about a different way of living life, one in which helping others brought joy. "You see," Diana explained, "when you give to others your heart feels lighter; when you're always trying to fill it up with something, it gets heavier. When your heart is heavy, it's not happy. When your heart is light as a feather, it soars! Would you like to try this?" Catalina saw that Diana looked like the picture of happiness, so she gave some merit to her words. Diana had just given her a lifeline so there must be something to this idea. She followed this young stranger to her home nearby. It was a small abbey that had very little in the way of treasures but the girls that lived there gave everything they had to help others. Nature understands this method; it gives of itself unconditionally. When bees suck the nectar from plants, it is bitter but the bees are able to turn it into the sweetness of honey, they don't wait around for payment. Without the depth of personal cost, goodness and happiness tread shallow waters. Catalina found the honey of life by giving up her own wants for the wants of others. She found the balance. I must tell you, I was so relieved! As I witness these experiences, I see how people find their life's purpose and it makes me feel good to share their stories.

5

Simon

School feels like the biggest waste of time; I used to enjoy it very much when I first came to this country but now it seems like it's just a place to keep kids locked up and busy while their parents are at work. Learning new things used to make me happy but now I can't say that I'm any better for it. Have I learned how to read? Yes, several years ago. Have I learned to do some math – yes, I have. Isn't this basically what I need out there in the "real world?" I just don't understand anymore why we are forced into this routine day-in and day-out when we could be out there doing something else. Anything else… I've learned more about life from doing real work than I have sitting at a desk and listening to directions from tired-looking teachers. I can't stand it anymore. I wish I could just disappear or something. The worst part, the part I really dread each day, is the part where I have to pretend I can fit in. I'm just not good at it. Kids tell jokes; I don't get the jokes – they're so lame. Kids ridicule everyone for stupid stuff; I don't get into that, either; I believe we should be nice to others. There are smart kids that think they're better than everyone else, and kids that are really good at sports. Some kids seem to have found things they like to do and they find friends that are good at doing the same things. The whole friend-thing is for the birds. I think I fall into the group that doesn't fit into anything; we don't actually group together, though, we're more like a scattered group of loners. When I was a little younger I learned to play with other children; it was just playing, not blending in. Each year it became more complicated and harder to blend. School seems to be a place where people learn to look for what is different about you. Let those that want to keep going to school to become somebody go ahead; let the jocks go on to play in the big leagues when they're done with school, but for those of us that can't find a single reason to be there, just let us go. Leave us alone. Let us just do what we want. As for me, I just want to be left alone to figure things out for myself, and I'm only in middle school. I don't see where this is going to end.

When Sister Maria Nicola asked me to stay after class today, I thought she was going to yell at me for not participating in her Scrooge skit during English class. She chose me to be Marley and she wanted me to read the part where Jacob Marley is explaining to Scrooge why he's there. "Why does Jacob Marley want to help his old friend Ebenezer, Simon?" I shrugged my shoulders and looked down at my desk. Let her call on somebody else, I thought. I don't care about Marley and Ebenezer or why Marley would want to help such a mean old man. For some reason our principal was in our classroom today watching us performing our skits about Ebenezer Scrooge. When I refused to answer Sister Maria Nicola, the principal shouted at me, "Answer!!!" so I said all I could think of "I think because a real friend must be someone who helps another without even being asked." Sister Maria Nicola smiled. The other teacher looked angry. I didn't care. I didn't know why Jacob Marley came up from his grave to help Ebenezer. I didn't care whether Ebenezer deserved to be helped or not and I certainly couldn't figure out why the old principal seemed angry with my answer. She was making all of us nervous, even our teacher. I don't know what her problem is; she always seems to be so mad, even when we haven't done anything wrong.

When I stood there in front of Sister Maria Nicola's desk after school waiting for her to explain the reason she asked me there, I felt like I just wanted to run away or disappear. I wanted to go home.

"Jacob and Ebenezer were kind of crazy people, huh?" she said.

I refused to look up. The scars on my right hand from when I fell off my bike last summer were much more interesting.

"Simon, look up at me, please." She sighed then relaxed a bit. "Thank you." After a minute she asked me another question I didn't want to answer. "Why do you think you're here, Simon?"

"You told me to stay here after class," I told her.

"Simon, why do you think you're *here*?" She thought that by putting an emphasis on *here*, I was suddenly going to have a different answer to that ridiculous question.

"I have to be," was all I can think of to say.

She was quiet for a minute then she asked me again "Why do you think you're here, Simon?" Was this some kind of a joke? I told her I didn't understand what she wanted. "Why am I here, *where*? At school? I told you, Sister, because I have to be."

She continued, "You're here at school because you don't have a choice. Okay. Why are you here in Pataskala?" How the heck should I know? I didn't answer and I was starting to get miffed. I look down at my hand again.

"Simon, I know you weren't born here, but I'm trying to figure out why you think you have to be here."

I shrugged my shoulders again. "I don't know. I was born in a place where I didn't have anyone and then I was adopted and this is the place where the people that adopted me live. So I have to be here."

"Where were you born?" At that point I looked up so she could see me clearly when I rolled my eyes. "North Korea," I answered.

"Do you still want to be in North Korea?" she asked. Again, I shrugged my shoulders.

"I don't know, Sister," I answered. "I wasn't allowed to live there anymore."

"So, you'd rather be here in Pataskala than in North Korea," she said. I shrugged again. The conversation was such a waste of time. What did this have to do with me not wanting to play Jacob Marley today?

"The people who adopted you – your parents – wanted you to be here with them in Pataskala, right?" She waited but I didn't answer; it wasn't really a question. "If you could have picked your own parents or a different place to live, who would you have picked? Where would you want to be?" I let out a big sigh and I didn't say anything, so she kept going. "Do you sometimes wish that you could make your own decisions about important things instead of being forced to be somewhere you may not want to be or to do the things you may not want to do?" *Duh*, I nodded my head. "That's probably the worst thing in the world, isn't it, being forced to do what we don't want to do, or being prevented from doing the things we want."

After a minute she said, "I want you to do something for me, Simon. I want you to imagine a different life for yourself. If you were in complete control of your life – no parents, no teachers, no peers, no one telling you what to do – what would you do? Where would you go? How do you see yourself living your life every day? Can you do that for me? I'm not going to ask you to write a paper about it. I just want you to think about it. Next week, I want to meet here again after class and I want to hear about what you've imagined. Okay? Just use your imagination and tell me how you envision your own life without someone forcing you to do things you don't want to do."

I shuffled my way out of the classroom and I wanted to forget about what she was forcing me to do for next week. I didn't want to think about it, and I didn't want to do it. I didn't want to do anything.............

6

Befana

Winks of early memories flicker in and out of my thoughts sometimes. When I see someone suffering terribly because of illness, abuse, injustice, or misfortune I am always tempted to wonder if this thing called life is worth the effort. At times, I'll admit, even I have used hardships to estimate the value of my own existence. I'm usually good at blocking out some memories that pop up every now and then, but then at other times I give in and think about it so I don't forget why my mission is important. The good Lord often chooses people who have had a rough time to help others who are going through something similar. We don't have to be perfect, we just have to care. When I think back on my life now, I can remember how I started learning to care.

In my mind's eye I can still see the place where I spent a few years of my early life. I couldn't have been more than seven or eight years old at the time. There were very few trees on the hillside; it was mostly rocks and crags with rye grass and dandelion shoots poking up through the scorched countryside. I can still recall where I used to sit at the top of a mound of tawny pebbles and throw them one by one into the gully below. When I used to get bored I would throw the pebbles way up high in the sky and try to reach the clouds hoping to pierce them and bring down some drops of rain. There was one day when I felt it worked. My efforts brought on one of the rainiest seasons that I can remember because I was living in a sort of cave on the hillside with an aging crone who made me call her *Padrona*, like she was a boss of some type. I remember the wiry gray hairs on her chin and a few stragglers of hair coming out of her cheeks, but her head was always covered with a black scarf tied very tightly behind her head at the base of her neck. I'd always wondered as a child if she had any hair at all on her scalp or just the migrant whiskers on her face. I don't know why, but she reminded me of a goose. So, in my thoughts I called her *oca*, the old Italian word for goose which I wouldn't dare call her aloud.

From the time I started to be a bit more self-sufficient, *Padrona* took me in; she would bring me rations of greens and small *pesce*, whatever she could gather outside or catch in the stream and we'd eat in silence in the dank hovel that sat hidden in the rural hills outside of town. At nightfall, *Padrona* would cover the entrance to our grotto with some rocks and we'd fall asleep on the corner slab covered with dry leaves, feathers and hay. There were many times when we went to sleep hungry but I wasn't allowed to utter a complaint for fear of receiving a few thrashes with the spindle. *Padrona* rarely spoke to me but she taught me to weave fabric on an improvised loom she'd fashioned out of sturdy olive branches and cordage made of vines. I must say that even in her dire circumstances, *Padrona* was a creative woman; what she did not have she would devise to suit our needs, like the blanket she'd woven from the bristly fibers of a plant she'd discovered. It was the itchiest, most irritating blanket known to humanity but it kept us both warm and dry during that miserable rainy winter. However, when my tender young skin reacted with blisters and an infection to those bristly fibers, I began to complain and that's when I received a few more whips with the spindle – the rash was nothing compared with the welts. *Padrona* no longer covered me with that blanket and I stopped complaining.

Though *Padrona* was stern and severe; her survival instincts were very keen. Yes, her nurturing qualities were limited, if not completely lacking, but I had a home for a while – I wasn't completely alone and abandoned. I knew not to speak unless she asked me a question. I was sharply aware that if I made any errors in my weaving or stitching I would be punished. But, I knew I could trust that her presence was the only thing that stood between me and certain starvation. *Padrona* was aloof most days, but when she did connect it was through harsh words or actions only.

One day she'd discovered an abandoned rabbits' nest. The kits seemed to be languishing, perhaps the mother had been overtaken by a predator. *Padrona* saw an opportunity for us to raise the small rabbits and provide us with meat for the coming season. I couldn't help it, the litter was adorable. I fell in love with those babies from the minute *Padrona* brought them back to our den. At the time I didn't realize she had brought them for us to keep, fatten up, and later kill them. I simply thought she'd brought something small for us to care for and play with, so each morning when I woke up I went to their new nest, fed them some wild grass and cleaned up their small pellets. There were three of them and I had even named them: the female was Pallina because she was small and round, one male I called Topolino because he looked like a little rat, and the other male I called Bobo because it sounded like a funny name to me. *Padrona* scowled when she saw my attachment to the little creatures and finally one day she warned me not to get too attached to them; as soon as they were big enough, she said, we would roast them with some wild peppers and chives. Her eyes and mouth watered with anticipation and I felt sickened. There was no way I could eat these little darlings; they were the closest thing I ever had to siblings. They looked to me for protection and survival, how could I betray them? I'd learned to nurture them and guard them as best I could, finding them a few thistles for treats and shielding them from foxes by constructing a pen around them made of sharpened sticks. When I approached the pen they would scamper to greet me, nuzzle against my cheeks when I held them, and let me carry them in my blouse when we went searching for berries in the groves away from the den.

As weeks and months went by, I felt like I had my own little children to care for and I could do a better job than *Padrona* because I would never, ever hit them with a spindle. I would never do anything to hurt them nor would I scold them for making a mess and peeing in their pen. They'd taught me how to smile, not by showing me, but by giving me a reason to, and I was determined they would not be eaten. When late summer was upon us and *Padrona* had gone out to collect wood for a good fire and some wild roots for dinner, I sensed that she had in mind to build a spit upon which to roast my little sister and brothers. While she was out I gathered up my fattened little bunnies in the itchy blanket and carried them over my shoulder to the woods near the *Spezzato* stream. As I sat with them next to the water I realized that this would be the last time I would see them; I had to free them. I started to cry. Bobo nestled onto my lap, Topolino sipped water from the stream and Pallina nibbled on the red wildflowers that seemed to grow out of the rocks. They seemed happy to be out and away from our musty den and in their natural environment. Whenever I thought of *Padrona* cooking them over a fire I became more determined to let them go. I knew I was going to miss them terribly but I couldn't live with myself if I didn't protect them. I held each of them one last time and cuddled them until they scrambled to be freed. I stood with big ol' tears in my eyes and climbed the hill away from the stream. When I'd reached the top, I looked back one last time. Pallina was still eating but the boys had wandered off in the tall grass. It was the last time I saw them.

When I returned to the den, *Padrona* still had not returned. I cleaned up the pen where my bunnies had lived and I shook the itchy blanket and covered up the corner slab. Just then I heard *Padrona* returning from her mission. She carried logs under one arm and some roots in her free hand. She came into the den and immediately walked over to the corner where the pen used to be. "Where are the rabbits?" she asked firmly. I looked at her but I could not speak. I hadn't given any thought to what I would tell her because we so rarely spoke, I didn't even envision a conversation about my decision. "I asked you a question," she growled, "where are the rabbits?"

I swallowed hard. I hadn't anticipated a problem, I simply thought that I was protecting my babies. I could see that *Padrona* was furious. I'd seen that look before when I'd fed our morsels of old bread she'd found in the village to the birds and we had nothing left to eat that day. *Padrona* had called me an *idiota*, *stupida,* and something like a brainless empty head, I think. There were many times when I'd received several lashes with the spindle and went without food for three days, but this time seemed different. I knew she would unleash her rage upon me and it soon came with one of the logs under her arms being tossed at my head. There was no name calling, no lashes with the spindle, no insults, and when I finally found my voice and told her that I'd set them free, I felt a coldness descend upon the summer air and it evaporated everything that I'd known as home. When Padrona spoke she'd said only this: *I don't care where you go or what you do now. You're more of a problem than you're worth. It would have been better if you'd never been born. Do you hear me? You should never have been born – what good are you? You're of no use to me, just one extra mouth to feed. Go away from here. I don't want to see you here anymore. Go!*

I walked out of the den and away from that part of my life. I really try to block that memory. That day, I went back down to the *Spezzato* stream but my bunnies were gone. Of course, years later I'd learned that rabbits kept like pets don't know how to fend for themselves in the wild. They were probably eaten anyway, but not by me and *Padrona.*

7

Stella

Some homes have a concept known as laundry day. It's a day when a Mom goes through everyone's closets and hampers, gathers up heaps of dirty clothes, takes them down to the basement and washes them in the washing machine, puts them in the dryer and then sorts them back into the baskets from which they came. It's the day when people who live in those homes have clean clothes to wear the next day. I thought it was an awesome concept when I heard about it because in my home there is no day that is designated in a special way like that. These other homes may also have a day known as cleaning day – the day in which each member of the family has assigned chores to do and everything looks spick and span when the chores are finished. The people that live in these homes may even enjoy a family fun day. I've heard about this from some of my friends; it's a day when the family does something special together like going bowling, or to a movie, or playing board games (instead of their usual electronic games) or going on a picnic or something. My family has none of these "special" days. There is never a day when all the laundry is clean. I cannot remember a time when our house looked neat, tidy, or shiny. I'm not sure what it would take for my family to have a family fun day. The very idea of such special days would be logistically impossible for us. There are eight kids in my family, two parents, one grandparent, and one and a half dogs. We didn't actually cut one of our dogs in half but we have a rabbit that *thinks* he's a dog so we treat him like one. The only thing we do as a group is eat and chatter. Yes, somehow no matter what everyone is doing that keeps them busy, whether it is school, sports, or jobs, we all manage to come together at 7:30 at night and eat dinner together. Dinner is nothing fancy because Mom and Grandma don't have the time or energy to concoct a special meal. Usually, what we eat is trough-like in nature. Everything goes into a big pot and boils – meat, vegetables, rice, whatever. It's all in there and no one questions it. Mom scoops it out of the pot and plops it into our bowls and we sit down to eat. It is on special occasions such as Christmas, Easter or Grandma's birthday, that mealtime consists of a special dish like lasagna, ham and mashed potatoes, or a big roast. Thanksgiving, of course, is celebrated with turkey and fixings. But always, no matter what the day, when we sit down to eat we first say thank you to God, and then Dad tells us to remember to say thank you to Mom and Grandma, too. It's loud at our dinner table for about 10 minutes. Everyone is talking at the same time, shoveling our mish-mash into our mouths, and rinsing our bowls so that we can run out of the kitchen first (this is so we don't get snagged into helping with clean up). Dad loads the dishwasher.

I have three sisters and four brothers. My sisters and I have two bunk beds in the room we share next to Grandma's, and the boys, except for Mikey, sleep in the renovated basement. "Renovated" means Dad drilled bolts of padding to the cinder block walls to insulate it from the cold. I think it serves another purpose. The boys share what we girls call the *padded room for the criminally insane*. My brothers are always wrestling, tumbling and rough-housing. The padding usually keeps them from getting hurt, but not always. Mikey is only three years old, so he sleeps in a trundle bed in Grandma's room.

That's my family; that's our home. We don't take vacations or go anywhere, we don't go to restaurants for dinner – ever, and we don't get to go to events as a family very much, except for free things that might be going on at the park or rec center or to watch the fireworks on the 4th of July by the river. My best friend, Emma, thinks we are the craziest family in town. I wouldn't disagree. She told me that my situation makes her feel better about her life. She only has three kids in her family and she said she thought that was outrageous enough. Emma is my best friend for two reasons: she loves me and she trusts me. I'm her best friend for two reasons: I love her and I trust her. What I love most about Emma is her sense of humor. She says she has to have a sense of humor because in reality she has a dark nature. What she says she loves most about me is that I am her bright side, the perpetual optimist. When she's irritated with something she looks to me like looking on the bright side. Our friendship works for both of us. At least, it has until recently. Emma has been a little quieter than usual for the last couple of months. She's usually quite the chatterbox but I suspect that there is something going on that she's not telling me and I don't understand why. We used to tell each other everything. When I'm at her house she takes me to the backyard garden and we sit in the little alcove where her mother has planted a dozen hydrangeas and she tells me that she doesn't think she wants to get married some day; that she wants to travel around the whole world and see everything there is to see. Emma goes to Granger Middle and I, of course, am homeschooled because my parents had enough children to fill their own classroom. I wish I could go to school with my friend. I love it when Emma tells me about "real life" in the outside world. She tells me about the crush she has on a boy in her school named Jack; she says that every girl in her class thinks he's the cutest but they all know he doesn't notice them too much. He's usually hanging around with his guy friends. Emma says one of the things she thinks is really special about him is that he's kind of a leader-type. All the guys want to hang out with him at break time and all the girls wish he'd look at them just once. Emma says she would be happy if only she could *talk* to him. She has no problem talking to anyone, but Jack is a different story.

She was so quiet today, so I asked her if anything was wrong but she said, no. Sometimes Emma and I walk down to the river bank and watch the mother duck urging her ducklings into the water for a swim. We often take some bread slices with us and break them into tiny pieces to feed the fluffy little babies. Today, we forgot to bring some bread along but it didn't matter, the ducks weren't anywhere in sight so we decided to sit on the bank and wait for something to happen. Emma always wraps her arms around her legs and props her chin on her knees and closes her eyes. She enjoys sitting like that when she's thinking. I slipped down to the water's edge to put my toes in the river which is what I do when I want to give Emma the space to think. Today, I noticed that the water has already started feeling very chilly, almost frigid. Thanksgiving will be here soon and I know we could probably get some decent snow any time now.

I noticed that Emma seemed to be taking a long time to think today. She almost seemed completely lost in thought. Our friendship has been very good at withstanding silence. We can be together for hours and never say a word, but today I was very curious about what was going through her head. I guess I could wait; she always tells me when she's ready. I can trust her. When she finally got up and walked over to the river to stand beside me she said, "Do you remember when I told my friends at school that I have a friend who never has to get up to go to school and that you can learn in your pajamas? Remember how you kicked up a real storm in a teacup because you thought I made it sound like your life was very lazy?" I looked at her to see where she was going with this. She waited for me to answer that I remembered.

"Are you asking me if I remember that you told your friends about me, or are you asking me if I remember 'kicking up a storm in a teacup?'"

"Both, duh!"

"I remember. But, I don't think I made that big of a deal about it. You did make it sound like homeschooling is easy. It's not. I'd like to think that it is more challenging than regular school. And I *do* get dressed. I don't learn in my pajamas!"

She laughed at me. "Storm in a teacup," she said, and we both laughed at her silliness.

"I remember, but where are you going with this?" I asked.

"I don't know," she answered. "I guess I was just thinking about what it would be like to be homeschooled. Why do your parents do it? Don't get me wrong, I like your parents, but what's wrong with them? Don't they need a break from all those kids?

Aren't they like other parents that like getting the kids out of the house for a while? I guess I just don't get it."

I laughed. "Believe me, Em, I think we try hard enough to drive them crazy, but they seem pretty fool-proof. I think they like the idea of deciding what their own children learn – they're our parents. They're responsible for us and they like to teach us. With them, everything is about family, what it means to be a family, how to get along with each other, and how to be good people. They think it's *their* job to teach us everything."

"I don't know if I could be home with my own family all day. Is family really all that important? I just think some people make it out to be more important than it really is. Look at how many people don't have a family. They're fine. Some people have screwy families and they don't complain. I just wonder if being so gung-ho about family is kind of outdated. I mean, is it really all that healthy to spend so much time together?"

I didn't answer right away. I'd never known a different way to live. Yes, my family has always been close-knit, but I didn't think being solid was unhealthy. I thought we were okay. Now, thanks to my best friend, I guess I have to wonder too.

8

Sister Maria Nicola

I had a letter from my sister, Genevieve, today. After my little talk with Simon and a meeting with Sister Maria Reyna I was a little rattled. I sought comfort in a letter from Gen, my younger sister whom I've always been fond of, but for whom my prayers are always beleaguered. Today, in this letter, she tells me she is writing from San Diego where she and her third husband are honeymooning. She is disappointed that I could not make it to her beach wedding but she hopes that she and Justin will be able to come to Pataskala to visit me. I know better than to hope for such a visit. No one comes to a small rural town like Pataskala, especially not when they live in a place like Chula Vista, Calif. I do hope she has found peace and contentment with this new husband. She says in this letter that she couldn't be happier. I pray to God that this is true. Gen's first husband, Matthew, adored her and went along with anything she wanted to do, just to keep her happy, just to *keep* her… But, Gen is a restless soul. She loved Matthew very much but "it wasn't a good fit" she'd said. "He was too needy." Then she'd married Will who was supposedly a better fit for her, but then she took up some old habits and left Will in favor of parties and the nightlife. Now, she's married to someone named Justin. She has told me very little about him. *God, give my sister some stability in life, help her to find peace in you,* I prayed.

Things are never simple, not for Gen, and not for me, even though I'd like to think I live a simpler and more stable life. I had worked myself up so much this morning and for the past few days to make sure that Sister Maria Reyna could find nothing to complain about during her observation, but of course, she complained. Not about Kelly, whose displays for attention were par for the course today, but about Simon who refused to participate in the activity. He is always so silent, so withdrawn, and so melancholy, I thought he might at least partake in a brief encounter with some interesting fictional characters. Sister Maria Reyna felt that I should have been more forceful with him.

"You cannot allow a child to be uncooperative," she'd said. "It is our responsibility to make sure they learn something whether they want to or not."

"Sister, I respect your opinion, but I feel confident that guidance is more effective than force. I spoke with Simon after class. I believe there is something going on with him that requires more support, than forcefulness. It's not a simple matter of pushing a child to be more cooperative, we must discover the cause of their reticence and encourage them. I believe that harshness can push a child like Simon further away. In a test of wills, I could have flexed more muscle and won today's battle with him, but I may have lost him in the long-run. We're losing too many students that way."

As long as I live and teach, I will probably never forget the look on Sister Maria Reyna's face when I'd finished speaking. I had the impression that she now saw me as the uncooperative student that needed to be coerced into cooperation. "You're not going to last, Sister," she'd said. "You're ideals are very noble, but if you wish to remain faithful to your vocation, these bumbling, foolish tactics of yours are going to be your downfall. You mark my word – you'll be out of here within a year. Those kids have no respect for what we do. I'd like you to take a firmer hand with them. That's not a suggestion. Do you understand?"

"Yes, Sister. I understand. I will make every effort to improve my approach." It's quite possible that my superior is right. My bumbling, foolish tactics *will be* my downfall with students like Simon and so many others. Has he responded to my noble ideals, my encouragement, my tactics? He has not. He's withdrawn into a place where he knows his mind can rest and be free of well-meaning, yet intrusive, teachers. Yes, perhaps Sister Maria Reyna was right after all; perhaps students need stronger guidance than an ineffective idealist such as myself can manage. I continue to be confronted with the same questions when situations like this arise – am I willful and convinced that I am following the right course no matter what? Or am I open to what God wants from me? Will I ever figure it out?

9

Befana

I like that there is someone out there who cares about each and every one of us. Have you ever met one single person on this earth who can claim to care deeply about every single person that ever existed? Most people care about the people they like and have a distant concern for other people. I like that there is at least one great big being that cares about everyone and everything. It makes my own life so much better just knowing that he's out there and that he does care. Knowing that God is there, and *believing* that he cares has changed my life. How? Well, now that's a story. This is the best way I can explain it. You see, back in the old days I was like a little mouse. I was afraid of everything. People could be mean and say harsh things or do cruel things. They couldn't be trusted and that scared me. I was afraid of wild animals whose natures seemed unpredictable. Their power could scare the warts right off my chin with their fierce looks, their growls, and their hunger. The weather used to scare me, too. You never could tell when a nasty storm was going to demolish your house, your garden, or your livelihood. And let's not forget about earthquakes; I tremble just thinking about them. All of these scary things added up to this – I was afraid of the unknown, the unexpected, and the unpredictable. There were so many times I would wake up in the middle of the night, for no reason at all, and my heart was popping around inside my chest. A potent fear would grip me like a great big pair of hands choking me around the neck. I couldn't breathe, I couldn't speak and I certainly couldn't go back to sleep. In the dimness of candlelight I'd peer around my hut (not leaving my bed, mind you) and look to see if there was something there that had snatched me out of a nice sleep just to poke at my fears. No one was there, nothing was lurking by; it was an unseen force that I could never quite understand. I'd shiver in my little bed until I grew weary and the distress would pass. My aloneness was tightly stitched to my fears, and together they spun a covering as uncomfortable and itchy as that bristly blanket I had as a child in *Padrona's* cavern home. I couldn't shake the jumpiness of those mid-night nerves any more than I was able to stop itching long after the woven blanket was off me. I guess it's not so much a fear of the unknown, because what I knew of people and animals and storms taught me to be afraid of them, it was my lack of trust that made my fears get bigger.

What does this have to do with God? Well, it started with my fearfulness which was like a door that kept me from getting close to people. The door was shut and locked. But on the night that I learned about God's Son being born, I had seen a light shining through my small window, the light that came from that big, bright star in the sky. I wasn't afraid of that light so I opened my door – just a crack – and asked the people who were following the star where they were going. I poked my pointy long nose through that crack and made a decision to started asking more questions about the newborn baby king that they'd told me about. The answers that came were about a baby who had come to save people like me, alone, afraid, poor and miserable and it was an invitation to put my foot outside my cozy zone. I stepped through the door of my own fears and followed that star, that magnificent star, like a compass for my life and as long as I've stayed focused on this path, I'm not scared. You could say it was an act of trust. What God can do with one tiny little act of trust is pretty amazing. He took my meager ounce of trust, added a whole lot of love and compassion and the result was an *Old Befana* that will follow him anywhere he leads me. Can people still be mean? Yes. Do animals still get that hungry *I'm-going-to-eat-you* look in their eyes? Yes. Do storms and earthquakes make a mess of life? Of course. But, now that I'm on the other side of the door, you see, where everything is well lit by his great big, protective arms, those things don't bother me as much anymore. Trusting him makes me feel safer. *Padrona* was wrong when she told me it would have been better if I'd never been born because if I'd never had a chance to live, I would never have experienced the love of this amazing God up there. I watch and see what he does; he takes care of everything! And if he asks me to help, I'm there. I'm *Old Befana* – I watch. I listen. I follow.

10

Salvatore

After my unintentional nap in the shed I realized that the storm had calmed down and I could hear the rain tapping gently on the metal roof but the thunder and lightning seemed to have passed. Good. My knee was throbbing and my head felt like hell but I didn't think I was seriously injured. It was only with the help of a bag of grass seed that I managed to push myself up onto my elbow just enough so I could pull the rake out of my forehead. The blood kept streaming out so I took a handkerchief out of my pocket and tied it around my head. I knew I had put a clean one in my pocket this morning. Sometimes I can't remember if it's clean or not but I remember this one was clean because I had ironed all the white ones at the same time this morning. The blue ones were still on top of the dryer. That was this morning, wasn't it? I also realized that I had no idea how long I'd been asleep in the shed. Even though my right knee was aching something horrible, I had to try to crawl on my good knee over to the door. If only I could have found that stupid flashlight, I could have worked my way back towards the door without getting into this messy situation.

I turned over on my back and by pushing on my hands and forearms I managed to sit up a bit. The door was open just a crack and letting a gentle stream of dim light into the shed so that I was able to see and remember that the tree was blocking my way out. By using my butt, my left leg, and my hands, I inched my way toward the door. I tried to push the door with my left foot but it was obvious, the bulk of the trunk was blocking the entire door and there was no way to open the door more than an inch or two. *There's no fool like an old fool,* I thought. I guess Joe was right; I should have gotten into the habit of carrying that phone in my pocket. I had no idea how I was going to get out of this mess and I knew he was going to be very angry and probably have me committed to some nursing home, or some special place for dementia patients. *You shouldn't be all alone, Dad.* To me, being alone isn't a place, it's a feeling. I don't feel alone in this house. It has been my home since I left Italy sixty-five years ago. I saved my money working in the meat district downtown and bought this home, this little piece of land, and filled it with a family. This is not the place where I feel alone. Being among strangers or people who don't care – to me, that is alone.

I looked around the shed, filled with some rusty tools, some unused shiny new ones that my grandchildren thought I should have, and stacks of pots, gadgets, gloves, trowels, and my old cap that I bought in Naples just before I embarked on the *Adalina* and sailed to America when I was no more than twenty. How can anyone feel alone when they're surrounded by everything that is as familiar as one's own skin?

When I visited my best friend, Louie, *may he rest in peace*, after his kids put him in one of those nice assisted-living places, he didn't have anything around him that he recognized anymore, so he stopped opening his eyes. I told Joe I didn't want to end up like that. Joe is the only one around now. My second son, Gino, never came back from Vietnam. The marines said he'd been captured, but they never found him. I don't know what ever happened to my boy. He was alone over there, in a strange place, without the people that loved him the most in this world. Annalisa never got over that. Until the day she died, my poor sweetheart believed our son was still alive somewhere in a foreign land and that he'd had to learn how to get along with his captors. She refused to believe that anyone would want to kill our gentle Gino. Her grief created a barrier with our other kids. Sammy left for college, became a lawyer - someone we could be very proud of and brag about - but eventually his successes, accolades, and ambitions turned him into someone we no longer recognized. He spent a lot of time with his wife's family (they were all lawyers) and he didn't even have time to come to his Mamma's funeral. He doesn't keep in touch except for the Christmas card his wife sends me. Our beautiful Allegra, the very apple of my eye, thought her parents were too old-fashioned, too stuck in the ways of the old country, too religious (whatever that means) and too blue collar for her lifestyle. She doesn't keep in touch very much, either. I try not to think about that because I choose to hang on to the good memories, if only for the sake of my sanity.

No, I've never felt alone here in my own home, with my own things, and my blessed memories. I am right where I need to be. Except that I needed to be in the house and not in the shed. I was starting to feel hungry. Perhaps I could lift myself up and use the shovel as a crutch, I thought. I knew I wasn't going to be able to put much weight on the darn knee, but one step at a time, I managed to hoist myself up onto the bag of mulch that I'd tripped over. From there, I used the box of birdseed to pull myself up a bit more since it was pretty full and sturdy. I had to chuckle to myself. This had to be the stupidest mess I've ever gotten myself into, if we don't count the time forty years ago when I was accidentally locked in the meat freezer at work for several minutes. Thank God my co-worker, Ellie came along when she did. I did feel rather alone then in the freezer but I refused to believe that I was alone now. Golly, working my way up to sitting on the darn box took all my strength and I was only getting hungrier. Staring at the gap in the door with the large tree outside was not helping my mood. I needed to close my eyes and think.

11

Befana

He and his classmates were too old for the playground anyway. He stood by and watched as the younger children scuttled out of the building like a colony of ants headed for one misplaced grain of sugar. Though the elderly second grade teacher, Mrs. Sharp, chided them to walk not run, their legs moved like Irish dancers, a firmly controlled sprint to reach their preferred playground equipment. But, my friend Simon was now reaching the end of seventh grade and recess meant less to him now than it did when he was a small child. He sat apart from the other students on a wooden plank that separated the playground from the sidewalk in front of the classroom, the barrier between work and recess.

He remembered the look on the old man's face as he'd watched him play in an empty lot when he was just five years old back in North Korea, where his school building had been fashioned out of an old factory which had once manufactured weapons and his playground was the gravel alley between one building and the next. His first experience with American recess came to mind now as he watched the smaller children; he was remembering the first time James Rossi brought him to take a look at the American public school he would attend, to speak with the teachers, and check out the playground, Simon had been surprised at the structures built solely for amusement. James Rossi had encouraged him to go ahead and play and get a feel for his new surroundings. It had been August seven years ago when Simon was starting kindergarten; school had not been in session yet, and few children were on the playground. Simon had stood by and watched a small group of children climb a ladder, sit at the top of the structure, then with hands stretched out in the air they slid down the smooth surface and landed on their bottoms in the mulch. It seemed a peculiar activity to Simon at the time. When the children finally left, Simon had climbed the ladder very carefully keeping his eyes on his adopted father, James, to make certain that this new parent was still keeping an eye *on him*. At the top of the ladder he sat down. He looked at the flat plane in front of him and he suddenly felt like a block of ice was wedged in his throat; he could neither swallow it down nor spit it out. He could not turn around to go back down the ladder nor did he feel secure enough to let go of the rail and slide down. Panic set in; he did not want to lose control of his bladder but he felt like he might not be able to stop it.

Cathy Jenson, the first grade teacher at that time, had been speaking to James Rossi and noticed the look of terror that had come over Simon's face. She calmly walked over to the slide, leaving James to continue speaking with the principal of the school. The young teacher knelt down at the bottom of the sliding board and reached out her arms to assure Simon that he could move safely down the slide and that no harm would come to him at the bottom. He wasn't afraid of the bottom, there was plenty of soft mulch and a smiling lady with open arms waiting for him; he was afraid of the journey, the feeling of letting go and moving forward without control or safety. Simon felt his heart beating fast like that day only a few months before when he was still living in Korea and he'd discovered that he had nowhere to go. His home had vanished.

12

Sister Maria Nicola

I wish I could say that I was comfortable with leading a double-life of sorts but after many spells of doubt I realize I am not. Perhaps if I wore a hairshirt as a means of atonement it would bring more comfort than lying to Sister Maria Reyna about my whereabouts when I leave the convent. Somehow I must reconcile the voices that tell me to live in the real world with the vows I have taken to live in the safety of my religious life.

From St. Asterius it's a short walk to the public library which lies on the other side of that rickety bridge. That crossover should really be rebuilt. Few cars travel over it now because of the new Route 12 but I always find children playing on or around it and to me it appears very dangerous, especially since this bout of unrelenting rains has caused the river to swell. By the time I reached the library and attempted to slip quickly and covertly into the ladies room my stockings were drenched and my black lace-ups were squeaking like a dog's chew toy. So much for being inconspicuous today. The elderly librarian who has spotted me going into the restroom on several occasions lingered for a time at the basin pretending to fix her hair and lipstick at the mirror. I may be getting paranoid but she seemed determined to catch me in the act of fraud and deceit. Once I stuffed my wimple and habit into my backpack and donned my old jeans, a faded Tool t-shirt and rotting sneakers I only waited a minute or two before pushing open the door of the stall and suddenly noticed that the old lady had no intention of allowing me any privacy. Missing the bus was not an option so I prayed that she wasn't there to spy on me. Doesn't she have to get back to work?

In answer to my prayers God sent in a pack of teenagers who weren't using their library voices and the old lady had to turn her attention to silencing them; it gave me a chance to slip out of the stall and outside into the relentless rain just in time to hop on the number 42 bus into the city. It was the last bus out of Pataskala and I had just a few hours to live my life, the one I believe I was actually meant to live, until I could catch the eight o'clock bus back to the library and change into being a nun once more. My vocation calls me to live a pious life, be on time in the chapel for Compline, grade today's stack of papers, and ask God's forgiveness for all my deceit and betrayal before I can lay down sleep for the night.

It was never my intention to live my life in such a disobedient and dangerous manner. Wouldn't it be so much easier if I simply complied with my vows, stuck to the strict routines at the convent, ministered to middle school children, taught them to pray, and made sure they understood the lessons about God's love and compassion through the many works of valuable literature? Sister Maria Reyna has made it very clear that she believes that I am ineffective in the classroom. The students often care very little for old works of literature; usually they're thinking about their game systems waiting for them at home, X Box 1 or Playstation 4, or whatever new gadget their parents have purchased for them. How on earth can I compete with the dynamic entertainment provided by the modern world and affluent families? I keep wondering what is wrong with me. Once a week I find myself sitting on a bus, feeling more at home in old, smelly clothes and cruising through the noisy inner city than I am in my starched, clean habit and speaking polite, reverent language amidst the Sisters of Benevolence in a spotless convent. And yet, all I want to do is be a nun and serve God. What on earth is wrong with me?

13

Stella

"Emma, it's me Stella. Can you talk right now?"

"Not right now, Stell, can I call you back in a half hour? I've paused Minecraft but I promise to call you back when I'm finished with my game, okay?"

"Well, can you meet me at our spot in a half hour instead?"

"Yeah, yeah, okay. See you – um, give me an hour. I'll see you at five." She hung up.

"Give me the phone, Stella, you're always calling that goofy Emma. She's a waste of time."

"Knock it off, Frank. She's my friend. And I am not always on the phone with her. If this family were normal we'd each have our own cell phone instead of being Neanderthals with one phone stuck to the wall for everyone to use."

"The Neanderthals didn't have phones, dummy," piped in Louis from where he sat reading *The Magician's Nephew* on Dad's recliner.

"Let me be and get back to reading…"

"That's enough," said Mom when she heard the pitch rising.

"Seriously, Mom, doesn't it ever bother you that our family is alien to our own culture? We don't have cell phones, not an ounce of privacy; we don't have video games or a decent computer. We exist in the new millennium like a species from the past. I can't invite friends over because we're so, so…. weird!"

Mom put her arm around me. "Stella, honey, does it ever bother you that no matter how many cell phones people have they don't know how to talk to each other anymore? They don't know how to tell stories about real things, or use their imagination because someone has invented some game to do it for them? Stella, you're right, we might be the weirdest family around. I wish it were easier to find a middle ground but our culture doesn't allow for average living, moderation, compromises, or stability... and forget privacy. Emma has a cell phone but she doesn't take time to talk to you when you call her."

"Okay, stop, Mom. I don't want to hear about the nouveau hippie ideas you and Dad have about how our life is filled with quality compared to the quantity everyone else enjoys. Today's not the day for that. I just wanted to talk to my friend without everyone piping in about one thing or another. Privacy, *right*."

"You're right. Sorry, Stella. Help me snap beans for dinner?"

"Fine, but I'm meeting Emma at our spot in an hour then I'll be back in time to eat."

"Well, now look who's sulking," Emma said as she approached the bank of the river. "What's up? You're pulling apart those pieces of bread and chucking them at the ducks like they're weapons. What's going on?"

"Nothing. I'm just tired. Wouldn't it be interesting if for just one week you and I could trade lives? You go home to my family and I try out your normal life, just for a week?"

Emma laughed out loud. "Yeah, right. As much as I complain about my life, I wouldn't want yours."

"Exactly."

We both sat there in complete silence for a while. I didn't really feel like grumbling away our time together and she looked deep in thought again. I guess today I just wasn't in the mood to be patient about anything and even Emma's silence began to bother me.

"What's been going on with you, Emma? Seriously, you haven't been yourself for a while. You used to talk up a storm but for the past few weeks you've just been clammed up. Is something going on?"

Emma didn't say anything. Not a sound came out of her mouth and she didn't even blink. It was eerie, like Grandpa before he died, he couldn't hear us anymore. He kind of looked like he was there but he didn't respond to anything. Emma seemed so lost in her own thoughts.

"You know what I'm starting to think?" I finally asked her. She used to jump at a prompt like that with a sarcastic remark, but the silence continued so I answered my own question.

"I'm starting to think that you are bored out of your skull with me, with our friendship. Let's face it; I have nothing interesting to bring to the table. Nothing new ever happens in my life. I don't have exciting things to share about what happens at school; I can't engage in a conversation about the latest stuff. I can't even relate to half the things you say because I don't get it. Look, if that's what it is, I completely understand. I must be the most tedious person on earth to be friends with and you're slowly dying of boredom."

She finally looked at me and smiled. "That is NOT it, silly. I'm not bored with you or our friendship. Forget it, okay. When it comes right down to it, you're not yourself either – you used to be more optimistic about even the most dreadful things. It's nothing about you, I promise. Sometimes I just get so confused about stuff in my life that I can't even find the vocabulary to talk about it. It's easier to slip into the diversions of games, TV, and internet stuff than to try and think. I don't know, when I'm with you I feel calmer and I can finally just *think*. You're good for me like that."

"Glad I can be of help."

"No, I mean it. You have a calmness about you, even when you're griping. You're the best friend I have, Stell. You're probably getting bored with me using you for a pillow to rest on."

Now it was my turn to laugh. "I guess I feel a little confused, too, Em. I've relied on you to be the fun factor in my life. Are we changing?"

Emma didn't answer. She sat there hugging her knees again and went into thinking mode. She took some of the bread pieces and fed the ducks. They didn't seem to be hungry anymore. Or perhaps they decided they were bored with both of us and swam away.

"You know, that's actually not a bad idea," she finally said.

"What's not?"

"Switching lives for a week. I saw something like that on a reality TV show. Maybe we should try it. You could move into my house, go to my school, sit there and listen to my slimy teachers, play with the gadgets we have in my house, use my cell phone, and see what it's like. I could put on a plain cotton skirt and wear a cap or something and live like the Amish in your house for a week. Now, that would be interesting – for about an hour." We both laughed.

"Are you being serious or are you just humoring me again?"

"No, I think I am serious. I think your life would give me time to think."

"What do we have to do to make this happen?"

"Get permission, I guess. Some kind of special permission from my school. Our parents probably wouldn't mind. Well, yours might; my life might corrupt you."

"Are we going to try it, for real?"

She stared back at the water again. I finally saw a flicker in her eyes – the spark of my old friend Emma. She seemed intrigued and filled with a renewed sense of purpose. I suddenly felt scared. My ideas are not always what they're cracked up to be.

14

Salvatore

Well, what do you know, it stopped raining. I could see a little sunlight peaking inside the shed through the crack in the door. I didn't know what the heck I was going to do, though. I still couldn't get out of the shed; my knee ached like the devil and my head was still bleeding but not as bad as before. I was tired, hungry, and had a foul taste in my mouth. I knew it was going to hurt but I needed to try and push the door open. With plenty of grunts and screams I tried to use my good side to thrust my weight against the door without putting any pressure on my knee but the door just won't budge. The tree was wedged solidly against it. Thanks to the effort, I hurt my good side, too. *My good side.* Annalisa used to tease me about what she called "my good side."

Allegra, if you want your father to say yes to the slumber party at Jeanie's house you're going to have to get on his good side, Annalisa used to say to our daughter. Every week that kid wanted to go to her friend's house, one friend or another. She wanted to be around her girlfriends all the time; I couldn't blame her with all the older brothers she had. But first, she had to get on my *good side.* Annalisa used to say that to all the kids when they wanted something. *Before you ask him for permission, you'd better get on his good side.* They would do chores, bring me my slippers, or fluff up the pillow on my recliner and that's how I knew they were getting ready to ask me for something. They knew better than to ask me for money, we didn't have much. But getting on my *good side* became a tradition in our house.

Once I asked my darling wife what this "good side" nonsense was all about. Did I have a bad side? She just smiled at me and didn't answer. Later that week Sammy came home from eighth grade with a note from his teacher. "Sammy is causing quite a bit of disruption and unrest in our classroom. He argues with me during class time, he talks incessantly, and he pesters the kids into doing things his way. Please have a talk with Sammy about proper classroom behavior. When I give him detentions, he argues that detentions are just a teacher's way of avoiding a problem instead of dealing with it. Mr. and Mrs. Lazio, please help your son to understand the meaning of authority. I greatly appreciate it. *Mrs. Walsh.*"

Annalisa had talked to Sammy about being respectful of teachers and to be kind to his fellow students. He claimed that the school had unreasonable rules and that people like Mrs. Walsh who showed favoritism to certain students should not be teachers. At that point, I'd taken off my belt and gave Sammy a few whacks across his bottom – not too much. He stood there and took it then said "And you think that's going to change anything?" I took away all his privileges for a month. Annalisa said Sammy had found *my bad side*. Well, he spent his teenage years always discovering my bad side. Until that day I didn't know I had one.

I peeked through the door to see that the clouds were blowing away. I thought if I could just squeeze my old bones through the crack with my good side which was just sore, not hurt, maybe I would be able to crawl over the tree and get back to the house. I thought it was worth a try. I felt strong enough to stand without the aid of the shovel so I thrust it through the opening and then pushed hard against the handle to try and force the door open just a bit more but the old shovel snapped in two and I lost my balance and fell once again. I was in too much pain to try and get up again. I sat by the door feeling hopeless; it was a good time to start praying.

15

Simon

I'd rather eats rocks than to do what Sister has asked me to do. Think about why I'm here? What 13 year-old kid has the answer to that stupid question? If I could have picked my own parents or a different place to live, who would I pick? Where would I want to be? How should I know? I don't know any other parents. I only knew Dasan. I only remember the hut. I knew my foster parents when I first came to America and now I've come to know the Rossi family as my adoptive parents. But what do any of us know other than what we actually have in our lives?

Do I sometimes wish that I could make my own decisions about important things instead of being forced to be somewhere I don't want to be or to do the things I don't want to do? Doesn't everyone? Maybe even Sister wishes she could do something different than what she's doing.

I'm supposed to imagine a different life for myself. If I were in complete control of my life – no parents, no teachers, no peers, no one telling me what to do – what would I do? Where would I go? How do I see myself living my life every day? That just doesn't seem like a realistic question to ask any kid. We just live and do what we're told until we grow up.

For me, thinking about all this doesn't seem to help; I only think of more problems as I go along. I try to avoid walking past Granger Middle School anymore on the way home, even if I have to go the long way around. Obviously, I didn't belong in public school but I don't think my life has improved since my parents put me in St. Asterius. They thought that I would thrive in an environment that is more structured and nurturing, they'd said. I haven't really had the opportunity to imagine a different life for myself, have I? Every time I turn around my life is changing because of decisions other people make for me. How do I see myself living my life every day? Not here, that's for sure. I didn't really like the other school. For me it was like walking into a house of mirrors (my parents thought it would be fun for me to experience that carnival attraction one time but it made me sick and I'd puked.) I had that same queasy feeling each day in first and second grade, and after all these years I still don't know how to feel good about where I am let alone imagine anything different.

All I remember from my early years is that my life with Dasan was simple. I got up when the rooster crowed in Chen's yard across the lane. I washed my face and hands. I ate four mouthful's of yesterday's cooked rice. I helped Dasan at the edge of the sea – holding the basket steady while he picked up seaweed from the shore. I helped him carry the basket to the market to sell what we could. Dasan would lift me up and put me on the table in front of him to draw people near. He said children attract attention better than old people. From behind, the old man would push my back with his leathery hands to make sure the peasants walking past our table would notice me and buy our seaweed. Once, he pushed a bit hard and I fell off the table. The seaweed landed in the dust. I had to pick it up and clean it with what was left of my drinking water in the bucket. By then, the people didn't want the seaweed. We made nothing that day. I went to sleep without my four mouthfuls of rice. I slept next to Dasan on a mat made from straw in the corner of our hut closest to the fireplace. I remember that his throat made noises like a hungry tiger while he slept. Dasan always pushed me to the edge of the mat against the wall to protect me, his strong arm always cradled me against his sharp ribs, his wailing snores would sting my ears, his hot breath would make my head sweat and my eyes tear, but I felt safe. It was home. Before we went to sleep each night, we prayed. Dasan taught me to say, *God made light and separated it from the darkness. When we find ourselves in the dark we must move forward to the light.*

The day the police came and took Dasan away to prison I watched him from the window and he looked back at me only once and pointed up to the sun. Was he going forward to the light? Is that what he was trying to tell me? I stayed in the hut until all the mouthfuls of rice were gone. I waited for him to come back but he never did. Then, one day I walked to the shore with my basket to find seaweed but the angry people shooed me away. The vendors at the market would not give me anything to eat even though they knew what had happened to Dasan. I'm not sure why Dasan was taken away. For a while I hid under some market tables and snatched up scraps of food that fell to the ground. At the end of a particularly long, hot day I'd fallen asleep inside someone's crate and that's when everything changed. I didn't have time to dream about something different. I only wanted to sleep in Dasan's arms and eat four mouthfuls of rice for my breakfast, lunch and dinner. That was all I ever remember wanting when it was taken away. I never wanted anything new after that.

Now, this nun wants me to imagine a different life for myself. I was taken by some guards to another home to live with other abandoned children because the market vendors complained about me. At the home, though I'd been given a small bowl of rice to eat, I still only ate four mouthfuls. I had to sleep next to children, some older, some younger, who either yelled or cried at night until the master came to silence us with his lash. I don't know how long I was there but when the rains began there were Americans who came to take many of us away from this home filled with unwanted children. I didn't have a chance to dream about a different life for myself. I went with some other children on an airplane and settled into a cleaner home in America with foster parents named Frank and Susan. There were younger and older children who either cried or yelled at night until someone told us to be quiet.

One day a man named James and his wife named Cynthia came into the home and tried to talk to me. They did not speak Korean but they smiled a lot and gave me candy. Then they took me to their home and told me that I was their son, this was my new home and my new room where I had to sleep alone at night without the sounds of crying and yelling children, without the sounds of tiger snores, without strong arms cradling me against sharp ribs. I listened to the sound of blowing wind coming from a vent beneath my bed. Sometimes the wind was warm and sometimes it was cold. I was given chicken nuggets and fried potatoes to eat, but all I wanted was my four mouthfuls of rice. It took a long time for me to understand my new parents and my new life. I hadn't really dreamt about the strangeness of sleeping on a soft mattress alone in my own room. I hadn't wished to have curtains with painted sea creatures covering my windows. It wasn't my hope to have a mother and a father that looked nothing like me. I never pictured myself going to a school with children whose language I did not understand and teachers that looked at me like I was a pitiable small puppy. I never had a chance to think of what I wanted instead of what I suddenly had.

The answers to Sister's questions really baffled me. I can read the books she tells us to read, answer the questions on the quiz, and write about what I think the characters in the book are doing and why they might act that way, but I cannot imagine a different life for a kid named Simon Rossi. In distant dreams I can remember that an old man named Dasan had called me Kwan. I never imagined being called anything else.

16

Befana

Life with *Padrona* stayed with me long after I was exiled from her unpleasant home. After she sent me away I could still feel the prickly blanket on my skin; I could still hear her harsh words attacking my sense of pride; and I could feel the blow of the spindle against my skin. As I grew, I wore the memories of my early life like stretchable clothing, a garment which I could never outgrow.

Children can carry so much with them, whether they are aware of it or not, but they also have a unique quality which fades away as they become adults; it is that quality which helps children to see or sense things that adults cannot. Children are open to the whole world around them, not just the world they can see but also the world they cannot. They can be quite sensitive to sights and sounds that most people do not even notice. Their minds do not automatically block sensations, ideas, wonder, or imagination. With this openness children can arrive at the truth long before adults. The problem with most adults I've come across is that they can become quite satisfied with the explanation to a question that fits their own ideas and in turn they tend to reject all other explanations, even the truth. This problem makes it very difficult for adults to wonder, to believe, to imagine or to accept. It's a difficulty that can often pit children and adults against one another. I've seen it happen often enough, but if a child can manage to hold on to what is good about life, he'll be okay.

At nearly five years old Georgie Ramsey carried his whole world in his pocket and it was quite a bit to carry. Georgie began to carry his world when, one day, as he sat at his grandmother's side, she finished knitting him a new blue sweater using a nice cable pattern. She was quite elated that she had been able to finish his sweater without having to go out and buy more yarn, for yarn was a luxury, she'd told Georgie. The little boy had clapped his hands and hugged his grandmother, thanking her for the new sweater. When Georgie spotted a length of yarn that was too long to throw away and too short to knit into a new sweater, he asked his grandmother if she would use the yarn to teach him to knit. His grandmother had laughed and said, "Boys don't knit, Georgie." The child frowned and asked "Well, then, what do boys do?" After thinking for a moment his grandmother answered, "Boys tie knots, little one." So she taught her grandson to tie the yarn into a knot, but, she said: "Don't tie knots for no reason. Let this be your story – your *yarn*," she chuckled at her own pun. Georgie looked confused.

"Here, let me show you," said his grandmother. "First, tell me what you love to eat most in the world."

"I love your homemade noodles, Grandma," Georgie answered. "Especially when you put butter and cheese on them."

Georgie's grandmother smiled. "Very good. Now, here, tie a little knot in the yarn" and she showed the child how to tie a knot. "That knot represents the noodles you love."

"Now, what is your favorite song, Georgie?"

"*You Are My Sunshine*," the child answered. Another knot was tied into the yarn to represent the song. The child sat with his grandmother for several minutes tying one knot after another into the yarn as he told his grandmother about all his favorite things. Finally, his grandmother asked, "What do you think you would like to be when you grow up, Georgie?"

"I want to be a cowboy," answered the child. Soon there were many knots in the length of yarn and Georgie's grandmother taught him how to roll the yarn into a ball so that he could keep it in his pocket at all times. Each knot represented part of Georgie's world: the things that made him happy, experiences that made him angry or sad, his hopes were tied into his yarn, his dreams became little nuggets of his story, his daydreams and night dreams - good or scary - were tied into the yarn, his worries and fears were weakened when he pushed them into a knot, his losses (like the day his poor old grandmother died) were fixed into his yarn. Everything that became a piece of Georgie's world was saved into a little knot and he carried them all in his pocket. Georgie even tied his favorite Christmas stories into a knot, like the story of the three Magi that visited Jesus with very special gifts.

One Christmas, a few years after Georgie's grandmother had died and he'd outgrown the blue sweater, the child had been hoping to find a toy airplane under the tree. Georgie's mother had insisted they still put up a tree each year, but his father had told him that those trees were a waste of good money, that fairy tales are anything but true, that Santa Claus is a myth, and that wishes don't come true – you have to be proactive in your life and stop wishing. "The older you get, the more you realize this is how life works," his father had said. He even taught the child that there was no such thing as God (despite the details his grandmother had shared with him). Georgie's father had told him that Jesus had probably not existed because his father believed him to be a myth generated by people who were hungry for power. If anything, he'd told Georgie, he was just a man and nothing more. When Christmas morning came and no toy airplane sat waiting for him under the tree, Georgie began to wonder if what his father said was true. Though he was disappointed at not having received the airplane, he sat near the tree reaching for the ball of yarn in his pocket. He'd never shown his yarn to his parents; it was a special secret between himself and his grandmother.

Georgie took out the ball and looked at it, trying to recall what each knot represented. It was hard not to remember that the first knot stood for his favorite noodles. He would never forget them because he missed those noodles now that his grandmother was gone. The last knot he had tied was for the anger he felt because either his father was lying to him or his grandmother had. His father had not even gone to the church to attend his own mother's funeral because he said the rituals were archaic, grandma is gone – finished. She didn't go to heaven and she didn't go to hell because there is no such thing. Georgie's grandmother had been sick for some time before she'd died. She told Georgie that there was a special place called heaven. It was her favorite place to think about and that someday when she got too old to stay on earth Jesus would take her to a new place where people don't have to be old and sick anymore and she would watch over him. That day Georgie had tied a knot for heaven. Now, as he looked at his ball of knots he wondered what to do about it. The knots were all real – the noodles, the dreams he'd had, the happy memories, the sad things, and all the things that made him angry – everything was tied up together and it was all a part of Georgie's world. His grandmother had been real, and she'd told him that things don't stop being real just because they're harder to see. There was a special knot for her. Could he possibly figure out which knot was for heaven? How could he go back and untie it if it wasn't real?

Georgie sat and stared at the tree in front of him. There was only one thing under the tree, something which had not been there the night before. It certainly wasn't an airplane. It wasn't a toy of any kind. It was a small figurine his mother usually kept in her curio cabinet, something she'd received when she was a child. Georgie wasn't sure what it was doing under the tree this morning. He picked it up and looked at it carefully. He knew his mother would be upset if he dropped it. It was a figurine of an old woman, carved of wood and painted long ago. The colors were fading from the body but the face was as bright and vivid as the day it had been painted. Georgie looked deeply into the eyes of the little old woman and wondered who she was, and why his mother was so fond of this statue. She kind of looked like a witch. (His father had told him that witches were *real*.)

As he pondered the little statue, his mother came up behind him and sat down on the floor next to him.

"Good morning, Georgie. Merry Christmas."

Still feeling disappointed about the airplane, Georgie did not reply.

"I wanted you to have her," his mother said, stroking the statue in Georgie's hand. "Merry Christmas," she repeated.

"It's not an airplane," Georgie said.

"I know," his mother said. "It's a little treasure I received a long time ago." His mother took the statue from his hand. "She travels more than an airplane, I can tell you that." She handed the old woman back to Georgie. "Her name is *Befana*. My Grandma Lucy gave her to me when I was your age. This little old lady flies all over the world during Christmas because she is looking for baby Jesus."

Georgie's eyes widened. "Did she find him?"

Georgie's mother smiled and stroked his hair. "Yes, Georgie. She found him. She finds him over and over again. Jesus lives inside everyone who believes in him. *Befana* wants every child to know that. So, when she travels around the world she brings, not only a few treats for children, but also his message of love and peace and she wants them to know that heaven is as real as you and me."

Georgie felt more than relief; he felt like he'd received the best gift in the world. He thanked his mother and gave her a hug. "Merry Christmas, Mommy. What did *Befana* bring you?" he asked. "Hope for the future," she answered, and she kissed the top of his head.

"Did she bring treats?" he asked.

"She certainly did. They're in the kitchen. Shall we go get some?"

Georgie and his mother enjoyed cookies and milk for breakfast, and I became a knot in Georgie's ball of yarn.

17

Sister Maria Nicola

Rain makes people walk faster, sunshine slows everyone down. The streets were not as crowded today as usual, probably because of the rain. Everyone was in a hurry to get to where they were going. It was all I could do to get from the bus stop to the 20th street alley before a deluge came down but I was already soaked to the bone because a Rav 4 had sped through a puddle and splashed me from head to toe. I arrived at my usual meeting spot ten minutes early. I raced down the concrete steps to the basement under Ted's Bar and Grille and noticed that Sandy wasn't there yet, she usually waited for me outside, rain or shine, but Krauss was there and he let me into the musty cellar.

"Where is everyone?" I asked Krauss. He shrugged his shoulders. He looked stoned and leaned in to try to kiss me. At that very moment, Sandy came through the door.

"Crappy weather. Son of a ..." she let the sentence drop.

"Where's Maggie and Sara?" I asked.

"They're picking up some stuff before they get here. They had a hard time last night. They went to the lodge but Zed had some bad stuff and got nailed. I hope they have better luck today. Boy, you sure got drenched, didn't you, Liz?"

I nodded. "An idiot didn't slow down, went right through a puddle and got me good."

"You know, sometimes I wonder about you, Liz," Krauss added and put his arm around me.

"Let's go sit down," I said. "Do we have any blankets in this hovel? My clothes are soaking wet."

Krauss snickered and said, "Take them off."

"Not today, pal," I answered. He shook his head and threw himself on the filthy cushions where we all usually sat. Krauss handed me a lit joint and scooted over to give me a little more room to sit.

Just then, Maggie and Sara came through the door. They were drenched as well. Sara was Maggie's younger sister. They looked like they could be mother and daughter. Maggie had a shock of gray hair, sallow skin and sunken eyes; too many years of meth, cocaine, or whatever the flavor of the month happened to be. Sara had fine, dark hair that hung straight in patches. The women sat on the cushions next to Sandy.

"I can't stay long today," I said. "I think someone might rat me out pretty soon."

"Who?" Krauss asked.

"It doesn't matter. But if you want me to keep coming, I'm going to have to be careful."

"Fine. What'd you bring today?"

"I got more than usual. Here." I handed them a bag out of my backpack.

"Where do you get all this? This is prime. You really scored big this time, Liz."

"It doesn't matter where I get it. Do you have my weed? I have to go. I told you I think someone might rat me out if I don't get back in time."

"Fine, whatever. Here ya go. Don't smoke it all at once."

I rolled my eyes and stood up gazing around the dank cellar. Only one light bulb screwed into the ceiling illuminated the cobwebs, black mold, and crusty white fungus on the brick walls. The smell of old urine, vomit, and bug spray didn't help the ambiance. "Did you guys ever think of meeting somewhere else? This place stinks."

They all laughed. "We tried to get a place at the Hilton, but they were all booked up," said Maggie, and they all laughed again. I looked down at Maggie and shook my head.

"You watch, Maggie, someday we will get a room at the Hilton. It's going to be better than this."

"Whatever," she said. "Thanks for the stuff. Don't get caught."

"I won't," I said, and I slipped back out into the rain and ran to the bus stop to wait for the next bus. I didn't know it at the time, but Krauss had followed me out. When the number 42 bus back to Pataskala stopped in front of me, I didn't notice that he had also boarded the bus. He'd decided to see where I go when I leave the basement.

18

Simon

The fastest way to get home is by taking the street in front of Granger Middle School but if I walk the next block over it takes forever to get home. Today, I didn't even care about getting home fast, even though it's been raining like the monsoons I remember back in Korea, I just wanted time to think about these dumb questions Sister asked me after school. It's not like I want to answer them, but I know she will call me in after class again and make me stay until I give her some answers. I think I've learned enough in her English class to know how to make up some fiction. That's what I've decided to do, make stuff up so I don't have to try to figure out the answers I just don't have. The trick now is to figure out the fake answers. As I walked slowly down Jensen Street. the sun started to peek out of the clouds. When I looked up I noticed that the house up the street had a tree come down in the yard. It was a really big tree. I walked a little faster to see it. The yard was big, too, so the tree didn't even reach the house but it looked like it smashed into the backyard shed.

There didn't seem to be anyone in the yard so I decided to go check it out. Throwing my school bag down in the wet grass I figured the only way I was going to climb to the top of a tree this tall is if it's horizontal. I started walking up the roots to the trunk and over to the branches in front of the shed. Just before I reached the shed door I thought I heard something inside. It kind of sounded like an animal. Maybe something got trapped in there. The more I listened, though, the more it sounded like something else, a grunt like Dasan used to make when he tried to get up from a chair but this sounded more painful.

I tried to pull at the door to peek inside when suddenly I heard a man talking. I couldn't really understand what he was saying but he sounded like he was hurt.

"Hey, is someone in there?" I cried out.

"Help me!" the voice said.

"Oh crap! I'll call 911," I answered, taking out my cell phone.

"No!" the voice said, "Please don't. Just help me out of here. Try to get the door open."

"Are you okay, man?"

"Yes, I'm all right. I just need help to get out of here. Can you get the door open a little more?"

"I'll try. This tree is pretty big, mister. But I'll see what I can do. I looked around for a way to use something stronger to pull on the door but I didn't see anything outside. I figured everything was probably in the shed with the guy.

"Hey, do you have a saw in there? Maybe I can cut part of this branch away." He didn't answer. "Mister, are you hurt? Maybe I should call for help. I'm not sure how to get this branch out of the way."

"No, please don't call anybody. I don't want anyone to see me like this. Please. I'll try to reach the saw. Are you sure you can cut the branch? You sound kind of young."

"Are you sure you're okay? You sound kind of old."

The man laughed but it sounded painful. I heard him rummaging around in there and making noises like it hurt him to move. I felt like I should ignore him and just call 911 and get out of here, but what else did I have to do today? I've never liked drawing attention to myself, either, so I get this guy. While he was rooting around the shed for a saw I started to break some of the smaller branches out of the way. It wasn't as easy as I thought it would be. After getting a bunch of the leaves and skinny branches out of the way I was able to climb into the space between the tree and the shed. Maybe if I leaned against the shed and pushed at the tree with my legs I could make more room, but that didn't work well either. That tree wasn't going anywhere. This was so bogus.

"Mister, did you find a saw or something?"

"Yes, I have one. I'm just trying to get back to the door. My knee isn't cooperating. Hang on."

After a while I could hear him near the door again. He didn't sound very good. He was breathing hard. "Are you sure you don't want me to call for help?"

"After what I just went through to get the saw? Are you kidding me? Here, be careful. If you get hurt, we're both in trouble, me more than you."

From the crack in the door I was able to pull the saw from his hands. I could see that they were all bloody. I didn't think he was as okay as he said he was. I had no idea what I was doing but decided to try and saw the main branch that was up against the metal door. After a few minutes of pushing the saw back and forth I'd barely made a notch in the wood. Good grief.

"Is there an easier way to do this, mister?" I asked the old man.

At first he was silent then he said, "A lot of things in life take time and patience. You just keep plugging away, just like life itself." I wasn't really looking for a philosophical answer. I wanted to know how to saw through this branch before it was dark outside. My parents wouldn't be home from work yet, but I couldn't stay here all night. I used both hands to push and pull the saw back and forth and that seemed to help. I was sweating like crazy and my hands were already getting blistered. The cut I'd made in the branch was only about an inch deep.

"Rest when you need to, son. Don't worry. Do you have any friends from school you can call to help you?"

"No." I don't know this guy and I'm not even sure why I'm doing this instead of doing what I know I should and that is to call professionals. Why didn't he call *his* friends?

"I'm going to take a break, mister," I told him. Even though he was very quiet I could hear that he was breathing hard. I went to the other side of the yard and called my mom at work.

"Cynthia Rossi, how can I help you?" she answered. My mom works at a big bank in the city. She's a loan officer. Most of the time she calls me to see if I got home from school okay so she seemed kind of surprised when she heard my voice. "Is everything okay, Simon? Is something wrong?"

"No, Mom. I'm okay. I just wanted to let you know that I'm helping somebody after school and I might be home little late."

"A friend?" she asked. She sounded surprised and excited at the possibility, but before I could lie she said that's fine and she was happy that I called.

The clouds were starting to look dark and evil again. I knew I'd better hurry up before it started to rain again. As I started sawing on the branch again I heard the man inside the shed moaning a little bit. If he *is* hurt, what am I supposed to do about that?

I wondered how long he'd been in there. "Mister, do you need anything?"

"Well, now that you ask, I am kind of thirsty. You might find a watering can out there. You can dump out the rain water and fill it with the water from the hose."

I looked over at the watering can. It was rusty; I certainly wouldn't drink from that and how was I supposed to get the can through the crack in the door? I shook my head and reached over to my backpack and pulled out a juice box I didn't drink today. My mom always packs a few for me, but all they do is make my bag heavier. I pushed the juice box through the door after I inserted the straw into the hole. I didn't know if old people could manage that. I remembered Dasan had a hard time with doing little things with his fingers. His hands would shake a lot. The old man's bloody hand was shaking too but he grabbed the juice box from my hand and thanked me. I kept sawing the wood but I was barely halfway through. Suddenly an idea occurred to me. Did I really have to saw the whole thing? If I tried to stand on the hacked section and stomp on it maybe it would break. I climbed up onto the branch and stood on the side that had been cut away from the trunk. There was a good chance I wasn't even heavy enough to break the branch. *You Asians would snap like a twig if we wanted to snap you*, I'd heard someone tell me just yesterday. I started to jump up and down on the branch and finally I heard a crack.

"Hey, what are you doing out there?" the old man asked.

"I'm trying to break this branch," I answered as I kept jumping up and down. Finally, the fractured branch gave way and splintered away from the trunk. I climbed back down and pushed the stupid branch as far from the shed door as I could, enough for me to open the door a few inches more and crawl inside. It was pretty dark in there; I could barely see anything, but off to the side I spotted the old man propped against a wheelbarrow and holding on to a shovel. It looked like his head had been bleeding pretty bad, some of the blood was dried to his face and his shirt but some of it was still shiny and oozing out of a wound on his forehead. This guy needed help. I didn't know what I was supposed to do for him. He didn't seem like he was doing so well.

"Hello," he said. "My name is Sal. Thanks for coming along to help me."

I stood there speechless and at a loss to know what to do. Finally I found my voice, "I'm Simon. We gotta get you out of here, mister. You don't look so good."

"I've had worse days than this, son. Let's try to get into the house before it rains again."

19

Befana

Months after I'd left *Padrona's* lonely hovel and her stingy heart, I made my way into the small village at the bottom of the hill. Years before, *Padrona* had taken me away from a house that was run by a group of spinsters; women who had never married or had children of their own who ran a home for abandoned babies – infants who were unwanted by their parents and were left outside to die from exposure to the elements or at the fate of some ravenous animal. *Padrona* was in need of help, she'd said. She'd told the spinsters she would provide me with a home and food and I would help her as she grew old. When she'd taken me into her cave I was too young to remember much of anything, but as I grew older I will never forget the life I'd led, put to work at a young age, given very little to eat, and subject to a great deal of hurtful words. I didn't know I was worth more than her judgment of me. It wasn't until I began to care for other creatures, like those small rabbits, that I began to understand what caring should be.

For several months after I left the cave I wandered around aimlessly, looking for food or a dry, warm place to sleep at night. Eventually, I made my way into a small village a few miles from *Padrona's* cave. As far as the villagers were concerned, I was just one more stray wandering the streets of town along with dogs, cats, and a couple other children that managed to survive exposure. Those were the days before compassion became a belief system. There were kind people here and there, don't get me wrong; the world would not have survived if everyone was like

Padrona, but there was no method of goodwill in place. If someone gave me some bread one day they might not want to do so the next; if I was permitted to sleep in a sheep's stable for one night I had to find another place to sleep on the following night. Kindness was measured, not limitless. Everyone knew how to be kind but they could be fickle about it – it wasn't a standard.

Finally, one day I met a woman named Livinia. She lived alone in a very small hut toward the center of town. She was about twenty-five years of age and she lived on the resources her parents had left her when they died. They had been cloth merchants, moderately successful in their trade, but after Livinia's accident they had used much of what they'd earned to pay for diviners, herbalists, and physicians who might be able to help Livinia walk again. She'd been thrown from a donkey and had landed on her head as a child. Her spine had been injured and she was paralyzed from the waist down from that time on. Livinia had called me over to her hut one day and asked me to fetch a pail of water for her from the town well. Evidently, her slave girl had run away with a neighbor's stable hand the week before. I took the pail from her hand and returned it full of water. She invited me to join her for a drink of water and to eat some bread and cheese with her. Then, that night she allowed me to sleep in her hut by the hearth after I helped her into her small bed by the window.

Had I become her new slave? I don't know. Perhaps. Slavery can come in many forms. A person can be a slave to their own bad habits, for one thing. I've seen many people go to their funeral pyres hanging on to a lifestyle that they justified and that became their downfall. Slavery is evil – whether it comes in the form of oppression against other people, or by voluntary submission to a self-destructive behavior. I don't think my servitude fell into the category of slavery. I allowed myself to serve Livinia because it seemed like the right thing to do. She didn't force me. I knew I could leave at any time. But if I did, who would take care of her? I stayed and helped her because she had no one else. I had no one else either, but I was used to that; I didn't have to stick around and clean her, and hold her head when she vomited. She was a very sick young woman. She didn't have long to live. At night I'd tell her stories that I made up about a family of rabbits. She would tell me stories about what life was like before she'd fallen from the donkey. She'd been loved and doted on by her parents. They had taken her on journeys to many places to buy and sell cloths of many colors and varieties. Once, they'd taken her on a ship to a land where women wore gold on their bodies. I wondered why her parents, clearly of some profitable means, chose to live in this town in such a small house. Why not live in a large city and build a grander home? Her father was born to the trade; his father had been a cloth merchant and his father before him, she'd said. Livinia's father was woven into the fabric of his family's traditions. This had been his family's home. "The thread of life," he'd told her, "can carry you to many places but home is the place where your heart feels loved." Livinia said that though her parents were gone her heart felt loved in this little hut because this is where she had first felt loved. I'd smiled at her tender story but I didn't really grasp it. I had never had a place I called *home*, nor experienced this feeling called love.

During the day Livinia would teach me to make small cakes and sweets. That young woman really had a sweet tooth, I'll tell you. But in her kindness she wouldn't keep all the sweets for herself; she would wrap the sweets into a linen cloth and tell me to go and share the goodies with the children in town. I did so, for a while but I soon discovered that some of the children could be cruel. They knew what I had in the linen knapsack. Sometimes they would snatch my sack and run. If that was all they'd done it would have been bad enough, but most of the time they would jeer at me, taunt me with vicious words, call me repulsive names, and tell me that I was uglier than a dead frog. When I stopped wanting to do Livinia's errand she'd asked me why and I'd told her about the other children. "Hmm," she'd said. "If children can be as cruel to you as they've been to me, it's because they haven't been taught to love anything bigger than themselves." I didn't understand what she'd meant at the time because loving myself wasn't something I'd ever considered. I never had a chance to find out what she meant; within a year Livinia had died. She'd told me to remain in the hut. It was now my home, she'd said. "Love has always lived within these walls," she'd told me, "stay here, and soon love will find you, too."

20

Sister Maria Nicola

When I saw his reflection in the glass doors, I became aware that Krauss had followed me into the library because I saw his face as he jumped off the bus. Usually, I'm the only one that gets off at Pataskala so it was obvious when someone else alighted as well. I made a dash for the non-fiction section which seemed to encompass the largest section of this small library. I wondered if he would actually follow me into the stacks. I peered through the gaps in the books and saw that he was looking around, waiting perhaps, for me to resurface somewhere in the main part of the room. I walked carefully along the back wall of the biography section and into the bathroom. I didn't think he had seen me. Quickly in the first stall I changed back into my habit and shoes and stuffed my sodden street clothes into the bag. I knew he would recognize the bag. In a flash I thought of lodging it in a locker overnight. I could come back for it tomorrow. I knew my clothes would begin to get moldy and smell but I didn't have a choice. I checked myself carefully in the mirror and started out of the bathroom. Krauss was pacing around the circulation desk. Agnes, the younger librarian asked him if he needed any help. He told her he was waiting for someone. The glazed look in his eyes and his unsteady gait must have alerted Agnes that he was high but she returned to her desk and seemed to keep a careful eye on him, probably suspicious of whomever he might be waiting for. I dared not walk past him but he was blocking the path to the exit.

Suddenly I spotted Stella and her friend Emma. On rainy days they hang out in the library at a desk near the mystery section. I sauntered over to them since this was the most natural thing I could do and I sat with them for a while.

"What kind of mischief are you ladies up to today?" I asked the girls.

They both giggled and answered, "Nothing," at the same time.

"Actually, Sister, we are up to *something*," said Stella. I wondered what it was now. I've known Stella's family for years. All the children have been homeschooled. Their parents are brave souls. Robert, their oldest, is high school age and working at St. Asterius two days a week as a bookkeeper in training. He is rather brilliant, our accountant Mr. Foley has said, and has discovered new ways to help the church and school reduce expenses and stay out of debt. I don't know what we'd do without him.

"Okay, I'll bite. What are you up to?" I was almost afraid to ask.

"We want to switch lives for a week," Emma told me.

"Excuse me?"

"We are always complaining about stuff," Stella answered as these girls were always tag-teaming a conversation. "Remember, Sister, when you told us about walking two moons in another man's moccasins? It was the Cheyenne proverb you told us about, something like that, and it made us think of what that would be like. I decided I want to walk in Emma's moccasins and she wants to walk in mine. Just for a week."

I wanted to burst out laughing but I remembered I was in the library and Krauss was still looking for me. My own students don't even listen to me and remember what I say but these two.... "Yes, I remember," I told them, "but *why* do you want to do this? What do you hope to accomplish?" As the girls tagged back and forth about their reasons for wanting to experience a different way of life, *a different childhood*, I watched Krauss out of the corner of my eye. He was growing impatient and he began to look through the different rows until he'd exhausted the entire realm of the Licking County library. At this point he looked irritated and perplexed. He couldn't figure out how I'd gotten past him. Finally, he left the building but I could see that he was still standing outside the door. I don't know why he'd followed me here and I don't know what more he's wanting from me but it seems I'm going to have to give my adventures some further consideration. I need to figure out which of the pair of "moccasins" I'm wearing are the ones that I'm outgrowing.

"At school, you're still going to be responsible for your own work, you know," I counseled the girls. "You may end up having to do twice as much work. Stella you'll still have to complete your own lessons for the homeschool curriculum and do Emma's work to get her full experience. Emma, you'll have to do the same." I could tell by the looks on their faces that they had not considered this possibility. No kid (or adult for that matter) wants to do twice the work for the same benefit. "Think about it," I said. "If you'd still like to try this I can give Mr. Anderson, your principal, Emma, a call and see what he thinks. If it comes from me, maybe he'll be more amenable to the idea."

"You're the best, Sister," they both said and hugged me.

"The rain has let up a bit, let's get out of here," I said. I figured that walking out of here in my nun's habit between two kids would be the best way to get past Krauss without much suspicion. As it turned out he didn't even look our way.

21

Salvatore

Yes, indeed. I had gotten myself into quite a pickle and now I'd dragged a poor kid into the pickle jar with me. For some reason I couldn't remember his name. Did he tell me? I couldn't remember that, either. Kids are very reluctant to tell strangers anything and that's a good thing, but the kid had squeezed us both through the narrow opening of the door past the old poplar tree, helped me into the wheelbarrow, maneuvered me out of the shed, and somehow pulled me up the two back steps of the house and into the kitchen. He helped me to the living room sofa and went to the bathroom to get a wet towel. He put the wet towel on my forehead and got some ice out of the freezer for my knee. He'd seen me at my most vulnerable and certainly at my worst but I couldn't remember his name. That's okay. I've been indebted to countless nameless people all my life, those living and those not, and it's all good. He only stuck around long enough to make sure I was okay but he refused my offers of diabetic cookies in the pantry or some money out of my wallet. Nice little Asian kid, very quiet; he wore navy blue pants, a white shirt, navy tie and vest – probably goes to St. Asterius a few blocks over. I wondered where he lives. I dared not ask. If I did it would probably land me in jail.

Before he left, he went into my fridge and made me a boloney sandwich and brought me a few bottles of water and set them on the coffee table. All he said on his way out the door was "You should be more careful, mister." Isn't that what old people usually say to kids? Things change.

I spent the night and most of the next day on the sofa. I called the guy that mows the lawn to come and see about getting rid of the tree. It will cost me four hundred bucks. Really? Four hundred bucks seems like quite a lot since the good Lord already took the tree down; all this knucklehead has to do is cut it up and sell it for firewood. He wouldn't even cut me a break after gouging me to mow my lawn these past few years. It's an insurance thing, he said. Fine, then. I'll get someone else and I sent him away. He gave me an idea. I called the insurance company. They're going to send someone out to take care of it and help me put in a claim. Do businesses think old people are stupid?

I managed to get to the bathroom using Annalisa's walker that still sat in the corner of the room. Holy Mother of God, my face was a mess. I must have scared that poor kid. I washed up, took off my clothes and put on my pajamas and bathrobe. I wasn't going anywhere anytime soon. I laid back down on the sofa when I heard the doorbell ring. I can't imagine it's the insurance fella already. "Who is it?" I yelled.

"It's Simon," came the answer.

"Who?"

"From yesterday," the small voice answered.

"Oh, the kid. Come in. I never did get up to lock the door." That was his name! Simon.

He walked in cautiously. "You should lock your door, mister."

"Well, today, lock it on your way out. Listen, kid, thanks again for helping me yesterday. I'd probably still be in that darn shed if you hadn't come by."

"I just came to see how you're doing, mister. I have to get home."

"My name is Sal, kid. Stop calling me mister."

"My name is Simon; stop calling me kid."

"It's a deal."

He seemed okay but he also seemed like he was kind of alone. Did anyone come around to see him? "Do you need anything, Sal?"

"Did you bring a pizza?"

"No."

"I'm kidding. Sort of. You want an afterschool snack?"

"No, thanks. I have to get home. Do you want me to make you another sandwich before I go home?"

"That would be nice, kid. I mean, Simon. Yeah, thanks. A sandwich is good when life throws you a pickle."

He shook his head and went into the kitchen. He came back out with a plate – he'd made me a sandwich and put a pickle on the plate this time. I looked at him and smiled. He seemed a little raw but there was something else about him that was different. Most kids I've seen act like they're permanently five years old, but there was something deeply authentic about this kid.

"Do you need anything else?" he asked.

"I don't actually mind the company, but I know you have to get home."

"I can stay for a minute," he said.

"Sit down, then, Simon. You can get yourself a sandwich, too, if you want one." He shook his head.

We hit that awkward moment when neither of us knew what to say next. "Well, tell me about yourself, Simon. Where do you go to school?" He pointed to his tie. The St. Asterius logo, a cross and sword, embroidered in yellow thread was surrounded by a white flag.

"Ahh… Do you like it there?" He shook his head.

"Mmm, school is school, isn't it? No matter where you go, there are things about it that are the same – teachers, homework, boring stuff, and other kids. It's not always fun."

"Tell me about yourself, mister. Oops, I mean Sal. Why were you in the shed during a bad storm?"

I chuckled. "Good question, Simon. I went into the shed so I wouldn't be outside during the storm. Lucky, too; that tree could have come down on my head." His eyes widened as he thought about that. "I just putter around in my garden sometimes. That's what old people do."

"I guess it can be the same for a lot of old people," he answered. "Puttering around, boring stuff, not much to do. Not always fun?" This kid had a way of turning everything I said on its heels. I stared at him for a few moments. He stared right back at me.

"Can I ask you a question?" he asked me.

"Sure, ask away."

"If you could live a different life right now than the one you have, what kind of life would you have? Where would you live? What would you be doing? Who would you want to be here?"

"That's more than one question, Simon. Those are a lot of very good questions. I guess my answer isn't very imaginative, though. I would want the life I used to have with my wife here and my kids, my job... It was a life, but it was in the past. This... this is... I don't know what this is. But, maybe it's just part of being old."

"Maybe, I'm old, too, Sal. I got to go home now. I'll stop back tomorrow and make you a sandwich."

I wasn't sure what he meant by that. I was going to tell him he didn't have to stop over again, but I stopped. I had a feeling he needed to make sandwiches.

22

Stella

We've called our project #*moccasinswap*. Stella did something with this project name called tweeting. I don't get all that jargon on social media because my parents said that it can sometimes lead to privacy problems and even mob mentality. My parents are not very understanding of what I feel like having to live in a world in which I am unable to participate fully. I don't think they're entirely wrong about stuff but I think they should prepare me for the world I will eventually have to live in, right? When I presented #*moccasinswap* to Mom, Dad, and Grandma, they all three looked at me like I was strange. Dad automatically shook his head and said, "Absolutely not." Mom didn't say anything at all, she just looked at me with a puzzled look on her face (like she did that time I rode my bike past the county line without telling them how far I intended to go) and then Grandma said, "Wait a minute, I think we should hear the whole plan first before we bring down the guillotine." I love my Grandma.

"It's just for one week," I explained. "I will continue to do all my homeschool lessons as usual but I will live in Emma's house and go to Emma's school and see what her day is like from beginning to end. She will do all her schoolwork and live here and see what it's like to be homeschooled and live with you guys. We don't plan on causing trouble. I will obey her parents and she promises to obey you because the whole idea is to get the real-life experience from doing this."

Mom's eyebrows went up. "Well," she said, "I do like Emma very much and I have always respected her parents as well. I know you will be okay with her family, Stella, it's just how you will adjust to her school that I wonder about. You've never been in that kind of environment before."

"I don't know if it's all that different, Mom. The teachers are in charge, it's not like I'm going to a wild animal zoo without gates and supervision. Emma says there are rules; there is a disciplinary code, and structure. You do the same thing only it's right here in our house. You've prepared me for that environment to some degree, right?"

Dad looked adamantly against the idea. He and Mom hadn't dedicated their lives to their own project of homeschooling every one of us kids only to let me out of the nest to *experiment*, not only with real school but with another family! He wrapped his knuckles gently on the table. "Stella, you've made your case. Let *us* discuss this. Go into the other room." Progress! Whenever Dad put it up for discussion it was a good sign. My father is not a tyrant – he is always a fair man even when I can't see it, that's what I love about him.

From the bathroom I get the best acoustics that come out of the kitchen. Perhaps the voices are carried along the plumbing pipes that connect the rooms to one another.

Grandma spoke first. "Stella's a good kid. She'll do whatever you say. If you decide against it, she'll obey you, but you might plant a seed of resentment, something she doesn't have now."

Dad said, "Let's consider why we decided to homeschool our children in the first place. One, we wanted them to follow a specific curriculum that may or may not be used in the county schools. We did our own homework first. The county schools report that many students have problems with reading. We have a stronger program. Stella's reading level is years ahead of her peers. Her math scores are very good. She excels in history and does well in science."

"Larry! She's only asking for one week! Her abilities will not be diminished because of her exposure to another system of education for five days! You're avoiding the real issue. You're afraid of the social element, admit it," Mom said.

"Okay, I admit it, that is point number two. We have been teaching our kids reading, math, history, science, all the subjects that are taught in county schools, but the one thing we've managed to do with our children here in this home is to create a loving environment where they can learn and preserve their childhood while they are still children. That is the difference, isn't it? I don't want Stella exposed to any kind of hostile environment – we've seen the news, the things that can happen in the schools. Is the environment in the town school a loving, nurturing setting where kids can just be kids? I love all our kids, but all three of us sitting here know one thing for sure: out of all the kids, Stella is the one with the biggest heart, the most loving and generous spirit. She's good down to the core. When the boys cause trouble, who's the one that steps in and tries to put out the fires? She's so *good* but maybe that's because she is a little naïve, too. I can only conclude that she is such a sweet kid because we've – well, mostly you and Ma – have done such a good job with our kids, shielding them from threats to their childhood. Especially with Stella; she's a very special kid and I just don't know if it's fair to present her with this kind of a challenge."

Even though Dad was afraid of going along with this idea, I wanted to run out of the bathroom and hug him.

"Larry, you're my son, you're a good man, and you and Beth are doing a wonderful job raising these kids. I respect you for that, and what you said is true, Stella is a gem. I don't think any one of us can take credit for that. She is the way she is by nature. And this is *her* idea. Listen to what she's asking: she wants to 'walk in her friend's moccasins for a week.' Isn't this what we want for all our kids, to understand what the world is like by walking in someone else's shoes? Don't we want to teach them that kind of understanding and compassion? Of course there are dangers, and I think the homeschooling idea is great but you can't teach this kind of lesson in a homeschool program and you probably can't teach it in the mainstream classroom, either. All you can do is expose kids to the *idea* of what others go through but you can't make them live it from the inside. This is a good opportunity for Stella, and let's not forget sweet little Emma, so she can learn something neither one of them can learn in either classroom."

It was all I could do not to go out and hug Grandma, too.

Mom said, "I think we should ask both girls to keep a journal about their experiences each day. Then, perhaps, they can discuss it with us so that we can enrich their understanding with a 'what did we learn from this experience' study. What do you think?"

I heard Dad exhale loudly. That's Mom for you, she's the teacher. She makes it sound like the decision has already been made in favor of my proposal, now let's see how we can turn this cockamamie idea into a lesson? I love my Mom.

I'm thinking there is another lesson here, too. Maybe every kid should eavesdrop on their family once in a while when their parents are unaware that someone is listening. Mostly what kids hear from parents on a daily basis is "Are those your socks? Did you finish unloading the dishwasher yet? How many times have I told you to set your alarm clock before you go to sleep?" Every now and then kids should hear what their parents really think about them. When Mom called out that I could come back into the room I didn't let on that I'd heard them talking; I just walked up to each one of them and hugged them after they told me about their decision. Grandma had that funny twinkle in her eyes. She knew I was listening.

23

Befana

You know you're old when you've stopped dreaming about the future. No one wants to get *that* old! It has nothing to do with age; people can grow too tired to dream, they can give way to illnesses that keep them from thinking about anything else but the end of pain, or they can focus on the past too much. Think about it: most of the time young people will say things like when I get older I want to be a doctor, teacher, nurse, whatever… They get a little older and they talk about saving money for a house, getting married, starting a family. Then, the day comes when they plan for their children's future, or grandchildren. And then the mid-life stage has them planning and dreaming about retirement and travelling – seeing and doing things they didn't have time to do while they were younger and working. The unmagical age is when they stop saying "*someday, I want to…*" that is when they have arrived at old age. You see, the trick to never getting "old" is to wake up every morning and imagine a new dream for the future. Keep telling yourself that someday you think you'd like to do something new. It happens – people in their eighties go back to school to get another college degree; they may even teach a class about a subject they've taken eighty years to learn well; they actually embark on new journeys. They keep using the word *someday*; it's quite a powerful word when you think about it.

There's an old story about God giving one of his friends (his name was Moses) a job to do when he was already long in the tooth – get those people out of Egypt, he'd said, and if that wasn't enough, *someday* he would have his aging friend climb a mountain to have a chat. Can you imagine that? Moses must have had good knees; better than mine! He isn't the only one that God nudged along. There was another fella named Abraham that had to move to a new home in Canaan when he was seventy-five. And good ol' Jacob had to move to Egypt when he was one-hundred and thirty. It's okay to keep thinking about someday, no matter how old you get. God wants us to keep moving along. That's why he has me kicking around the world year after year after year. I don't have to climb any mountains, thank God, but I do have to visit people and try to help them find what I've been looking for.

From what I've heard there aren't a great many women who get recorded as reaching ultra-advanced ages or being life-long travelers for unending periods of time. I seem to be a rare breed for many reasons. Yes, it's often men who get their names etched into the bedrock of time and regularly assigned to tasks that require them to travel. My early years spent in cave-dwelling left me with some pains in my joints and shortness of breath so I never did much travelling in my lifetime. By some standards, I was already an old lady by the time I hit twenty. Back then, my secret wanting was for home and family but it wasn't meant to be. I once remember thinking that I wanted to be able to do something that helped me fit in to the culture around me, to be able to blend in with the wives and mothers and maybe have the people in the village think of me as the best baker in town, not the weird old recluse. Though my cynical little heart didn't know it at the time, all those years of scratching out a lonely existence caused me to want to have new experiences with other people *someday*. A lack of family made me want to learn how to care for others. Seclusion caused me to want to be included in other peoples' lives. If my life had been different, maybe I wouldn't have been so eager to follow a dream in my old age. If I'd had everything my neighbors had maybe I would have been too busy to notice a bright star that beckoned me to follow. If I'd been truly satisfied with my routine life, then perhaps I would not have taken up an uncertain journey in the middle of the night; maybe I wouldn't have been up for this task of endless travel. It took me a lifetime to learn how to dream; when I was young I didn't dream of wild adventures, so people thought of me as an old lady and now that I am "old" I feel like I get younger every day because my life is filled with endless possibilities and new adventures. With each new experience I'm a part of someone else's life, not just my own and I'm learning each day how to care about others. That happened because someone cared about me first: the only one that ever cared – and that was the caring God.

I'll say it again, when old *Padrona* told me that it would have been better if I'd never been born, she was wrong. If there was no other purpose to my life than learning about this thing called love, then it was worth it all right. I'm not sure *Padrona* ever learned that.

Someday, I'm going to see where this journey takes me. I know there is a destination to every journey or it's just aimless wandering, right? Everyone agrees that life is a journey and journeys are only worth it if you're going *some where*.

24

Simon

The old guy, Sal, told me he called his son, Joe, and that his son brought him some groceries. I'm glad about that. I was starting to think that the poor old guy doesn't have anybody to help him or do stuff for him. He was so strict about me not calling for help because he didn't want anybody to see him like that and I thought maybe he was some kind of nut or recluse. He hasn't said too much about his family and I don't tell him about mine. I'm not sure why I like stopping by his house to check up on him. That's what he called it: he said I was *checking up on him* but he was smiling when he said it so I don't think he minds. Besides, he really seems to like it when I make him a sandwich. He always smiles when I bring him a plate with just a plain old baloney sandwich on it. It's weird really, the things that make old people happy. He asked me what makes me happy. I couldn't answer him. What is it with people: Sal, my teacher, and even my parents, asking me all these dumb questions I don't know the answers to? Why can't they just leave me alone?

The thing I like about Sal is that even when he asks me dumb questions he doesn't sit there and give me the long, hard stare waiting for me to answer. If I don't answer him I think he forgets he asked me a question and he goes on to something else. Yesterday, after he asked me what makes me happy, he started telling me this long story about when he got his first bicycle.

"Do you have a bicycle?" he asked me.

"Yeah, but I don't ride it," I told him.

"Why not?" I didn't answer and so he kept talking, "I was younger than you, oh, by maybe a couple of years when I got my first bicycle. It wasn't new; it was old and rusty. My parents couldn't afford to buy me a new bike. This was back in Italy, a long, long time ago. I think my Papa actually got it in exchange for a sack of lemons from a man he knew whose father died. It was the dead man's old bicycle. Anyway, my Papa brought it home to me and told me that he had a gift for me. The bike was still outside when he came through the beaded curtains of our house and said, Sal, *vieni qua.* He said, *you're what, ten years old now? Good boy. I have a present to give you. Come here.* He led me outside to the alley and said, *there it is – una bicicletta. You're old enough to go to work with me now. You don't have to walk; you can ride the bicycle and carry the lemons in the baskets. See the baskets on each side?*"

At that point, Sal looked like his eyes were seeing the past alone and he waved his arms and pointed to things that were not there in his living room but somewhere way back in his past. He'd point into the past and "show" me where his father's land was situated alongside Via Rustica, and then he'd chuckle about his father's donkey, Boni, and he'd rub the bandage on his head. I think the pain from the cut in his forehead brought him back to the present and he seemed surprised for a second to see me sitting there.

"What was I saying, oh yes, the bicycle. The day I got my first bicycle kind of marked the end of my childhood, you see. At ten years old, I didn't have to go to school anymore. The law said only until the fifth year.

"What?" I asked. "Are you kidding me? Dude, that would be nice."

"*Dude,*" Sal answered, "it wasn't nice. I had to go to work instead of school. I got up before the sun came up and went with my father to our lemon groves. I picked lemons all day. I raked and tilled the soil. I had to dig up stones and fix the wall around our property. Pshh, I had to climb the trees and prune the branches. Every day, I had to ride that darn bicycle laden with hundreds of lemons for 2 or 3 kilometers. I would have been happier in school, sitting on my butt learning to spell words and add my sums. I didn't get to play with my friends anymore. I had to work. I did that kind of work until I was seventeen, then my Papa, he died. The lemon groves, he shared with my Uncle Alfredo, but my uncle didn't like farm work so he sold the land and with his half of the money he came to America. For a while I had to get a real job so I could save up some money and come to America, too. My uncle had found work in the steel factories in Pennsylvania. I did that for a while but it was an *inferno*. Do you know what that is, Simon? An *inferno* is hell. I met a guy in the factory that had some connections for jobs around here. There was an old shoemaker's shop just down the road, I apprenticed there for a while and then got my own shop. Yes, that's what I did. And you know what? I bought myself a shiny new bicycle to use for going to work. I didn't get a car until the kids started coming along in the 50's. We needed a car to put the kids into. But by then I needed steadier work, too, so I got a job in the meat markets."

This was so much more than I needed to know about Sal. I only came by to make sure he was doing all right and maybe make him a sandwich. I wondered sometimes if he was even aware that he's living in 2015. All he ever talks about is stuff that happened a long time ago. I've heard some stories about Italy, some about when he was in the army, and some stories about the only time he went on a vacation when he was thirteen, my age, he said.

His mother had wanted to go and visit a *living presepio*. I'd never heard of a *presepio*, living or otherwise. He said his Papa piled up his nine kids into the wagon and he and his wife rode up front with the two donkeys – Esmerelda and Boni– the journey took all day long until they came to a place called San Severino where this *living presepio* was supposed to be on display. That night his Papa covered the wagon with an old canvas sheet and the nine children slept beneath it with their Mamma. His father slept outside with the donkeys to make sure they were okay and his family was safe. In the morning, they all walked down the path called *Strada di Vita*, lined on each side with grape vines and fruit trees until they came to a stretch of land outside a monestary and that is where they found the *living presepio*.

When I told Sal I didn't know what a *living presepio* was he chuckled and said, "Oh, my boy, it was a nativity set with real people and animals. All of us kids went straight for the animals; to us it was like a petting zoo. My mother went to talk to the lady that played Mary and she even asked if she could hold the Baby Jesus. Mary seemed relieved and let my Mamma hold the baby for a long time. My Papa went over to the makeshift "inn" where there had been no room for the Holy Family and he talked to the wood carver who pretended to run the inn. The man was very talented; he fashioned small stable animals and charged only 5 lire for a set of wooden barn animals for all of us to play with.

The wood carver had a funny little statue of *La Befana* sitting next to his table. Papa asked how much for the *Befana* statue but the wood carver told him 'she's not for sale.' Papa told the wood carver that the legend of *La Befana* was part of a story that had once saved him from going too far down the wrong path." Sal was quiet for a moment. He put his head in his hands, took a deep breath and then spoke again.

"My Papa and his brother Alfredo were being trained to… how can I say this… make people disappear." Sal looked at me intently with a sad look in his eyes. "How old are you, Simon?" Before I had a chance to answer, he continued slowly. "You look old enough to hear this. I don't mean your age; I mean your sensibilities. I don't see it in too many kids anymore. But, anyway, my Papa and Uncle Alfredo were living during bad times, very bad times in Italy. The government was going from bad to worse, very corrupt, and the decent people in small towns didn't know which way to turn. When *Il Duce* came to power he had a big axe to grind with the church. He didn't make any bones about how much he didn't want the church to interfere in his business. Where we lived some of his followers started taking matters into their own hands. They started rounding up church-going people that spoke up against *Il Duce* and taking them out of the town somewhere, I don't know what they did with them. Papa and Uncle Alfredo joined up with them. It was either join them, or fight them, he said. One Christmas, my grandmother, suspecting that her sons were doing something unforgiveable, grabbed both of them by the ears and took them to a small chapel in our village called *La Cappella dei Santi Martiri*.

For a long time she just sat there and told her sons to sit in front of an ailing Christmas tree. After several minutes had passed she told her boys to empty their pockets. The boys resisted. My grandmother said, 'If you don't empty your pockets right here, right now, I will leave you here and you will not be allowed to come home. Still, the boys resisted. My grandmother said, 'Fine, before I go I will tell you a story and then you must stay here. I will not lay eyes on you again.' My grandmother told them the story about King Herod, how he was so thirsty for power and so determined to kill the Baby Jesus that he sent his soldiers to kill every baby boy born in Bethlehem and the surrounding area. He wanted to wipe out any trace of this infant savior before he had a chance to live. So many innocent children were killed because of one man's greed for power.' Papa said my grandmother was crying when she told this story. '*Il Duce* is trying to do the same thing as that stupid king, *you fools*. To go against the church is to go against Jesus – make no mistake about that and if you're mixed up in that I will leave you here; you'll no longer be my sons. Those men, the Magi, had the courage to go against a powerful king, and find a different route home so they wouldn't have to help him. Now, don't you ever forget the story of the old woman *Befana*; she lived during a time when she could be killed for following Jesus, too, but she wanted to follow the Magi and find the Baby Jesus. Even a poor old woman had more courage than my two sons. You empty your pockets, you can come home. You keep to your business, you go your own way.' Papa and Uncle Alfredo sat there without saying a word and then they both went to the tree and emptied their pockets of rope, knives, and lists of names. They put their secret badges under the tree as well. It was one thing for powerful men like the Magi to have courage; that was to be expected of men, but a poor, defenseless, elderly lady? Italian boys have some pride – they could not be proven to have less courage than an old woman.

They'd grown up with the story of *La Befana*. They had nothing against her. They had nothing against Jesus, or the church really. They were just following the tide and the time had come for them to decide what was more important – to follow a fascist ruler or the respect the church. Simon, every man, young or old, has to face a crossroad at some point in his life. My Papa explained this story to the wood carver. The man nodded his head and gave Papa the statue for free. 'She's not for sale,' he'd said. 'She goes where she is needed.' When he finished his story, Sal reached over and picked up a statue of an old woman from the lamp stand. "Here she is. This is that statue of *La Befana*. We call her *Old Befana* because her legend is so old; I don't think *she* gets any older! I want you to have her."

I held the little statue in my left hand and stroked her smooth wooden features with the fingers of my right hand. She didn't look very special as far as statues go, but there was something interesting about the way she smiled. She did have kind of a feisty look – Sal called it courage.

"You hang on to her for me, will you Simon?" Sal asked. "It's not a superstition thing, my boy. She doesn't bring good luck or anything like that. Do that thing you kids do on the computer – look up her story on the net. You'll see what I mean. Her story only points to the Christmas story. There is nothing about her that stands alone. Now, you'd better get home and do your homework. I've kept you too long today."

I put the little statue into my shirt pocket but I didn't get up right away. "Can I ask you a question, Sal?"

"Sure. What's on your mind?"

"Why do you like baloney sandwiches so much? I've heard they're pretty gross."

"What kind of sandwiches do you like, Simon?"

"I don't actually like sandwiches that much."

"I'll tell you a secret. I don't like baloney sandwiches, either. I never have. When my kids were little, they were the ones that liked baloney sandwiches. When I would come home from work for lunch they would take turns making me a baloney sandwich. I ate the sandwich, not because I liked baloney, but because I loved my kids so much. It used to mean a lot to them that I pretended to love the sandwich they made me. I never told them otherwise. Joe is fifty-three years old now; he still thinks I love baloney and buys it for me at the supermarket. I eat the darn stuff because I have a son who cares enough to go to the store and buy his old dad some baloney."

"I won't tell anyone," I said. "What do you like instead?"

"Ahhh, I like mortadella and provolone, maybe some salami or prosciutto, but you can't find any good stuff around here."

I got up to leave. "Thanks for the statue, Sal. See you tomorrow."

I put my hand on my shirt pocket over the place where the little statue sat. Weird little thing, I thought. I was curious about her story. She had courage, Sal said. She could have been killed for following Jesus. The old man named Dasan back in Korea; he'd gone to jail. He'd followed Jesus, too.

25

Stella

"*Annnd*?" I urged my friend. Emma could be quite exasperating when she dragged things out. She agreed swapping lives for a week would be fun. I went through the hoops to get my parents' permission. Her parents had kind of laughed and said, "Interesting...," now she was keeping me on pins and needles about what her school principal had to say.

"Well, it's complicated, Stell," she'd told me when I asked her for the third time.

"It doesn't seem that complicated; it's either yes or no. What did the Mr. Anderson say?"

"He didn't actually say anything like yes or no; he gave me a five page form for my teachers to sign and that my parents have to sign. I have to read and sign it and then I have to write up a description of my "project" as they call it, state my reasons for wanting to carry out this project, and make a list of what I plan to do. Then, you have to do the same thing – get your parents' signatures plus you have to provide the school with a copy of your shots record and get a signed character reference from somebody; I would ask Sister from the library since she knows your family and she already talked to Mr. Anderson. Is this worth it, Stell?"

"I don't mind doing what I have to do to get this project going. Did you get all the signatures?"

"Yep. Everything is signed but I still have to write up my description, reasons and plan. I have a lot of homework this week and I don't know when I'm going to find the time to do all this."

"You sound like you've lost interest. Is there something else you're not telling me? Have you changed your mind? We can sit down together and hash out the description, reasons and plan together and it won't take as long, but I have to know if you are backing out."

"No, I'm not backing out. It's just…" I really don't like it when she lets her sentences trail off like that. She doesn't say anything until I repeat it like a question.

"It's just, what?"

"It's just that after one week, Stella, you can step back into your family and take up where you left off. They're your family for heaven's sake. You do family stuff with them and you do school stuff with them, it's all the same people – you're all solid, like you said. My life is compartmentalized. My family and my school don't mix. Sure, I can come back into my family but school is a whole different ball game. You kind of have to earn your friends there and if I step out of the game, do I have to start all over again to earn my way back in?"

"And then there's Jack, right? He may forget about you while you're out for a week? I get it. If you don't want to, it's okay. You won't hurt my feelings, honest."

"No, I still want to, and yes, I think of Jack. But I'm not worried about him forgetting about me. I haven't even made any progress with him noticing me. I would love a chance to get to talk to him and maybe go to Betty's ice cream shop with him. Other kids in my class do that all the time."

"Does he ever go there with another girl?"

"No. He just hangs out with his friends. You know, the more I think about it, the more I want to do this swap. Maybe getting away from my life for a week will give me a new perspective when I come back."

"You are not afraid he's going to notice *me*, are you? Because if that's the case I can assure you I am 100% unnoticeable."

Emma laughed. "No, good grief. Even if he did, I trust you. It's just…"

Sigh. "Just what?"

"Nothing. Forget it. Let's get this paperwork finished so we can move forward. There are only a few weeks of school left anyway before break."

There was something about Emma's tone that concerned me. She sounded worried about something but she wasn't saying anything more. I could be wrong; it could just be about her crush on Jack, but something told me there was more to it. Even the closest of friends don't fess up about everything. Good friends supposedly tell each other *everything*, but first they sift through all there is to share before they tell their friend everything else. And, just look at how many best friends stop speaking to each other because they don't agree on everything. Some things they don't agree on are very important but some things just aren't worth losing a friend over. I hope I would never have to choose between something important to me and my friendship with Emma. I don't think I could ever make that choice. Grandma always says we should make the right first choice then future choices are a bit more obvious. Choose your friends wisely so you don't have to make tough choices later. Choose to do the loving thing first and you can live with the other choices you have to make. It's not always easy, Grandma says, but try to choose the path that does the least amount of harm so your tears won't be so heavy, your regrets will be few, and it's easier to ask for forgiveness.

As I sit and write my own description for our project, my reasons (which I'm borrowing from the conversation I overheard in which my parents and grandma had good reasons for letting me do this) and my plan to succeed, I wonder if Emma and I have a strong enough friendship to withstand such an intimate intrusion into each other's lives.

26

Sister Maria Nicola

It has been the kind of day that feels like a successful mistake. All of my attempts at encouragement and goodwill ended in mistrust and relapse. I feel that I've lost so much more than I ever gained at any point along the way. I keep asking God if I'm really as much of a disappointment to him as I feel I am to myself. He doesn't answer right away. I get the feeling that he wants me to choose one path and stay on it instead of trying to divide myself between my passions and my vocation.

Krauss confronted me as soon as I entered the basement the following week. Sandy, Maggie, and Sara were already there when I arrived. Their eyes all aimed barbs of suspicion in my direction as soon as he said, "So, what is your game, Liz? And you'd better tell the truth because we're all experts at lying enough to spot a liar when we see one."

"What are you talking about? What game?"

"Yep, always start with ignorance, that's classic – not original, though. Strike one. Last week, we all decided I should follow you, where you go and what you're up to. No one around here knows where you crash. They all see you around but nobody knows where you come from or where you go. So, I got on the bus and I followed you to some hellhole out in the country and into a library, of all places. Funny thing, too, you disappeared into the book shelves somewhere and I never saw you again. So, I'm going to ask you again, what's your game, Liz?"

"Just because I take a bus to other places doesn't mean I have a game. I have other connections in many places that don't concern you. Too bad you're always too stoned to see what's right in front of you." I heard Sandy laugh but I didn't break my eye contact with Krauss.

"Liar's method number two: always follow up ignorance with distraction. Don't answer the question directly but redirect it so that you don't have to answer. You're digging in deeper here, Lizzy. These are typical manipulation techniques. If you can't get the upper hand in a poker game then throw the ball to left field and maybe everyone will look over there instead. Strike two. I'm asking a third time: what is your game?"

"You're mixing your stupid metaphors, Krauss. I said get off my back. I told you I don't have a game and if you're going to keep at me you'd better have something more solid than vague suspicions about a non-existent game to harass me about. So, either ask me a direct question or back down. Your ridiculous instincts may just be some bad meth and paranoia. If you want a better answer then ask a better question, or get out of my face."

Krauss turned and looked at Sandy, Maggie and Sara. Their lukewarm concern was palpable. They didn't like aggression, either, but they were so used to it by now that violence only pushed them farther down the spiral where they could fool themselves into thinking they're getting away from it. I only saw Sandy out of the corner of my eye; she was looking at the door, the way out.

"Okay, Liz, have it your way." Krauss grabbed my arm so tightly I thought my wrist would break. "Once ignorance and distraction don't work the trained liar goes on the offense. Beautifully done, but strike three." Krauss pulled out his knife. "Now, let's see if I can keep my metaphors from getting mixed up and ask you a better question. Where do you come from and where do you go?"

I didn't flinch. I stared right into his eyes. I could feel my stomach collapsing but my resolve did not. "Go ahead and hurt me. If you think you're so smart, go ahead. If I am a narc or whatever you suspect then someone knows I'm here and they'll know what to do with you because they have your name and you can't get away. If you want things to go on as they have been, then let go of my arm and mind your own business. Where I come from doesn't concern you as long as I bring you what you need. Where I go when I leave here is my business. I don't ask YOU, *not any of you,* where you go when we leave here. Find someone else to supply you, harass them like you're harassing me, find a new hideout, do whatever you want, but get out of my face and don't you *ever* threaten me again. That's my direct answer to your questions." I could see the molten anger behind those bloodshot eyes. Krauss wasn't fooling around. He was very angry that he'd followed me and lost me. He wanted answers and he wasn't getting them. He wanted to save face now but he had to decide between his needs and his wants. He compromised; before letting go of my arm, he slashed my arm and pushed me against the wall. I took the bag I knew he wanted out of my backpack and threw it on the floor. I held my arm and left the basement, making a mad dash for the bus before it pulled away from the stop. I hoped that I'd thrown him off of my destination by suggesting that there were other places besides the place to which he had followed me; I didn't want him to follow me there again. I knew if I didn't return to the basement again next week he would seek me out starting with my library. I couldn't risk bringing this part of my life too closely into the other part.

I never dared carry anything in my backpack except for what I needed. Fortunately though, I had placed a towel in there just in case of rain again. Now, I used the towel to wrap my arm and hold it tightly to limit the bleeding. I don't think the knife went in very deeply; there was no way I could go to a hospital without raising even more questions I did not want to answer. I squeezed my eyes shut remembering poor little Simon standing in front of my desk this afternoon clearly not wanting to answer my questions, either.

"Did you think about what I asked you, Simon?"

He remained silent. For some reason this poor kid doesn't trust me. I wonder if there is anyone at all that he can trust.

"If you could have a different life right now, what life would you like to have?"

He shrugged his shoulders as he'd done so many times before.

"You know, Simon, if I could choose a different life for myself right now I think I would want a life that isn't quite so predictable each day. What about you?"

"I don't mind life being predictable," he'd answered.

"Do you want the same thing tomorrow that you have today?"

"I don't know. No offense, Sister, but maybe tomorrow I can come to school and my teacher will ask me only the questions based on today's lessons. I don't know what people want from me. If I could have a different life I would want one that made some sense. May I please go home now?"

I felt so sorry for him. *I don't know what people want from me,* he'd said. I'd suddenly felt like I was harassing him. There seemed to be plenty of that going around today.

27

Befana

When a person is tough, a lot of people get the idea that that person isn't very sensitive or they are without feelings. That's about as close to the truth as east is to west. At least that's been my experience with people who are strong – they are not without emotion and they are not purely thoughtless. It's like Italian biscotti – these are some pretty tough cookies but they can be sweet and they can become soft, but there is no question about it, they are hard cookies. I used to make them all the time because I liked giving cookies to babies who were teething. Biscotti are cookies that are baked twice. People in my day used to bake some types of bread and cookies twice so that they would become tough and less perishable; these hardened baked goods travelled well.

Tough people, you could say, have been hardened like biscotti, too. Some people are naturally strong, I think. They might be afraid but fear doesn't stop them from pursuing what they want in life; they might have worries but anxiety won't hold them back from taking charge. Life puts everyone through, shall we say *hell*, at one time or another. That is where the additional hardening comes in; these people whose personalities are strong to begin with can become hardened when they go through the pain. Being born strong doesn't keep you from feeling pain any more than having a weaker personality means you feel nothing but pain. Everyone has the choice to be kind, not to use their strengths or weaknesses in a bad way.

Ginella and her husband Renato tried for many years to have children. This was back when people didn't have much help with those kinds of problems. In general, people had to put their faith and trust in God. They were convinced that if God wanted them to have children, they would have them, and if he didn't, they would remain childless; they learned to accept things. Ginella wanted children very badly and she refused to accept the fact that she would never be a mother because somewhere in her heart she felt like she was already a mother; her children had simply not arrived yet. One day Ginella and Renato decided to take a small holiday by the sea. Ginella had always wanted to visit the coast and out of love for his wife, Renato took her to a village in the south of Italy that bragged about its magical sunsets. At dusk, Ginella and Renato held hands and watched as the sun appeared to dance gently and unwind in its final moments of the day. It would gradually change colors and melt into the waters of the sea relinquishing any claim it once had on the day. This beautiful experience, night after night, gave the peasant couple an appetite for eating foods that came from these waters so each night after the sun went down, Renato would go to the local fishermen who were hauling in their nets and he bought a basket full of freshly caught urchins and clams. Under the starry sky, Ginella and Renato drank wine and cracked open the rock-like shells of the creatures and ate raw sea urchins and clams while listening to the minstrels singing evening songs in the distance. This holiday habit brought the middle-aged couple closer than they'd ever been and when they returned home from their lovely getaway, Ginella realized she was pregnant. Within a few short months Ginella's abdomen had grown to the size of a watermelon. The midwife explained, "You are carrying more than one child, I'm afraid. At your age, this could be dangerous."

Ginella grew tired and could no longer carry on with her daily chores. Renato hired some young village girls to come and help his wife. Some of the girls were lazy and helped to do one or two chores, then soon became bored and left to find other work, but one girl, in particular, was robust and she took control of the entire household. Her name was Sabrina and it was lucky for

Ginella that this young woman had a strong back, a spirited personality, and a take-charge attitude because when Ginella went into labor and the midwife came to deliver the babies, there were not one, not two, but three infants born to this once-childless family. The difficult labor took its toll on poor Ginella and shortly after delivering the three children she died. Renato, was heartbroken at losing his beloved wife. He didn't know what he was going to do with three children. He was in desperate need of help. He knew that this young servant girl was kind and capable so he asked Sabrina to marry him. Sabrina agreed to marry the older man; she became mistress of the household, and raised the three young boys: Maurizio, Franco, and Donato as her own. Sabrina worked hard each day to maintain the *masseria* while Renato managed the workers and the fields. The babies were a handful, to say the least, but as they grew older they entertained each other and required little attention from their step-mother or their father. Yet, tragedy hit once again when their father, now in his sixties, had a heart attack and died in the fields. The workers were rather greedy and decided to take over the land and move into the *masseria* with their wives and families. This action forced Sabrina into a showdown with the tenants. She did not own the land by law but she was mistress of the house and she fought them tooth and nail. The workers were not afraid of this bold young woman. They forced her into the stables and took her life without batting an eye. The three young orphans were then forced into labor. It was Maurizio's job to tend to the animals and clean the stables each day. Franco was made to thresh wheat and gather it into large sacks, and Donato had the task of ridding the large fields of weeds, insects and rodents.

Though the three children were triplet brothers they were each very different in personality: Maurizio was considered stronger than the other two but soon his outlook became weakened by his circumstances. Fiesty and impulsive, Franco showed himself to be a bit unreliable and his brothers warned him that they needed to stick together. One day, while they rested in the shade during the middle of the day, Donato, who was considered the tender-hearted one of the three, began to cry about the heat and the difficulty of his job. Upon hearing the sobs of the child, one of the worker's wives, Elena, came out to give them their plate of bread, cheese and olives. Of all the intruders upon their life, this woman felt sorry for the children and took it upon herself to show these young orphans some kindness. When the other wives had settled in for an afternoon *pisolino*, a nap, she brought them food, sat with them, spoke with them, and encouraged them to the best of her ability. When Franco folded his arms in anger about the harshness of his job, Elena put her arm around him and told him that there is not one situation on earth that lasts forever. *Things always change, you can count on that*, she told him.

"Come here," she said, "let me show you something." She led the boys to the outdoor fire pit where a large pot of water was heating up to a boil to do the day's laundry. She asked Maurizio to bring her an egg from one of the chickens in the coop. She asked Franco to bring her some of the dried *Asteraceae* leaves from the pail in the pantry, and she asked Donato to bring a good sized butternut squash from the garden. The boys went off to gather the goods while Elena brought a plate, a cup, and a bowl from the kitchen. When the boys returned to the fire pit, Elena told them to sit down and watch. She placed the squash into the water and the boys watched the hard, bulbous vegetable float and then sink to the bottom of the pot. Next, Elena put the egg into the water and the egg bobbed around as the water boiled. Finally, the kind woman scooped some of the boiling water into the cup and placed the dried *Asteraceae* leaves into the water. Then she pulled out the squash and put it on the plate and placed the egg into the bowl. She set the three items in front of the boys. First she asked the boys, "What did I do to all three of these things?"

The boys answered, "You put them into the water."

"Yes," Elena told them, "and what kind of water?"

"Very hot water," the boys answered.

"You are correct," she told them. "That water is *very* hot and dangerous, and it would burn you if you touched it. You know that it is something that can hurt you, right?"

The boys nodded their heads.

"But look at what happened to each of these things. The squash was very hard and became soft. Touch it." The boys touched the squash and found it to be quite mushy. Then Elena asked them to consider the egg. "The egg was just liquid inside but the boiling water made it hard. Peel the shell and see for yourself." The boys peeled the shell and saw that the egg was hard. "Now," Elena told the boys, "take the cup of tea and taste it." The boys passed around the cup of water flavored with the leaves, each taking a careful sip of the very hot tea. When they had finished they looked up at Elena wondering why she was asking them to do such strange things.

She looked at each child intently and asked them, "Which one of these things do you want to be? Do you want to be the squash? Would you rather be the egg? Or would you like to be the tea?"

The children were confused by the question, but one by one each one agreed that the tea tasted good so they wanted to be the tea.

"Good," Elena told the children. "You see, the squash is something that started out very hard and strong but when it faced something difficult, something dangerously hot and overpowering, it became soft and lost its strength. You don't want to be like that, do you? If things are difficult for you right now, you don't want these bad conditions to weaken you. You are all good boys and you want to grow up to be good men. I know you don't want to be like the egg, either. The egg started off soft and runny, but when it faced the intensity of the heat and the power of the boiling bubbles, it became hard. You don't want life to harden you so that you can't show kindness to anyone. I've seen how thoughtful the three of you can be. You don't want that to change and become ruthless men. I know you've been through such sorrow, losing a loving mother you never knew, a kind and gentle father, and a steadfast step-mother. Now you are under the thumb of callous men who would enslave small children, but from this experience you do not have to grow up to be like them. You can become healthy, young gentlemen and retain your sweetness and vigor just like the tea. Have you noticed how the leaves have not changed? They've simply given their goodness to the water. Do you understand? You, too, can retain your goodness even in difficult and overpowering circumstances and when you become men you can share your goodness in any circumstance in which you find yourself. You can be like the tea. Now drink up!"

The children looked at the soggy squash and the hardened egg. They decided not to become too hard nor too soft. They wanted to be as Elena described them, loving like their mother, gentle like their father and strong like their step-mother. They wanted to be like the tea, a good blend of good qualities: strong, sensitive and caring. Kindness can go a long way to nurturing the hearts of the young. From that day forward, the boys resolved to drink the tea every day.

28

Salvatore

I told my son as much of the truth as I thought he could handle. That's what those know-it-all child experts tell you to do with your kids. *Only tell them what is age-appropriate*, they advise. Even though Joe is in his fifties, he's still my son and when he asked me what happened to my head and why was I walking with my cane again, I thought for sure he would use any answer I gave him as an excuse to sell the house out from underneath me and put me in a home for old people. That's how kids his age respond to parents that fall. I'm not that old. Okay, the population of people younger than me continues to grow but I don't think I'm old enough to be useless yet. So, I steered the conversation to be age-appropriate for both of us.

"Dad, what happened to the old poplar tree in the back yard?"

"It was in the way; I decided to get rid of it."

"In the way of what?"

"It was just in the way. I called the guy and told him to come and take the tree away."

"And what happened to your head, Dad?" he asked with that skeptical tone in his voice.

"Well, son, the tree didn't fall on my head or we wouldn't be having this conversation."

"I came into contact with the wrong end of the rake. My head is fine. I appreciate that you care; I really do, but you know that even when I was thirty I would come out of the garden with bumps and bruises. Everything is fine. Don't I look fine?"

Before Joe could continue to grill me, the doorbell rang. It was 3:30 so it was probably Simon. Joe went to answer the door. Simon looked up at Joe and said, "Sorry, I..."

"It's okay, kiddo," I yelled out, "come on in; meet my son, Joe."

Joe pointed to Simon and looked at me with a big question mark in his eyes.

"Joe, this is Simon. Simon, this is Joe." Simon headed straight for the kitchen as usual to make me a sandwich, ignoring Joe as he went past him.

"Who is this kid, Dad? Why is he here and why is he going into the kitchen?" Joe was whispering so I had to cock my ear in his direction. I can't hear whispers and he knows it.

"Simon is a nice kid that stops by to visit me on his way home from school." Before I could say anything else, Simon came into the room carrying my baloney sandwich on a plate. He put it on the coffee table and said, "I need to get home early today, Sal. You have company. I will see you tomorrow," and he was gone as fast as he came.

Joe just stood there with his mouth hanging open for a minute. Finally he said, "Dad, what's going on? Who is he?"

"I told you already, he's just a nice kid that stops by and makes me a sandwich."

"Okay, Dad, that's odd, okay? There are laws about such things. You can't just have a kid come in here and make you a sandwich. Can't you make your own sandwich?"

"Of course I can make my own sandwich. I was able to make my own sandwich when you were a kid, too, but you seemed to like to do that for me. Let it go, Joe. The kid likes to make me a baloney sandwich as much as you did."

"That was different, Dad, I was *your* kid. You can't just ask somebody else's kid to come in here and make you a darn baloney sandwich."

"I didn't ask him to come in here and make me one. Why are you getting so worked up about this? If you want to make me a sandwich then come by and make me one once in a while. Now, let this go."

"I am not going to let this go, Dad. What if his parents get upset about him coming over here? You could get into trouble. Think about it, would you have wanted us to go into a stranger's house when we were kids and make some old guy *a sandwich*?"

"We're not strangers anymore. We've gotten to know each other. I get the feeling the kid likes to be around *old people*. Some kids like old people."

Joe threw his head back and looked up at the ceiling as if the best way to get me to see his point was hanging up there.

"Look, would it make you feel better if I tell the kid to get his parents' permission first?"

"Yes, that's a start. My God, Dad, sometimes I really wonder about you."

Sometimes you don't wonder enough, I thought.

"Sit down, son. Split this baloney sandwich with me." Joe shook his head, no, but sat down anyway. "How are you kids doing?" I asked him so I could change the subject.

For a minute, he stared at his half of the sandwich and didn't say anything. "I don't know, Dad. Sometimes I wonder about them, too. JJ and Lorena try to scramble their schedules so they can be home with the kids. Liv keeps going from one job to another; she never seems to settle down. I don't know what to make of kids anymore."

"What about Tony?"

"Tony seems like he's doing a little better but even when he was smoking pot he was good at hiding it from us. Ahh, Dad, how do things get so crazy?"

"Are you going to eat that?" I'd finished my half and I could tell he was going to play with his food like he did when he was a kid. He handed me the other half.

"Things have always been crazy for kids. I told you about what happened to my Dad and Uncle Al. There are always dangers out there for kids. You know that as well as I do. I think there are dangers out there nowadays that weren't as common back in my day. There have always been things we couldn't protect kids from, like bullies and violence and abuse and all kinds of threatening situations where people can steer them wrong. I don't know, I feel sorry for kids these days because of so many other things that they shouldn't have to face, things like growing up in a world that changes too fast from one day to the next. It's not stable.

Joe nodded his head. I patted his knee. "You and Joanie have done a good job with your kids. I know it hasn't always been easy, but you've set a good example. They've grown up into fine people. Your example will pull them all through in the end, more than any words you ever spoke to them. I worry about kids that, I don't know, don't have anything to hang on to. There are a lot of kids out there being pushed out of their childhood too soon, even by well-meaning adults. Not enough kids have been taught about faith, you know. They've been encouraged to believe in magic stuff but not in miracles. They've been deprived of a sense of wonder and imagination because they've been given devices to occupy them. Why haven't we protected their innocence or their conscience? We haven't kept kids any safer by teaching them all about the dangers out there, only to turn around and create new dangers for them, or redefine what is dangerous?"

"You're starting to sound like your age, now, Dad. Careful. Is that what you're trying to do with this kid that makes you sandwiches? Give him some of your hard-earned wisdom?"

I shook my head. "No, son. I don't think that's what he needs. He seems a bit wiser than most kids I've come across; maybe he's even wiser than me. I think I'm getting more out of this arrangement than he is."

"Well, be careful, Dad. Make sure you meet the parents."

I had to laugh. "Don't you mean *you* want to meet my friend's parents? Things turn around, don't they? I'll tell him, don't worry."

"You should make friends with people your own age."

"Yeah, well, they keep disappearing on me. Say hi to Joanie. Tell her it's okay with me if she wants to come by to visit once in a while, too. I won't bite. I wouldn't mind seeing my grandkids, either, and the little ones. I'll teach them how to make a sandwich."

29

Simon

"I think he might have finally made some friends, Jay. I came home from work a little early yesterday and Simon wasn't home yet. When I asked him about it he'd said he stopped by a friend's house." Mom and Dad were talking in the family room when I came downstairs for dinner.

"I hope so, Cynthia. I knew that changing schools might help. I know it was a big adjustment for him at first but I think he seems to be adapting, now, don't you? He's such a quiet kid; sometimes it's very difficult for the quiet ones to find friends. Maybe we can have him ask his friend over here for a barbeque or something. What do you think?"

"Let's give it time, Jay. This is a big step for him; give him a chance to come up with the idea for himself. He may need more time. Let's not rush him, okay? He's making progress!"

"I want to take him to a Cavs game before the season is finished. They're doing really well this year. 'Think he'd like to go?"

"Ask him. It would be good for you two to spend more time together. By the time you get home from work he's usually upstairs doing his homework then goes to bed. I think he needs you; I'm not sure he knows how to ask."

"Is dinner ready?" I interrupted their conversation. I didn't like it when they talked about me instead of *to* me. But, then, I don't really like it when they talk to me because all they do is ask questions.

"Are you hungry," Mom asked.

I shrugged my shoulders. "I guess so."

"Dinner will be ready in ten. Why don't you come sit down with us, Simon, before dinner is ready. We can just chat a bit. How was school today?"

"Fine."

"Do you think Sister Maria Nicola is good with kids? I was talking to Martin at the club and he said his daughter Leah hates Sister Maria Reyna. Leah thinks that this nun absolutely hates kids. She shouldn't be teaching at all; she's very impatient and doles out too many punishments, offers little praise, and assigns way too much homework. Leah wants Martin to take her out of that school and send her to Granger. What do you think, Simon? Is your teacher okay with kids?" Dad asked again.

"She's very patient," I answered.

"She seems to have quite a passion for literature, I've noticed. At Parents' Night that was all she could talk about, but I have to say, she made it interesting. It wasn't at all like she was talking about two-dimensional characters printed in black and white; I almost had the impression that she was talking about old friends. Does she motivate the class to love literature, Simon?"

"I guess so."

"What about you; do you like literature?" Dad asked. Oh, the lame questions. If I made them, my parents would sit here and wait all night for me to answer, pressing me with even more questions. Can't we just eat dinner?

"I don't know. Is dinner ready?"

"It should be," Mom said and got up to pull her *famous* tuna casserole out of the oven.

"Tell me about your friends, Simon." Out of the corner of my eye I saw Mom giving Dad a disapproving look but Dad sat there and stared at me until I answered.

I sighed and shrugged my shoulders. I guess I should get them to stop worrying about whether I'm making friends or not. I told them the truth. "I have a friend named Sal. But, we're just *kind of* friends. There's not much to say."

Dad smiled and nodded his head. "Okay. Well, maybe someday we can meet this Sal. What's his last name?"

"I honestly don't know. Can we eat now?" Dad's smile turned into a frown. Maybe he thinks "Sal" is an imaginary friend. I don't care. I can't tell my parents that Sal is eighty or ninety or a hundred years-old. But, I think of him as my friend. I don't care if he's old. He's easy to hang around with. He does okay on his own, he doesn't seem to want anything from me. He just talks and pretends to like those disgusting sandwiches.

"Hey, Mom." Both of my parents looked up, startled. I'm not the one that usually initiates a conversation at the table.

"Yes, Simon?"

"Do you know where we could buy provolone cheese and some Italian-like lunchmeats?"

"Umm, I think I can find some in the city. Why?"

"My friend, Sal, likes them."

You'd think I'd brought home a straight-A report card, a house full of friends, and a million dollars all on the same day. Both of my parents put down their forks and smiled from ear to ear. Mom looked like she was going to cry. "Of course I will look for them. I will pick some up tomorrow!" She looked too happy; I don't think I've ever made her this happy since I moved in here. I asked to be excused. I heard them chattering like chipmunks as I left the room. "See, I told you! Okay, let's not get too excited... Maybe I'll pick up some Italian rolls, too..."

30

Befana

The Big Dipper is directly above us. There's a Little Dipper on the other side of the room. At night, Simon takes me out of his shirt pocket and sets me on his nightstand next to his bed. The stars on his ceiling are glow-in-the-dark stickers that his parents put up to decorate his room. They even designed the constellations by arranging the stickers according to a chart in a book. Some of the stickers look like they're getting old; they're peeling and ready to fall. I guess that can happen to real stars, too. I like it when Simon shines his large reading lamp on them for an hour or so before he goes to bed so that when he turns the lights out the stars glow almost as brightly as real stars. There are no cloudy nights in Simon's room, the stars are always shining. I've always found stars to be very comforting in a way that the light of day cannot make me feel; no matter how glorious the sun may be it does not have the same effect on me. The stars never shine so brightly that you cannot look up and gaze at them for as long as you please. Their light is more gentle and soothing than the sun –and of course, they twinkle. I love to focus my squinty eyes on the twinkling stars. Even the glimmer of a bright star can gladden this old heart and my eyes get misty when I think of the star that shown on Christmas night. At the moment, Simon decided to get on his computer and look up my story, like Sal told him to. He read:

"The story of *La Befana* began in Italy during the Christmas season. *Befana* is often depicted in a rural world because during the cold of winter, she visited at a time of greatest difficulty for the farmers and Italian peasants. The tradition of the Epiphany and *Old Befana's* visit originated in biblical accounts about the journey of the Three Kings and their mission to follow the Star of Bethlehem; the old lady, *Befana*, decided to follow them to their destination. In the original story the Magi, in seeking the newborn king, were guided by this compelling and intense star. As the story goes, one night this old lady stopped the entourage to find out where they were going - she had not heard of the newborn king until that moment. They told her about the star, the prophecy that a new king would be born in Bethlehem, and that he would come to save the world. When the entourage left, she wanted to follow them to see the Christ Child but she was never able to catch up to them. From that day on the old woman, with a heavy bag of treats on her back, passes through the houses of all children and delivers the treats to each child just in case this child is the newborn king." The article had a picture attached that looked nothing like me. It portrayed some kind of loony hag. Really now.

At this point Simon picked up my little statue and looked and me. I still don't think he knows what to make of me. He whispered that I look like a little witch. Well, it's been said before – many times. He also said that there is something very mischievous in my eyes. I'm not mischievous, am I? I don't remember having done anything naughty, not even when I was younger. Well, maybe I did. What child ever considers his behavior to be bad? None that I've ever met. I don't think Simon is mischievous at all. He does not seem to have a nature that considers doing anything bad to anyone. He just seems very distant, like his mind lives in a different world than the one which he is forced to occupy. Suddenly, Simon has started laughing. He has found a depiction of me, written in Italian and translated into English. Simon read the description to me out loud.

"*La Befana* is an ugly old woman; she has a hunch on her back, a big nose, and a pointed chin. She wears raggedy old clothes and a shawl over her shoulders, a long skirt, and a scarf on her head. But despite her dreadful appearance she is good in her own way and brings gifts to children."

Humph. Well, that's not a very nice description. I don't have this problem with smaller children who can't read. They just think I'm a silly old lady. *Ugly, hunchbacked*? It's not a very flattering depiction of me but Simon has stopped laughing. "*Manyeo*," he says out loud. "You look like a *manyeo*, a witch, but I don't think you are a witch at all. Witches are mean and do bad things to people, but you bring gifts. You are not a *manyeo*. You're just a funny looking old lady."

Well, thank you. I'll take that. He set me down and continued reading, finding a poem by someone named Pascoli:

La Befana vede e sente;	*La Befana sees and hears;*
fugge al monte, ch'è l'aurora.	*She flies to the mountain, the aurora.*
Quella mamma piange ancora	*A mother still cries*
su quei bimbi senza niente.	*about those children with nothing.*
La Befana vede e sente.	*La Befana sees and hears.*

If I could produce tears, I'd be wiping them from my eyes right now. What haven't I seen, what haven't I heard throughout my travels? Mothers crying, children suffering, fathers desperate to help but feeling powerless. I've witnessed people in all stages of life weeping and yearning for compassion, for understanding, and for happiness. That is why the Baby Jesus came into the world – to give hope to the hopeless. This life on earth is not all there is to life. It's a speck of light in an eternal universe. The bigger, better stuff is out there. That's what we're striving for, no more tears, no more suffering. Peace and Joy on Earth as it is in Heaven.

Simon closed up his laptop, turned off the lights and set me on his nightstand. That night, for the first time in years, he dreamed of a life he cannot remember when he's awake.

31

Stella

Maris doesn't have a clue that things are going to get a little weird around here. She just thinks, *yay, Stella will be out of my way for a while and I can rule the roost.* Little does my next youngest sister know: Emma is not about to be *ruled*. It's always a power struggle between Maris and I. She actually has the bossier personality, but I have the responsibility our parents have given me to maintain order over my younger sisters in our little hen house we call a bedroom. It's a battle every single night until Grandma in the next room bangs on the adjacent wall and tells us to pipe down. Grandma's old fist doesn't deter my sister, Maris.

"You are out of here tomorrow and I can't wait," she says. "You make my life so miserable. I wish you would go to Emma's house and not come back! At least Emma doesn't think she's the boss of me. Finally, I will be able to relax in my own room without you breathing down my neck." Usually, I respond with a lot of defensive comments that begin with: *but Mom and Dad said...* but not tonight. Tonight, Maris is right; I'm out of here tomorrow. I will not be making my sisters' lives miserable for a whole week. I will be the one who will be able to relax without responsibility breathing down *my* neck. And seriously, I wish I could go there and not come back, too! These dear sisters of mine will still have each other to cause havoc. That will not change in my absence, of that I'm sure. Suddenly, I feel sorry for Emma. What has she gotten herself into? Even poor Emma is clueless about just how weird things can get around here.

Tonight, Mom suggested that I keep a journal about my experiences during the coming week. I don't want to wait until tomorrow to begin. I want to write a little something tonight.

#Moccasinswap: Preface to Journal:

I'm nervous and excited. I don't know how different my life will be while walking in Emma's shoes. All I know for sure tonight is that all of my routines are about to change. This bedtime routine with my sisters has become old a long time ago. The battles for the upstairs bathroom will finally come to an end for a while. I might come to enjoy more privacy so much that it will be difficult to give it up when I return. I don't entirely know what to expect but peace and privacy are some things I hope for. Part of me feels a little scared:

- o *Emma will get so freaked out in my life that she'll put an end to this project by tomorrow night.*
- o *I don't have Emma's social skills and I may end up experiencing the most embarrassing week of my life.*
- o *I know without a doubt that I will be a fish out of water – everything will be new and strange to me even though I'm going to a school in my own hometown and seeing kids that I sometimes see around town for a short amount of time.*
- o *I have no idea what to expect of real teachers.*
- o *I will make a mistake that Emma will have to pay for.*

The more fears I write down, the more I come up with. This journal entry might not be the best idea. Tomorrow is going to be an interesting day no matter what happens because it won't, for one minute, resemble any day I've lived in my life so far.

Morning came in a flash and my feet hit the ground running. My bags were already packed. My books and this week's homeschool lessons were already outlined. I have everything I need. Dad will be dropping me off at Emma's house in a half hour and then he's bringing her here just in time for her to go to church with my family. Emma said her family doesn't always get to church, sometimes they do, but *for show* they might go today since I'll be with them. I found that statement to be funny. How does anyone go to church *for show*? Church isn't a place to model your clothes, or put on an act, or be entertained. I told Emma that I thought church was a place where we shut up and listen to God for a change instead of blabbering away like we do the rest of the time. She just stared at me like I'd said something in another language. "I suppose you're right," she'd said. "I never hear him say anything to me, though. We just go because Mom said it's a good thing to do once in a while."

I took a deep breath and thought, *here I go*. Yikes, for the first time I realized how crazy this idea might really be. Everyone else had looked at me like they thought it was a strange idea. Only now do I feel like they might be right after all. I passed by Emma in her driveway. "Good Lord, Em, you've packed up your entire room. Where are you going to put ....?" I stopped short of finishing my question. It's her problem; it's her life for a week. We gave each other a hug and wished each other luck. Dad squeezed me tight. "You be good, okay, Peanut?" He hasn't called me that for a long time. "I will, Dad. You know I will." He rustled my hair. "I know." And in a flash he was gone. He and my best friend drove off and I entered Emma's house with my overnight bag.

"Where is the rest of your stuff?" Emma's Mom asked me.

"I travel light," I answered, thinking maybe I should have packed more stuff. Emma's Mom smiled. "Well, go ahead up to Emma's room. You know where it is. Make yourself at home. It's only you and Bill going to church this morning. I have to take Sue to a Girl Scout trip to the dairy farm, and the Rory is still at his friend's house. I'll see you this evening when we get home. This is going to be an interesting week for you, isn't it? I think it will be interesting for us, too. It's nice to have you here, Stella."

"Thank you, Mrs. Thompson. I think it will be nice to be here, too. *Very nice.*"

"I guess for this week you should call me, Mom."

"Oh, wow, okay Mom. It's getting interesting already!"

32

Sister Maria Nicola

Pacing is a curious behavior. Why do people pace back and forth when they are nervous, or waiting, or thinking? Does retracing one's steps repeatedly have the effect of moving us mentally forward when we feel stuck in our situation? I have always been a pacer for as long as I can remember. My sister, Genevieve, however, has always been a runner. She runs from one job to another and one marriage to another. She runs to catch planes and trains and cabs and she runs into a lot of people that she befriends for two hours and then she runs some more, and many times, like today, she runs into trouble.

I am grateful that Sister Maria Reyna has given me a few days off to fly to Chula Vista to be with Genevieve over a long weekend. My sister's phone call consisted of three words: I need you. When I returned her call, the receptionist answered, "Orange County Detention Center. How may I direct your call?" Gen needs me – again – so I caught the next plane to California.

"I'm here to see my sister, Genevieve O'Malley... or, I'm sorry, her maiden name was O'Malley, I know she's been recently remarried. I... I'm so sorry, I've flown here from the Midwest and I'm a little rattled. My sister was brought in day before yesterday, if that helps."

The sergeant at the desk looked at my habit and took some pity on me, as other sergeants have in the past. "Let's see what I can find out for you. Would that be Genevieve Martinez, Caucasian, 33 years old...?"

"Yes, yes, Sergeant, that's her, thank you. May I see her?"

"Sign in here. Sergeant Walker here will take you to the Women's Detention area. You can wait for her there."

Pacing allows me to ruminate and work out the discomfort of having been searched by Sergeant Walker.

"Sorry, Sister," the poor Sergeant apologized.

"It's okay. You're doing your job," I reassured her, but now that I'm waiting in the visitor's quarter for Sergeant Walker to escort Gen into the vacuous room, I'm smoothing out my habit, biting my nails, and walking between two walls eight feet apart. Dozens of thoughts started going through my head all at once. If I am unable to show up this Wednesday afternoon to bring stuff to Sandy, Maggie, Sara, and our beloved Krauss, they're really going to think something's amiss. I gave my students an assignment to research a unique Christmas story and they were supposed to be working on their rough drafts in the coming days. Sister Maria Reyna seems angry with me about something which we have not had time to discuss. I'm surprised she let me come here on a moment's notice. I told her it was a family emergency and she said my students would benefit from someone who can run a tighter ship for a few days. I've also been thinking about Simon – *I don't know what people want from me*, the poor kid had said. How many times did I hear my younger sister say the same thing for so many years? *Elizabeth, what do Mom and Dad want from me? What does anyone want from me?*

Now, here she is, back in this situation again. Mom and Dad are both gone. It's just the two of us. Oddly enough, Gen has never asked me what *I* want from her. Maybe it's time to find out. When she came through the door she looked like something yanked out of the second circle of Dante's *Inferno*. I walked over to her and she backed away slightly. Sergeant Walker took her post by the door. I touched Gen's cheek which was streaked with trails of black makeup, tears, and snot. She was wearing her least favorite outfit in the color that looks worst on her: an orange jumpsuit. Her hair was matted down with a sticky blend of hairspray and sweat on one side, giving her features a hideous cartoon-like look of a female cartoon villain. This time, her hair was colored blond. Sometimes it's red, other times she has it colored in shades that do not come naturally to humans.

"You look terrible," I told her with a waning smile on my face.

"So do you," she replied. "Is that black and white outfit all you have?" Then she finally smiled. We always begin our reunions this way.

"Can we sit?" Sergeant Walker's eyes remained on us the whole time and she nodded.

"What happened?" I asked my sister.

"What usually happens." Gen grabbed at her hair on each side of her face and gave me an exasperated look.

"We have a half hour, Gen. Give me the short version."

"I married Justin a few weeks ago. I thought it would be good this time. He's so cute, and smart and so much fun. He and I are so good together, especially, you know…"

"You can skip that part, Gen. Why are you here and not with Justin? And what kind of a name is Justin for a Hispanic?"

Gen laughed. "His real name is *Jose*. But, he goes by Justin because he said his real name doesn't fit him. I'm here because my husband likes to party, and as you well know, so do I. I'm here because I've been told that I was so doped up on cocaine that I tried to kill Justin and then myself. That's why I'm here. My husband, *Jose*, pressed charges. I don't actually remember all the details. I remember that we went to San Diego on our honeymoon and we partied down there like was no tomorrow, and then we came back up here and we went to his friend Sky's house and we partied some more. All I can vaguely remember is that at one point I saw Dad. He was walking out the door again after he'd beaten Mom for the last time and she had to go to the hospital for a long time, and I wanted to hurt Dad so bad; I wanted to kill him. I went after Justin instead. I wanted to kill him, I guess. I don't remember what I did. I just remember thinking that this explosive feeling inside of me was not going to go away until I killed him, until I killed Dad."

"But, Dad is already dead, Gen. You know that. Dad is gone. You can't kill him."

Gen laughed in an unhinged way. I've never seen her this bad before.

"I know, right? He took that away from me, too. He died and now I can't even kill him like I want to. So, I just have to spend the rest of my life wanting to kill him, over and over again."

"Or, you could start by forgiving him so you don't have to feel like this for the rest of your life."

Gen reached out and smacked my face with one, really hard blow. Sergeant Walker was on top of her in a split second, hand-cuffing her behind her back. "Time to go back to the cell," said Sergeant Walker. "You can't assault your visitors."

"Please, Sergeant, one more minute, please." I wiped the blood springing from my mouth. "Please, she's cuffed now, please. Just another minute."

"There," Gen said, "do you forgive me?" She laughed and then she started crying. "Do not talk to me about all that forgiveness crap, Elizabeth. It may work for you and your holier-than-thou life, but it will never work for me. Do you understand me? Our Dad destroyed our lives. We can't get that back! Never! We can't bring Mom back; we can't bring our childhood back. All we can do is live with the pain every single day until we freakin' die! And I want to die right now! I want to die, Elizabeth. I don't want to feel all this pain anymore. Nothing can help me." Gen's grief was unbearable. I stood up and put my arms around my sister. Sergeant Walker stood close by as Gen leaned into my chest. "I want to die; please help me find a way to die, Elizabeth. I don't want to live like this anymore."

"Sshhh. I do understand; you feel like dying is the only way out, but Gen, you need to put an end to this lifestyle – *that* is what needs to die. You need to bury the past where it belongs. Sweetie, I'm here to help you. You have to let go. Stop running and let it go. I can show you a better way. You need help and you need to surrender your life and stop thinking you have all the answers. Can you trust me, Gen? I need to ask you just one question, okay? Just one question: what is it that you think I want from you?"

She stopped crying and looked up at me with the hurt in her eyes I'd always seen when she and I were little girls. "What do *I* think *you* want from me?"

"Yes, what do you think I want from you?"

"I think you want me to be like you. I think you believe that the only way for me to go on is if I live like you do, like I have to take on your life in order to redeem my own. That's what I think you want from me, and I can't do that! I've never been like you, not even when we were kids. You seemed to just bear with everything; good ol' you, strong and confident. But, that's never been me. I thought you could get me out of here, but the more I come to my senses, the more I realize there is nothing you can do for me, *Sister*. Now, just go, leave me here. I don't have any intention of turning my life around and surrendering to your delusions of a loving God. I've done what I've done. I have to accept the consequences. I stabbed my husband because I wanted to kill him. I don't even regret what I've done. I can't live your life, Elizabeth. I can't save my own life by living yours. It's too late for that." Gen was calmer now. Sergeant Walker lifted her up out of the chair to take Gen back to her cell.

"Gen," I said quickly before she was led through the door. "I love you. You've always had that; you always will. There is nothing you can do to kill that, either. I will always love you."

33

Stella

#*Moccasinswap - Journal Day One:*
I don't feel like there is much to write about today. I went to the small church in town with Mr. Thompson at 11:00 am. Their church is different than ours. They read scripture and the pastor talks about what everyone just read. Mr. Thompson kept turning around and looking at who was in church. At one point, he elbowed me and asked, "Do you know that family with the disabled girl?" I told him I did. Her name is Terry Ann and she lives down the street from me. Her family does an awful lot for her; she's in our homeschool group for social time when we do special events together, like the Easter egg hunt, or the Christmas cookie exchange, but Mr. Thompson had stopped listening. I did what Mr. Thompson did; I looked to see who was there. I only saw people I've seen around but didn't really know by name.

The rest of the day was kind of dull. Shortly after I arrived, Mrs. Thompson left with Sue. I went up to Emma's bedroom and unpacked my overnight bag. I hung up a few blouses so they wouldn't get too wrinkled. At home I don't have to worry about wrinkled blouses but at a real school, I think I should at least try to make a decent impression. Unpacking took all of three minutes and then I sat there until it was time to leave for church with my dad-of-the-week. When we came home, he told me to help myself if I was hungry; he said he was going to catch a game of golf; he'd see me later. I was at home, all alone, in Emma's house. I picked up Emma's cell phone and dialed my house number. The line was busy, of course (one of Emma's major complaints about trying to reach me). I walked around the house, kind of like what I think a ghost would do. It was so quiet. There is never a time in my own home that is this quiet, unless I happen to wake up in the middle of the night and go down to the kitchen for a drink of water, but in the middle of the day? Never.

I opened the fridge. It felt weird to be in Emma's house and think of it as home and to get into her fridge and her bedroom without her. In the fridge I found a couple packages of string cheese, a dozen juice boxes, a loaf of bread, and a box with some leftover pizza. The grapes in one of the bins looked pretty good but the gallon of milk had expired (that doesn't happen in my house). This refrigerator seemed rather sparse even for a family half our size. I realize we have an army living in our house but the fridge always seems to be filled with stuff Mom buys at one of those warehouse grocery places in the city, like a five pound bag of carrots, whole chickens, a block of cheese that could feed a small village and a bushel of apples. On the shelves of Emma's pantry I found a box of dried fruit leather, several cans of tomato soup, mac and cheese bowls and a few cans of tuna. I settled on some string cheese and some grapes.

At around seven, everyone came home. They brought in Chinese food from Number 33 Take-A-Way. I only ate a little bit. It was kind of salty and there was some kind of aftertaste that lingered until well after I'd gone to bed. After dinner everyone seemed to disperse into their own private corner of the house. Rory was in his room playing video games; Sue went to her room to play on her tablet, and Mr. and Mrs. Thompson went outside on the porch with a bottle of wine. I sat in the living room and turned on the TV. I couldn't believe I had the TV all to myself without having to fight for the remote control, or beg to watch something other than sports; I even had the whole sofa to myself, or the recliner, or the velveteen easy chair in the corner. I found these choices to be rather nice so I went from one piece of furniture to the next, which was more exciting than actually watching TV. I scrolled through hundreds of channels and found nothing I wanted to watch so I turned off the TV and went upstairs to Emma's room and picked up her book (she's reading a romance book for the third time called "When Night Falls On Your Lips"), weird title, weird book. She's told me about it several times because it's her "favorite book in the whole world." Not my cup of tea. I fell asleep at 8:15.

34

Befana

As a child I was made to feel pretty worthless, and as I grew older and people avoided me I started to feel like an unsightly wretch. Why do we do that to ourselves, I wonder? Why do we base how we view ourselves upon the opinions of others? We seem to do it all the time. Children rely on their parents' approval to see their worth. They put great stock in how teachers view their efforts at school. And they even go so far as to believe what their fickle friends say about them, and worse, how their enemies see them. How can we ever see ourselves as good if others criticize us, mock us, or belittle us? Is it possible for us to see our value if someone is always pointing out our failures? I was never able to take what others saw in me and see something different, something better. I was guilty of believing the negative attitudes that surrounded me. This world is funny like that; we are willing to believe what flawed human beings think about us instead of what a flawless creator fashioned us to be. It isn't easy to get it right. Of course we have flaws, every one of us does. But we are not the sum of our flaws; it is our likeness to the creator which gives us our beauty and dignity. But, without him, we are not very beautiful, or dignified, I'll tell you that! A person can look unappealing on the outside but be filled with goodness and love on the inside, while another person can look lovely on the outside and allow themselves to be filled with bitterness on the inside.

I remember one time when I was a young woman of about twenty-five, I had a regular visitor; her name was Sevia. She came to my hut because she wanted to learn how to make bread the way I made it – with spices and sun-dried grapes. I would go to her house and she showed me how to make sweet treats out of dried figs. This went on for about a month or so. We were back and forth from each other's homes and spent time talking about things that, now in retrospect, were not the building blocks of friendship, but of regrets. I told her about my past and living with *Padrona* in the cave. At first, I thought she was sympathetic, but soon I'd noticed that she responded by saying, "Oh my, poor little you. What a terrible thing to happen. You deserved better." It's not *what* she said, but *how* she said it that made me begin to wonder. It would be followed up with "Boo hoo, poor little you. You shouldn't feel sorry for yourself so much."

I didn't actually think at the time that I was feeling sorry for myself. I just thought that friends shared their stories and garnered some support. One day she'd even gone so far as to mock my language skills. I hadn't attended any kind of schooling. She'd had some, but that was enough for her to laugh at my speech and ridicule my opinions as if I were very ignorant and her opinions were correct because they agreed with the majority of people in town. Then came the day that she showered me with empty compliments and the feeling that I couldn't trust her began to grow. How can someone make you feel so stupid one minute and compliment you the next and then expect to be trusted? I didn't have the courage to tell her that a real friend shouldn't act like that; I simply left her house and did not return. When she'd knock on my door I didn't open it. Soon enough, she went away and didn't try to come back.

The experience had the effect of leaving a very bad taste in my mouth, like the time I'd tried an uncured olive from the trees outside *Padrona's* cave. The olive was ripe and it looked tasty but boy, oh boy, was it bitter! I couldn't get rid of that taste, even while I was asleep – the memory of it was very harsh. If Sevia, a young woman in touch with the world around her, had unreliable opinions about me, then why would I want to place myself in that kind of situation ever again? If that was the nature, or even the *possible* nature of friendship, then that type of relationship wasn't for me. I didn't want to make friends anymore because of what I discovered about myself in the short time I'd spent with Sevia. Until I met her I wasn't aware that there were things about me that *could still* be mocked; I thought I'd left that behind in *Padrona's* cave. Because of Sevia's attention to my shortcomings I'd recoiled from even wanting to know anything more about myself. During the early years of my life I'd judged *Padrona* to be a very mean person (because of what she wanted to do to the bunnies) and so I did not want to believe there was something wrong with *me*, it was easier to disregard *Padrona's* attitude because she did not have my respect. However, I thought Sevia could be my friend and she had caused me to doubt myself and perhaps even confirmed the way *Padrona* had once made me feel – like I was truly worthless.

Why do we judge our sense of worth from what others have to say about us, or in how they make us feel about ourselves? Okay, I may have a pointed nose, a bit of a hunch on my back, and some have even gone so far to say that I have a crooked spiky chin, but a whole person is more than their physical appearance. The whole person is more than their bodies, their thoughts, their speech patterns, or even their mental capacities. Most of the time we can't even see the "whole person," we only see what we want to see. Our sense of worth doesn't come from those people who are as fragmented as we are; it comes from the one who made us. The caring God is the one who can see the total me. When I look at myself through the eyes of others, I can only see what they see in me and it isn't always good, but when I look at myself through the eyes of a caring God, I see someone a lot prettier, someone with a decent sense of humor; I see someone that cares about not hurting other people, and I see a little old lady that sparkles like a star – that is what I see when I look at little *Old Befana* through the eyes of my creator. Why would I choose to see anything else?

I am thankful that what is here before our eyes is not all there is for us to behold. I came to understand this by coming across so many people who were broken by life's injustices and yet they found inner peace and joy. I don't know that we can do that on our own. The caring God is there to hold us together when we cannot hold ourselves together. I was broken by years of sadness, abuse, loneliness, rejection, and loss. This caring God opened his arms to console me, give me dignity, ease my loneliness, and welcome me into a loving relationship –a gift that I try to share with the people I find along the way. I try to do for others what he has done for me.

35

Salvatore

I've heard people say, you're never too old to learn. I suppose that is true. I think the problem for some of us older people is that we don't think we have anything new to learn, we've seen it all. Or worse, we don't put ourselves in a situation that might be a learning experience. Old age becomes an irritating comfort zone. It's irritating because we don't want to be there in the first place but it's comfortable because we don't want to venture outside of it. We can't go backward, and we don't want to go forward; we know what's waiting there, so we sit still, too afraid to move half the time.

If you make friends with a kid, look out, you will learn something. Simon didn't come by the day after he ran into Joe. I'm not sure if Joe's visit made him feel unwanted, or unneeded. But, when he came by on Friday, he was holding a brown bag and he had an impish little smile on his face.

"Are you hungry, Mr. Sal?" he asked as he came through the door.

"I didn't eat lunch," I answered. "I'm waiting for my sandwich."

"Well, have I got a sandwich for you!"

He handed me the brown bag then sat across from me watching to see the look on my face. I opened the bag, pulled out a long roll wrapped in foil. As I pulled the foil away from the roll, the smell of Provolone cheese was the first thing to hit my nose, followed quickly by Genoa Salami, Prosciutto, and Mortadella. I opened up the bread to see the contents with my own eyes. There were some nice, thinly sliced tomatoes and a little lettuce on top of the provolone wedged neatly inside an actual small loaf of Italian bread which was crusty on the outside and soft on the inside.

"Where did you...?" I started to ask but then I noticed that the kid was smiling from ear to ear. God bless America – a Korean kid who hates American baloney sandwiches as much as I do manages to find an Italian deli and brings me a sandwich made in heaven. Simon nodded his head and waved his hand to urge me on to take a bite. As I sank my teeth into the sandwich, I closed my eyes and savored the moment. I added a few noises to show the kid how appreciative I was. He beamed.

"Good?" he asked.

With a mouth full of first-rate sandwich fixins I nodded my head and closed my eyes again. I was afraid that if I look at how happy this made him I would find a way to spoil the moment. Sometimes, my children have told me, I have a way of ruining a moment by smiling too much (they think I'm faking) or smiling too little (they think I'm disappointed) so it was best if I kept my eyes closed and my mouth busy eating this sandwich. After two or three bites, I opened my eyes and saw Simon sitting across from me, still smiling.

"Go bring me a knife from the kitchen, my boy. You have to try this."

Simon came back with a knife and I cut the sandwich in half and shared it with him. I sat there now and watched as he took a bite out of his half. He closed his eyes while he chewed the sandwich. When he opened them again he was smiling and nodding his head. He gave it a thumbs up while he continued chewing. Neither of us said another word until we finished my afternoon surprise.

"Sal, what are you supposed to drink with a sandwich like that?" he asked me.

"Hmmm, you're not old enough. You're thirsty, too, huh? See if you can find some orange pop in the pantry. I hide it back there because I'm not supposed to drink it. I don't want Joe to see it."

Simon came back with two bottles of orange pop and two glasses full of ice. After drinking down our sodas we both sat back and enjoyed the moment in silence.

"This was the best afternoon I've had in ages, son. Thank you for that sandwich. You really made my day. It means a lot to me." After a few moments Simon asked me,

"What's the hardest thing about being old? I mean, I know there are health problems and stuff like that, right?"

"Huh, well... let's see. There are many things that are not pleasant about being old. I guess the hardest thing for me would be this: I remember moments like they happened yesterday – giving my kids horsey back rides until my knees were sore, teaching them to ride their bicycles, knowing that just holding them in my arms could make them feel safe. I can remember those moments so clearly because they brought me more joy than I ever dreamed possible, but I also remember that while I was in those moments I would never in a million years have suspected that the day would come when looking back on those moments would make me feel sad. I guess remembering them can make me happy until I realize how far gone that life is in the past and I will never experience those feelings of joy again." Simon looked down at his shoes.

"Okay, your turn, kid, in your opinion, what's the hardest thing about being young nowadays? I wonder if things have changed."

The kid never answers my questions and I didn't think he would answer this one, but after thinking for a minute he said, "I think the hardest thing about being young, for me, is people's expectations. I'm never sure what others want from me. My parents have expectations, so do my teachers, but worse than anything is what other kids want from me – and I don't know what it is; I don't know what they expect, and it seems like I'm always getting it wrong."

I didn't know how to respond to him right away. Finally, I said, "It's getting more confusing than ever, I imagine."

He nodded his head, yes. "I should be going," he said.

"Before you go, let me say this. Think about it when you get home. Try not to worry about expectations, okay? I think, as you pointed out, everyone has different expectations and it's hard to know what they are. Not only that, but expectations can change from one minute to the next. Try this instead: forget about expectations and always aim for the highest good. Do the right thing. Do you know what the right thing is? Sometimes it's hard to figure out."

"Yes, sir. The only right thing is the thing that leads us to God." Simon waved his hand, turned and left. That was an answer I wasn't expecting. I guess I'm the one that learned something new today.

36

Sister Maria Nicola

"There you are!" I did not find Sandy or the others in our usual meeting spot. I walked around the side of the building and saw them standing near O'Geary's Pub on Main St. "I went to our usual place and no one was there. What's going on?"

Maggie looked me up and down then turned and walked away. Sara turned and followed her. "Sandy, what's going on?" Where's Krauss? Why aren't we meeting in the basement?

Sandy blew smoke out of her nose and mouth simultaneously and looked me up and down. "You didn't even show up last week. What's going on with you? Of course, after your little tiff with Krauss no one really expected you to come back. I guess we're just surprised you're here today. We've kind of disbanded. Krauss was busted two weeks ago. He went on some kind of a rant after you left and scored some heavy stuff from a narc. He's in jail. Looks like he'll be there for a long time, too." She laughed a throaty, phlegmy laugh and asked again, "So, what happened to you?"

"I had to be with someone, well, actually it's my sister. It's bad. She's in jail, too. I wanted to help her but I don't think I can. It's such a big mess. I wasn't able to get here. I was with her." I choked. I wasn't sure how much more I could say. After I'd returned from California, some of the Sisters asked me if I was okay. I didn't feel I could tell them everything. Opening up one small part of the story can lead to divulging far more than you ever intended. I'd only told Sister Maria Reyna that I had a family emergency and I hoped I wouldn't have to say anything more. I simply told my Sisters that a family member was very sick and needed our prayers. That sufficed. We prayed together.

Sandy put her arm around me and led me back around the corner to our basement. It was just the two of us. When we settled on the mattress and she gave me a hit from her joint, I put my head on her shoulder and started to cry. I felt like I could talk to her.

"It's my sister," I began. "She's in so deep. She is so lost. I can't do anything for her. She tried to kill her stupid husband. Now she's in jail and there is nothing I can do for her."

"What would you do for her if you could?" Sandy asked me. "Look at yourself. You're no better off than she is. What are you supposed to do for her? We're all lost, Liz, every stinking one of us."

I looked at her with tears streaming down my cheeks. "You're right. I don't think I'm of any use to anyone today. I do believe in hope but sometimes it's hiding behind a very big mess."

"Why don't you crash with me tonight? You don't have to go to *wherever* it is you go. Just stay." She brushed my hair back with her fingers and kissed me on the forehead. I sat up.

"I can't stay," I said. "I have a tyrant waiting for me. If I don't get back, God knows what would happen. Seriously, I should go now." I stood up and took two steps toward the door. I turned around.

"Sandy, have you ever thought about what kind of a life you'd like to have instead of this one? What would you do, where would you be if you could just change everything right now?"

Sandy laughed then let out a muffled scream. "What kind of life, indeed? Sheez, what would I do? I'd… Christ… I don't even know where to start! I would want my kid back, for one thing. I want my Rosie-girl. She's about seven now. They took her because I'm unfit. I'd want the kind of life I could hold together, that's all I want. That's it."

"Wouldn't it be nice if we can figure out a way to do that?" I asked. "Think about it. Please meet me here next week. I'm glad Krauss is not around. Don't leave me alone without finding you. I need hope right now."

"And you're looking at *me*? Get real. I don't have any hope to give you."

Sandy couldn't see it from where her life was sitting but in all honesty, today, she felt like my only hope for making some sense out of things.

37

Simon

"Did you forget something?" Katie asked me during lunch. I shrugged my shoulders and didn't reply. That's usually enough to send people along; most of the time they don't care enough to pursue anymore conversation with me. I kept looking down at the table but Katie sat down across from me. The cafeteria was louder than usual today. It was raining outside which meant we couldn't go out for recess after we finished eating so we sent our noise levels out to the playground and beyond without us. Katie unpacked her lunch and offered me half of her sandwich. I shook my head.

"Oh, come on, don't be that way, Simon. My Mom makes pretty good peanut butter and jelly sandwiches. Please take half. Last week I forgot my lunch and that goofball, Robbie, of all people, shared his sandwich with me. It was a PB&J, too, but not as good as my Mom's. Here, try it, at least."

I looked up at Katie and she genuinely seemed to want to share her sandwich. I thought about my visit with Sal last week and the best Italian sandwich (the only Italian sandwich) I'd ever eaten. Maybe I did need to taste new things once in a while. My Mom tried making me PB&J's, too, but then she started leaving for work earlier in the mornings and told me I was old enough to make my own lunches, now. Most of the time, I remembered to make one; today, I'd overslept. I took the half sandwich from Katie's extended hand and thanked her. She didn't take a bit of her own half yet; she was waiting for me to try my half so I took a bite. I think my eyes must have popped open because she looked at me and chuckled. "Pretty darn good, huh?" Then she took a bite.

I nodded my head in approval. This really was the best PB&J I'd ever tasted. I ate it slowly because I didn't want it to be gone too quickly. Katie finished her half in just a few bites. She continued talking while she chewed.

"Want to know the secret?" she asked. I nodded. "My Mom mixes some sugar and cinnamon into some butter and spreads that on the bread first, then, she spreads the peanut butter and jelly over it. Oh, my gosh, it's so good. She knows it's my favorite sandwich in the world, but she gives me baloney sandwiches, every other day. She says that I'll appreciate the PB&J's more if I have to eat baloney once in a while."

I couldn't help it; I laughed. What is it with baloney sandwiches?

"Oh, my gosh, Simon! I don't think I've ever seen you laugh! What did I say?"

"Nothing. Just the baloney sandwich thing struck me kind of funny."

"Do they have baloney in Korea?" I shrugged my shoulders. I don't like to talk about Korea. I have very few memories of it anymore, anyway.

"I don't know," I answered.

Katie grew quiet and took out her apple slices. She offered me some. I only accepted one and waved off the rest.

"You're always so quiet, Simon. You don't have to talk to me if you don't want to. My Mom says I do enough talking for everyone. No one actually has to be listening or respond; I just keep right on talking. She thinks I'm a blabbermouth, but I'm really not. I have my limits. I don't talk about people, and I don't talk about what other people have told me. I have standards. Do you not talk because you don't like people, or because you're afraid of what to say to people? Never mind. I said you didn't have to talk to me. I think that quiet people need someone to talk *to* them once in a while, even if they aren't comfortable doing any of the talking. Am I right?"

I nodded my head. In truth, yes, it gets a little too quiet in my world. She's right, I guess I am afraid of what to say to people so I'm not all that comfortable doing any of the talking. But she's not right about me not liking people. I've just found that I have very little in common with kids my own age, no matter what school I go to. It's not that I think of myself as Korean and the rest of the kids are American because I've been in America longer than I lived in Korea. As strange as it seems, I don't think of myself as American, either, because I am *different* than the average kid around here. It's not just about the way I look or speak, it's more about knowing how to interact with others. Most of the kids I know have been to preschool before they started school, or they have brothers and sisters or play groups they experienced before coming to this crazy place called school. I was a small child living alone with Dasan, and when I came to the U.S. and was adopted, I was an only child and started school in a strange new place. I looked up at Katie. I think she'd lost interest in talking to me. She was putting her lunch trash in her bag and getting ready to leave the table.

"Thanks again for sharing your lunch," I told her. Suddenly, I noticed she was staring at my shirt pocket. I pulled my sweater shut.

"What do you have in your pocket?" she asked.

"Nothing," I answered quickly. "It's nothing. Just a gift an old man gave me."

"Can I see it?" she asked.

I didn't answer out loud. I just shook my head and looked down at the table.

"Please?" she begged. "Please, I promise I won't do anything to it; I just want to see what it is."

"Maybe tomorrow," I said, and I got up and went into the boy's bathroom. Katie had left the table by the time I got back. If I wasn't *different* enough, carrying around a statue of an old lady in my pocket would surely put me over the top. I know how these things go.

38

Befana

This young man named Simon is having a very rough time, more than he lets on to anyone. I'm glad that people are taking an interest – his teacher, his parents, even one or two kids at school, but the one he seems to be responding to the most is old Sal, the one that introduced me to Simon. His teacher knows that he is very smart, but very quiet. She's also noticed that he is not doing as well as he did at the beginning of the year. His grades have dropped and he is withdrawing more and more. She tries to draw him out but then he retreats even more. His parents have noticed that he speaks less and less when he is with them and he chooses to spend more time alone in his room. They were initially excited about hearing of a friendship with someone named Sal but every time they ask Simon about him, or about inviting Sal over to the house, Simon clams up tight and goes to his room. Now his parents are becoming concerned about this "friendship." Who is this Sal, and what kind of influence is he having on their troubled son? The kids at school find Simon's demeanor to be anti-social and that always spells trouble in school or in any social environment. What Simon doesn't realize is that the more he retreats the harder it is to deal with others. Retreating does not make life any easier. This, I know from personal experience.

What is beginning to worry me the most about Simon is the time he does spend alone. Even when there is no one around he isn't engaged in activities that many kids his age enjoy. He is not playing video games. He is not "surfing the net." Most of the time when he goes to his room he is lying on his bed and staring at *me*.

That's all he does is stare – he won't talk to me, either. I can't read minds, you know. His thoughts he keeps locked up inside his head and he doesn't share them, even with the vacant air around him. At least when I was all alone back in my hometown in Italy, I used to talk out loud inside the privacy of my little hut. But, not this kid, he doesn't even trust nothingness to be loyal. I can't reach him. I can be here for him, but if he doesn't put his thoughts out there, I can't touch his thoughts. Even the spiritual world has some rules.

Today, before dinner, he was sitting up in bed and sketching pictures in his notebook. He always draws the same kinds of things: geometric shapes – circles, triangles, and odd-looking multi-sided figures. Out of each shape there are elongated little circles that shoot out of the abstract forms. He fills up pages and pages of these same designs. Sometimes, he will stare upward at the ceiling as if he's looking for new inspiration, but then he looks down and draws the same figures again. When his mother called him down for dinner, he didn't even appear to hear her. He continued to draw his pictures as if he is all alone in the world. Finally, she knocked on the door and entered.

"Are you okay, Simon?" she asked him, but Simon was still in his reverie and did not respond. "Simon, I asked if you're okay. Didn't you hear me calling you for dinner? I've been calling you...."

Finally, Simon looked up at her and shut his notebook. Without saying a word, he set it down on the bed and walked past his mother to go downstairs for dinner. Before heading down after him, she picked up his notebook and looked inside. Flipping through the pages she saw sheet after sheet of similar drawings. She sighed and said in a quiet voice, *"Dear Lord, please help me. I don't know what to do. What is wrong with our son?"* I know that she and her husband have taken Simon to a therapist but the child psychologist told them to be patient with Simon. *Some children adapt to huge changes at a different pace; Simon is adapting slowly. Don't push him,* he'd said. But Cynthia Rossi is worried that there is a reason Simon might be adapting more slowly than usual. She is afraid to push him but she thinks he needs to adapt soon – for his own sake, not hers. Out loud she said, *"I just want our son to be happy, Lord. Please help him to be happy."*

Now that his mother has put her thoughts out there, I tried to reassure her that everything will be fine. God hears her prayers. I hope she understands the message I am meant to convey. He hears us and he does answer us. He will help Simon; one way or another; she may not see it but he is already helping Simon.

39

Stella

#*Moccasinswap* - *Journal: Day Two*

Today was an absolute blur. I went to Emma's eighth-grade class at Granger and showed up twenty minutes early so that I could find her classroom. Her homeroom teacher, Mrs. Horner was alone in the room making some preparations before the students arrived. She seemed very preoccupied and not wishing to be disturbed so I quietly made my presence known.

When she asked me if I was Emma's friend, I told her yes, and gave her my name. She said she was perfectly aware of why I was there, she told me to wait outside with the others and when the bell rang she would show me my seat, or I could ask one of Emma's classmates.

I carried Emma's schedule with me throughout the day and went from one classroom to the next for each class. I don't know why they have to switch rooms all day long, it seems so disruptive. I found each classroom without any problem except for the gym for PE class which was on the other side of the building from everything – so, I was late for that class. I endured a number of stares and snickers from the other students but Emma's friends, Toni and Eve, at least came over and sat with me during lunch. They asked me quite a few questions about homeschooling and "why anyone in their right mind" would want to do that nowadays; it seems so old-fashioned. I told them that it wasn't so bad and that my mother is a trained teacher; she has a degree in history. They shrugged their shoulders.

After school, I gathered up all the assignments I needed to pass on to Emma since part of the deal is that we are still responsible for our work (and we agreed to do both our own and each other's – just to see how they compared).

When I met up with Emma after school at the river, the first thing she did was yell "How on earth do you live in that small room with those sisters you have?" She complained that there wasn't enough room for all her stuff, let alone her clothes. She noticed that when she came back from the bathroom (after standing in line) that Maris was wearing the outfit she'd laid out for herself! Why does she think she can do that, she asked me! I told her that Maris has boundary issues. Emma said my brothers were exceptionally loud all day long and it was impossible to concentrate on the lessons she was required to do with all that noise! My Mom and Grandma were very sweet and sympathetic and they invited her to help them make chocolate chip cookies with them because "cookies are good for the soul."

She told me that she used to think that my life might be kind of "interesting" but that now she knows that interesting does not mean the same thing as outrageous and that's what she thinks of it now. How did I put up with it every single day?

I smiled as Emma went on about her difficulties fitting into my moccasins. I reminded her to keep a journal of her experiences. She said, "Ha! Are you kidding me? Who has time or energy to journal? I didn't have enough time to think before, but now, forget it."

I tried to share my thoughts about her life, how quiet it is and how I find it to be very busy sometimes, but she didn't seem interested. She told me she knows what her life is like already, she doesn't need a play-by-play from me. She was positively exasperated and tired. I told her to go home (to my home) and go into the garage. It's quiet there, most of the time. What I can't understand is how she lives with so much quiet time but, poor Emma, I knew this would be an adventure for her. I'm the one that has found some peace and quiet I did not know existed.

I did get to see this kid named Jack that she thinks is so wonderful. He is cute, I'll give her that, but he seems rather full of himself. No wonder Emma is afraid to talk to him. How is anyone supposed to squeeze past that big bubble of arrogance to say hello.

Lastly, I didn't get a chance to ask Emma if I could borrow some of her clothes. Evidently, Toni and Eve said I looked like I belonged in a Huck Finn novel. If I was going to make it at this school – even for one week – I needed to get with it.

I guess I was a little exasperated, too, but for once, I had no one to share my feelings with.

40

Sister Maria Nicola

I want the kind of life I can hold together, Sandy had said. Every person on this planet knows that it is difficult to hold one's life together. There are so many facets to life and holding them all together is like trying to pick up a jigsaw puzzle and keep it in one piece. Married people know that it is supremely difficult to hold a marriage together and help each other. Parents know that holding a family together takes a lot of work and energy and patience. Teachers try to hold their classrooms together. Faith is another part of life that takes work and holding together, but not one of these aspects of life are we ever meant to hold together alone. Human beings were never meant to do it all alone. For everything, we need God.

Yesterday's class lesson: C.S Lewis – how do the children "hold it together" once they pass through the wardrobe into Narnia? They suddenly find themselves in new territory without a map.

Question 1: How would you personally feel if you went through a wardrobe and found yourself in an unfamiliar and often dangerous place?

Question 2: How do you keep from getting too scared when you are in a difficult situation?

Question 3: What happened to the children after they encountered the lion?

Question 4: Why was the lion so important to this story?

Question 5: Have you ever had a "lion" make a lasting impression upon your life?

The answers to my five questions were varied. First I had the students write their answers on a piece of paper, then I asked them to share their answers with the class. Finally, I asked them to turn in their papers (because we all know that not all students want to share their answers out loud.) Most students could not seem to make the connection I was asking them to make. Many of them gave me answers that included imaginary weaponry they use in their game systems to solve their problems and the "lion" turns out to be some 3-dimensional virtual superhero. I can't exactly lecture them about sticking to realistic answers when the basis for Lewis' story was purely filled with fantasy. One student raised a red flag about the "lions" in her life being bad, and not superheroes at all. But, Simon's paper concerned me the most. There was neither reality nor fantasy in his response. To each question he answered by drawing a shape with small ovals around the shape. Each question contained a different shape, but all the shapes were surrounded by small ovals. He had no words with which to reply to the questions. I decided to get his parents in here for a chat.

Today, when both Mr. and Mrs. Rossi came in to speak with me about Simon, I began by placing Simon's paper on the desk between us, the one filled with shapes and ovals. I could tell by his mother's reaction that she had seen this type of thing before. His father looked amused but also concerned and said, "I used to do silly stuff and doodle on my papers when I was a kid, too. But, you're right, Sister, he shouldn't be answering questions with shapes."

"Mr. and Mrs. Rossi," I said gently, "I want to reassure you that Simon is a wonderful young man. I never experience any behavior issues with Simon. He is always on time for school; he is always polite and quiet, perhaps too much so, and until a few weeks ago, he has always been very conscientious about his work and has excelled. The reason I've called you in here is that in the past several weeks, Simon's work has regressed. He does not complete his math assignments, he rarely turns in essays anymore and on his tests and quizzes, he either leaves questions blank or he puts an x through the all the options. I guess I am wondering if you've observed any changes at home. Has something happened or has Simon experienced something that can help me understand why he may need some extra help right now?"

It was Mrs. Rossi who now replied, "I'm actually glad you called us in, Sister. To be honest, I have noticed that Simon spends more and more time alone in his room. I don't know what he does up there except draw similar pictures to what you've shown us here. He's always been a very quiet child, but he's shying away from any conversations lately. I was going to ask you if you know of a student, a friend of Simon's named Sal? Is there a student named Sal here at your school? We were wondering if maybe this friend is having some negative influence on Simon."

"No, I'm sorry, Mrs. Rossi, there is no Sal in our school. You're aware that we're a very small school. We know all the students – I know of no one named Sal; it might be a nickname but I'm unaware of anyone that goes by this name. Quite frankly, Simon does not have many friends here, and certainly, no one named Sal. Has he talked about this person with you?"

"Only once," Mr. Rossi replied. "He mentioned him only once with regard to the Italian sandwiches that this friend likes. He seemed like a real friend to us but when we questioned Simon further, he clammed up on us and wouldn't tell us anything more."

"Hmm, that's interesting. I'll see what I can find out. I know the principal over at Granger, Ed Anderson. Perhaps there is a student named Sal who attends there. I can get back to you on that. In the meantime, we need to figure out what we can do to get Simon back on track. Is there anyone you know of that he will talk to? I tried to talk to him one day after school, but like you said, he clams up rather quickly."

Mrs. Rossi reiterated what she had told me at the beginning of the school year about Simon having seen a therapist and how Dr. Everson had told them that some children just take more time than others to adapt to new environments. I suggested that maybe they would like to have Simon back to see this Dr. Everson and discover if something has happened to slow down the pace of adaptation. At the end of our little meeting I think we were all more worried about Simon than we were before. I don't like it when I have to worry parents; it seems that most parents have enough worries, but something is wrong with Simon and I think we need to work together to help him, not let him "adapt at his own pace" all alone. He needs support and guidance. Clearly, Simon is not adapting; Simon is giving up.

41

Salvatore

Allegra called this morning. She wanted to know if I would be up for a visit during the winter holidays. When did we start calling them winter holidays, I wondered? But, I kept my mouth shut and told her I would enjoy seeing her and her husband.

Well, Dad, Steven and I are no longer together, she'd told me. They've been married for fifteen years, for heaven's sake. No longer together? What does that mean?

What happened, I asked her.

We have different goals, she said.

I felt bad for my daughter. Different goals? Is that all it takes to bust up a marriage anymore, *different goals*? I asked her about the divorce.

We're not divorced quite yet. We are legally separated. At least we didn't bring any children into this scenario, she said so nonchalantly.

When she wanted to marry Steven I told her to make sure this was what she wanted – she seemed to have *different goals* back then, too. I had my concerns, but Steven seemed like a good man. What more can a father ask for his daughter? Over the years Steven's job has taken him all over the world; he's hardly ever home. Do they really need a legal separation? Her job as a hospital administrator keeps her pretty busy and both of them decided that they couldn't incorporate a family. I always had this notion that families were gifts we were supposed to love, not incorporate. Who incorporates a gift, for Pete's sake?

Not to look a gift horse in the mouth, though, I asked her why she wanted to come visit me after all this time. She said we needed to talk. She feels concerned about my determination to continue living by myself. I told her I would love to see her, but I'm doing just fine and we don't need to talk about that. We have so many other nice things we can talk about. I told her I've missed her. She cleared her throat and then said she would see me in a few weeks.

Before I let her hang up I came straight out and asked her a question:

Allegra, what happened between us? A long time ago we had a much different relationship; did I do something to make you become so distant? It would be nice to know.

She didn't answer right away and then she said simply, *life changes things, Dad.*

So then I asked her, *If you could have a different life than the one you have now, what kind of life would you have?*

She asked me what kind of a question was that. I told her that someone had asked me the same question recently. She said she wasn't sure but she'd think about it and see me soon. Then she hung up.

When Simon came in today he caught me looking through some old photo albums. He sat with me very quietly as I looked through each page. If I offered up a story about a picture or two, he'd sit there and listen. If I didn't say anything, he remained quiet also. My lovely wife loved to use our old Kodak camera to take pictures when the children were small and at each stage as they grew older. We have several photo albums full of pictures. After looking through two of them I pushed them to the side.

"You have a nice family," Simon told me. "It is good that you have pictures to remember them."

"Do you have a bunch of pictures, Simon?" I asked him.

"No… well, not like this. The pictures that my adopted parents have taken are all on the computer. There are some printed out and framed."

"But no pictures of when you were a little guy in Korea." He shook his head.

"Do you remember much about your parents, son?" Again, he shook his head.

"Just because you can't remember them doesn't mean they're not a part of you. They're with you every day. They live in your very self, how you laugh, how you talk, how you react to things. We inherit more than we realize. I believe that, don't you?" He shrugged his shoulders. I expected him to get up and leave like he does when he doesn't want to talk about something, but he didn't; he sat there quietly and just looked at the pile of albums.

Finally, in a low voice he spoke up and said, "I remember my grandfather."

"Oh," was all I could think of to say.

"He took care of me when my parents were no longer there. I don't remember what happened to them. He didn't have much but he gave me all he had."

Again all I managed to say was, "Oh."

"I miss him very much."

"I'm sure you do, son. He must have been a very fine man. All he did for you helped you become such a nice young boy."

"I don't think people understand," he said. "I don't think they *can* understand."

I didn't know what he meant or how to respond. He seemed to be thinking more than communicating. I waited and listened. After a few minutes he stood to leave.

"My parents are bugging me about meeting my friend named Sal."

"Oh," I said again. "I suppose I should change my shirt." I smiled but he looked so despondent. "We'll figure it out, son, don't worry." Simon left. He thinks of me as a friend. Well, I'll be… I thought it was just me that considered him a friend.

42

Befana

Sweet little Vittoria was only eight years-old when I found her sitting on a wooden bench in a small flower garden enclosed by a short stone wall. She was pulling the petals off of a sunflower, one at a time and in clockwise order, and for some reason, sniffing each petal before throwing it into a basin of water next to the bench. She was an only child and though her parents doted on her night and day, she often found herself quite alone in the garden with very little to do. Her parents tried to fill her life with every good thing, new learning experiences, plenty of joyful moments, and the things that make children smile such as toys, games, activities and entertainment; they surrounded her with plenty of playmates and cousins, but little Vitty always felt like something was missing in her life. She would pout and fold her arms in front of her when her mother told her to stop sulking around the house and enjoy herself. She would sit and whine until her father sat on the floor with her and read to her or played some games, which he did every time his daughter would pout. When the child was invited to her cousins' homes or to a play date with friends she would brood in a corner while the other children frolicked and played. Vitty had made a career of sulking, no matter how hard anyone tried to cheer her, she refused to be cheered. By the time she'd reached five years-old she was known as Vitty the old bitty. The more her parents tried to amuse her the more this child would feel sorry for herself. And so the years passed.

On this particular day when I met little Vitty, her mother had tried to distract her from acting churlish by giving Vitty something creative to do; she'd given her a clay and paint set so that Vitty could sculpt and decorate something beautiful, but Vitty continued to act like a petulant child and refused to be consoled by arts and crafts. She threw the clay against the wall and spilled the paints on the floor. Her mother was patient but in her heart she felt that Vitty must be a spoiled child because she did not seem to appreciate anything. Her mother felt exhausted from years of trying to please her daughter only to discover that she could not be pleased. "Well, Vitty, if you're going to continue to pout go outside and sit on the bench and count your blessings," her mother told her. "Don't come back inside until you have found a way to be grateful for all you have." So, when I found Vitty, she was pulling the petals off the sunflower plants and sniffing each petal before tossing it into the water basin. She did not have a clue what her mother meant by "counting her blessings" so she counted the flower petals instead, and realizing that each of these petals had no scent, she tossed them into the basin.

Vitty continued this activity until all the sunflowers were without petals. She'd counted dozens of petals and not one of them smelled yellow, like she thought they should. When she discovered that all the sunflowers were now bare and ugly and all that remained was a pitiful looking bulb, she began to weep silently. She knew she was not allowed back in the house until she had found a way to be thankful for all her blessings but she did not know what they were. How could she count them? In her own young mind, the mysterious missing piece in her life was larger than the sum of all her blessings and she didn't see how counting the basic things in her life that she was naturally supposed to have would lessen her frustration.

Vitty went from flower patch to flower patch pulling up daisies, zinnias, black-eyed susans, and coneflowers by their stems and then sitting down on her bench and plucking away all the petals from each flower. She would sniff each petal and toss it into the basin just as she had with the sunflowers. After a couple of hours, Vitty was finished counting the petals. In actuality, she'd lost count after thirty because she could count no higher. The basin next to her bench was now filled with wilting debris of once-beautiful flowers. In the next moment, Vitty looked around at the garden. It no longer looked like a beautiful garden, she thought. It looked barren and useless. What was the point of having a garden if you could toss away the flower petals so easily and find it looking wretched? Vitty started to cry, not only out of sadness, but out of sheer anger as well. She had enjoyed sitting in the garden when it was filled with colorful flowers and fragrant scents; and now that it looked pitiful she hated it. She jumped down from the bench and began to stomp on the ravaged plants; they were useless, everything about the garden was now worthless because flowers without petals are ugly. Flowers are supposed to have petals; that's what makes them flowers!! Vitty jumped up and down in anger until, finally spent of her frustration, she plopped down on the ground and began to sulk with determination. She folded her arms in front of her (her favorite pose) and cursed the garden for being so fragile. What good is a garden if anyone can ruin it?

In her brooding state of mind, Vitty suddenly heard a small sound. At first it sounded far away like a distant motor but then as it drew near it reminded her of a soft hum, a distinct murmur of insect activity. Vitty looked near her elbow and saw that a bumble bee had come into the garden and was hovering near one of the coneflower plants. The child turned slowly and watched the bee as it whirled and whirled around the plant until it found the object of its purpose: a small bud. As bumble bees are apt to do, it niggled around the bud until the child could see that there was a new flower that would open soon. Vitty gazed around the garden. All the plants she had stripped of flowers had tender stems with new buds. Soon the garden would be filled with lively colors and sweet aromas; bees would spread the pollen around and butterflies would dance lightly on the petals and all the basic things would fill the garden once again and for reasons she did not yet understand, Vittoria felt happy – and for the first time, she smiled.

43

Simon

Old-fashioned clocks have always fascinated me. The clock at school looks very old-fashioned; it has a red second hand that ticks away each minute, a short black hand that sits on the hour and a longer minute hand that moves with each passing minute. You can actually watch time passing by. You can't do that by watching anything else. Dasan used to know what time it was (more or less) by looking at the position of the sun up in the sky. My parents have a couple of modern digital clocks – one is on the microwave in the kitchen and others are on the TV and computer. Other than that they rely on their phones to tell them what time it is. I asked them if I could have an old-fashioned clock for my bedroom, so for my birthday last year they bought me a large wall clock that looks like a pocket watch and the chain is looped and nailed to the wall; it's kind of cool. It may be a lame thing to do, but I like watching each second of time ticking away and wondering how many seconds of time each person has before they die. It's a morbid thought, I know, but if you knew how many seconds you had, would you watch them to see how many you had left or would you ignore them? I think I would watch them. At school, I've taken to watching the clock on the wall to see how much time there is left before we can go home. When Sister Maria Nicola caught me watching the clock one day she said, "Simon, time passes much more slowly when you watch the clock." I disagree with her; I've found that by looking away from the clock and then looking back that time doesn't pass much at all.

Sal has some really old-fashioned clocks; one is a cuckoo clock he found in a thrift store. It still works pretty well, he said, but that doesn't matter, what matters is that it represents a time when people made things that were meant to last. He also said that this *Befana* statue has been around for a very long time; she was made to last and so was her special story. She lived during a time when there were no clocks. She must have known how to tell time by the sun, too, like Dasan. Sal told me that she spends a timeless eternity seeking the Baby Jesus. I thought that the idea of a timeless eternity would be even more fascinating than watching the time tick by on a clock but it can't be possible to watch eternity.

"I don't think there is such a thing as a timeless eternity," I told Sal. "It doesn't seem possible."

"Oh, really," he'd said. "How do you know? We only pay attention to time here on this earth because our planet goes around the sun and sometimes it's daytime and sometimes it's nighttime. The only way we can keep track of everything is by using time, but there is more to life than what we can see, and life in eternity may not have any use for keeping track of time. There must be a place where time doesn't need to be measured."

I thought about that. I thought about Narnia, and stories like that where other places we can't see exist and time isn't important. *Old Befana's* story exists in such a place, Sal had said, and time isn't that important for her. She journeys around the world and counts her life by experiences not by age.

"Do you do that, Sal? Do you count your life by experiences and not by age?" I'd asked him. It was the day I found him looking through old photo albums and he'd started telling me about his wife and his kids.

"I guess I do, son," he'd said. "The number of new experiences we have can slow down as we get older, but time doesn't. I've had some friends that don't live in their homes anymore. They spend time in places where they can't see the sun, the moon or the stars anymore. They don't know if it's summer or winter, if it's raining or sunny and warm. They stay inside a building that is always the same temperature and the artificial lights go on and off depending on what time the nurses decide to regulate them. These friends of mine see the clocks ticking time away, just like you and me, but the only experiences that affect them usually have to do with medical issues, when the nurse comes in to give them meds, or bathe them, or bring them food. I don't want to live like that." After a minute he continued, "I think of getting trapped in a tool shed with a rake stuck in my forehead as a valuable experience." He had chuckled when he said *valuable*. "What do you think about wiling away time without experiences?"

I told Sal that I didn't think that passing the time without experiences was a good use of time. Even though I agree with him on that, I know I don't fit into that pattern of measuring my life by experiences. He'd patted me on the back for saying that. "A good use of time," he'd said, "is when you are experiencing life with everything it has to offer: the good, the bad stuff, and the stuff that makes you think and feel something. The best thing you can do, kid, is balance those thoughts and feelings because not all experiences are going to tickle."

I had to think about what Sal said. When I came home that day I felt like he was right about one thing at least. The experience of getting him out of the tool shed was valuable, even for me. It was bad because he was hurt, more than he let on, but it was good because I was able to do something to help. Bad experiences don't always turn out to be good like they did that day and good experiences don't always remain good – someone can always ruin them.

44

Stella

#Moccasinswap - Journal: Day Three
It's only Tuesday and I don't know if I'm going to have the energy to get through an entire week of Emma's life. It's exhausting! Getting ready in the morning is hard enough. I must have changed clothes five times before I found something that I hoped would not offend Emma's friends. I was able to get into her jeans and I decided on a tank top which I'm pretty sure would make my Mom and Grandma raise their eyebrows, and I finally found the right shirt to match it. I had to let my hair down instead of pulling it back like I usually do. Emma's friends said that pony tails are for five year-olds. They also told me I needed to wear some makeup because my slightly olive skin tone looked like the same color as my dirty blond hair. Evidently, I needed to "accent" my features. They spent all of our free time telling me how I can improve my looks. I'm not sure I'm entirely comfortable with the makeover that seems necessary to fit in with the kids at school, but if I hadn't gone to a real school I guess I'd never realize that my natural looks needed improvement, so now instead of taking ten minutes to shower and get dressed it takes me an hour and a half before I feel "complete."

School is tiring, too. The first bell at 8:30 signals the start of the day in home room. I haven't really made any friends at all except for getting to know Emma's friends a little better. Emma's beloved Jack is in her home room; he is also in her English and Math class. I've never seen anyone so completely preoccupied with his own persona before. He likes to stir things up with the other students and when he does he seems to visibly inflate! I've noticed that the teachers find it easier to leave him alone instead of confronting him on every single issue. He is always talking to his friends and they seem to watch and wait for him to turn his attention in their direction. It's weird. I haven't quite figured it all out.

During the day it's a mad rush from home room to PE and then to History. I've decided not to try to run to the locker each time between classes because it takes too long so I end up carrying most of the morning books with me from one end of school to the other. Once I'm in class it is hard to concentrate because there are so many learning styles offered before I can even focus on the lesson itself. I have to choose how I'm going to learn the lesson presented by the teacher. Am I a visual learner? An auditory learner? A kinesthetic learner? A solitary or social learner? A verbal or logical learner? Or some fancy combination of the above? Once I determine my learning style for that class then I can begin the lesson which is directed by the teacher. By the time I'm finished, I don't feel like I've learned the lesson, I feel like I've just been used as a mouse in a cage as a part of an experiment to see how my brain works.

Between trying to discover the right shoes to wear to match with the right eyeliner, having the correct responses to "what did I think about 'The Bachelorette' last night, navigating my way through a vague learning process and finding the ins and outs of system known as education, I am exhausted!!! No wonder Emma just wants to sit and hold her knees and "decompress" when I see her after school. Whenever I'm around her friends I feel like I'm wearing something like a shock collar to gauge my responses and I can't stop myself from fretting about saying the right or wrong thing, even if I tried. Long after I leave the school I'm still twitching.

Emma thinks my life is too dull and dysfunctional because she can't find herself in my big family. She says she loves my Mom and Grandma because they pay attention to her so much. (She told me she can't figure out how they can pay so much attention to all my dumb siblings?) Emma's family doesn't have half as many kids, not by a long shot, but her parents seem to be in overdrive – the same way I feel at Emma's school – when they come home from work; they're exhausted and don't seem to mind if the kids do their own thing. What completely different lives we have! How did Emma and I even become best friends, I wonder? Do we even have anything in common? If my life is so dull and dysfunctional and her life is so wired, how did we find the same *friendship frequency? I have no idea. I'm glad there are only four days left. "Being Emma" is a constant puzzle and it requires constant attention to detail – the face she puts on at school takes a lot of work.*

I'm glad Mom suggested I keep this journal. If I didn't check in and write from my own heart, I might lose Stella altogether in the vastness of Emma's moccasins.

45

Sister Maria Nicola

With Advent upon us and Christmas season rapidly approaching I thought it might be nice to have the students discover some Christmas stories from around the world. In class today I began with my usual enthusiasm for what I believed to be a guaranteed hit with my English class.

"Marcus, open your thesaurus," I began, "and read aloud the synonyms you find for the word 'advent.'" He let out a disgruntled puff of air and opened the thesaurus on his desk. "While Marcus is reading the synonyms aloud, I'd like the rest of you to jot down one synonym that jumps out at you, something you never thought of when you heard the word 'advent.' Begin."

Marcus read the words: arrival, coming, appearance, approach, entrance, occurrence, debut, emergence, introduction, materialization, rise, showing up, unveiling, start, dawn, actualization..." The list continued for a few minutes as Marcus grew weary of reading the list of synonyms. I noticed the students were writing down a word here and there as instructed. Then I continued, "Imagine for a moment that you were sitting in this classroom one day and you were bored." (A din of chuckles followed from students who were actually listening to what I'd just said.) "Now, imagine that something wonderful made an appearance, something we'd never even heard of before it arrived, or something that we might be expecting that suddenly materialized, or our dear Principal, Sister Maria Reyna unveiled something brand new that we'd never seen before... take ten minutes and write down what that wonderful something would be! Tell me, in your own words, why the advent of this new thing you've imagined is important enough to celebrate every year for the next few thousand years!" I could feel myself smiling with excitement but the students expressed some lukewarm interest. Then, little by little, I could see their faces changing as they thought of something they would love to have appear before them, in this very classroom, to liven up their day and then they began to write.

I walked around the classroom, treading softly down each aisle, glancing at my students' papers as they wrote about their imaginary advent visitors. I must admit I was a little surprised; quite a few students had begun writing about people from outer space, or robotic artificial intelligence, or characters they know from the games they play, but some – the few serious students – began to write about real people from the past, or family members they had lost and would like to see again. I walked by Simon's desk fully expecting to see some shapes being drawn on his paper, but instead of his recent doodles he was writing about Korean legends in which kings were often presented at the top of a lofty mountain, or gods came down from the sky to be with the people. He imagined that these kings or gods would make a sudden appearance at a time when they were least expected. And, what if these godly kings appeared wearing rags, what would people think? Would it get their attention? In Christianity, he wrote, the Christ child is both a king and a God delivered to his people to save them and he's born in a poor stable. It fits together with what he'd heard as a child, he wrote thoughtfully. I believe there is more to Simon than most people realize. I do believe this child is special; his parents know this, I'm certain of it, but he just seems so vulnerable, so fragile. It is very difficult for kids with special insights to fit in with other kids that are hip and trendy. I hope the time will come when he begins to open up and find some friends. I've seen too many people I care about spiral downward within themselves and turn toward lifestyles that keep them in a frightening world of sadness.

I thought of my sister, Gen. At one time she was so much like this child, very sensitive and afraid to show her vulnerability. I remember one Christmas when I was ten and she was seven, she'd gone into her safe place and stayed there for a very long time. Our father had just stormed out of the house after teaching our mother another "lesson." Our mother had come home from the grocery store with several bags of food, none of which contained Dad's favorite beer and sausages. He was livid. Mom had told him that he was much kinder when he wasn't drinking his beer and she thought he might enjoy some steaks for Christmas instead of his usual sausages, but she never got to finish that thought. Dad had pushed her up against the refrigerator and hit her repeatedly while he told her to march right back to the store and return the groceries, *and don't come home until you have what I want.* During these frightening times it was my habit to retreat to the farthest corner of the room I shared with Gen and delve into another mystery novel while Gen crawled into the closet, plugged her ears, and drew pictures on the wall of the closet with her pencil. It would be easier to erase the pictures if she had to, she'd said. Her pictures generally featured a house with four windows. In each window there was a face – usually a father's angry face, a mother's crying face, and the faces of two children which showed no emotion but typically blackened with her pencil. Once, she'd drawn a path from the house to a mountain and the children hid behind the largest knoll. Gen would never talk about what she felt; she simply drew pictures in the closet. Sometimes her pictures would entail imaginary figures that had nothing to do with reality; it seemed she would get lost in her own imagination.

She tried to appease our parents so they wouldn't fight by bringing Mom some dandelion flowers she'd picked from the cracks in the driveway and she would collect the metal caps from Dad's beers and glue them on pieces of cardboard into a smiley face to give to Dad and try to make him smile. On this one occasion, however, Gen had tried to run after our Dad with one of her beer cap pictures. He'd grabbed the picture out of her hand, ripped it in two and tossed it on the ground. From that day on Gen never made pictures or drew anything more inside the closet. After that day when problems would heat up around the house,

Gen would run down the street to hide somewhere and not return until the coast was clear. I don't know where she went but she seemed to sense when it was safe to return. It was Christmas of that year when Dad walked out and never returned. Gen and I sat by the window of our small bedroom looking up at the stars, hoping that something magical would happen on Christmas morning, maybe Dad would come home a changed man, maybe Mom wouldn't cry all the time, maybe we would at least have some little presents under the tree, but when we awoke and tip-toed out to see if anyone had left us anything, there was nothing once again. We found our mother on the sofa, her eyes blackened from the assault of the previous evening, and the contents of her stomach dripping down the sides of her mouth onto the sofa cushion. She had taken too many sleeping pills. On this occasion she had survived the attempt at ending her life, but eventually she would succeed.

I heaved a heavy sigh and glanced once more at Simon's paper before I continued walking down the aisle. I felt confident that Simon had a good home; he appeared comfortable around his adopted parents; he'd always done well on his work, but something was wrong now, I could feel it in my bones. I had no idea how to gain his trust or the slightest inkling about how to invite him to confide in me. All that I'd tried so far seemed ineffective and I know from experience, the more you try the more you can push someone farther away. Simon seems to need an outstretched hand, or a shoulder, or a lifeline, but he doesn't seem to be very receptive and I believe his parents are quite concerned. So am I.

46

Befana

In my experience it is never easy to completely let go of something, whether it's a grudge, a bad habit, or most especially the past, and when you've been around as long as I have, you find that carrying any of those things around can become not only a bulky effort but a disfiguring one as well. These things can contort your features because regrets and sorrow look nothing like anticipation and gratitude when they're outlined into your eyes, or form lines around your mouth where your smile should be.

Back in my youthful days I didn't have anything like a looking glass. It was difficult to see my true reflection when I was younger, except for the muddled likeness that appears in the ripples of a river. I wasn't exactly a beauty but it could be said that I did not have a frightening face, either. My features were rather typical for someone of that region of the country. When my face was young it was smooth and my hair looked shiny and black. I had dark eyes and a prominent nose; like I said, nothing frightening, but there was also nothing remarkable about the way I looked. I was easy to ignore. As I grew older – and older – life seemed to change my appearance; I don't just mean aging, I mean *enduring* life. Where I once had softness and plumpness in my cheeks I eventually grew a calloused grimace like my cheeks were being sucked in by a powerful force within me. Between my dark eyes a deep track of irritation became a permanent crease between my brows, and the burden of survival had caused my shoulders to hunch forward and my back to twist and bow. Life is the artist that paints and sculpts our features with either harsh or delicate strokes. In my case, I allowed it to chisel away the pluckiness of optimism.

In recent years, however, I've learned that we don't have to reach old age looking like a beaten, wrung-out lump of hide. It's the load we carry that carves out those unattractive qualities – the grudges, the bad habits, and hanging on to unhappy memories. I didn't know this when I was younger but that's why my journey to follow the Baby Jesus and the man he became, changed my life. He came along to shoulder these burdens for us, take them off our hands and carry anything that is too heavy for us - and guess what? You can get to old age looking a little more like a polished apple. The one who gives us Life is the artist who can give us a make-over. That's what I've learned, folks, and it's the truth! My fear and loneliness have been lifted and now I can see myself as Jesus sees me – a person full of possibilities.

I once knew a farmer whose orchard was too close to the side of stony mountain. Every day the farmer would go out to his orchard and find that large rocks had tumbled down the mountain and damaged his fruit trees. Branches would break away from the trees, the fruit would become badly bruised and smashed, and the trees began to languish. The rocks were everywhere and the farmer could barely till the soil around the trees. The orchard looked like a war zone and the farmer was beginning to despair. One day when he'd reached the end of his rope, he finally looked up at the sky and said, "God, why do you keep bombarding my orchard with all these big rocks? Can't you see that they are destroying my land? Look at my trees, they used to be beautiful and now they are all ruined. What do you want me to do?" The farmer kept staring up at the sky wondering why God wouldn't answer him. "Is there some kind of a wall between us, Lord, is that why you won't answer me?" he asked, and shook his head in dejection. And that's when God's answer hit him – *is there some kind of a wall…?*

The farmer looked around at all the rocks; he pulled his cap off his head and eyed his orchard and then he laughed. He slapped his knee with his cap and got up from his self-pitying rut. He began to gather all the rocks in the orchard and piled them in a straight line around his land, rock after rock, boulder after boulder until he had a fine wall surrounding his property. Each day as more rocks tumbled down the mountain, the farmer would build his wall higher and higher. Soon the wall was so high that it protected his orchard from just about everything, and the trees began to flourish again. The farmer's reputation for the best fruit in the region became well-known, so renowned that the farmer became quite prosperous. Even the marauders and thieves could not breach his wall to steal his fruit. What was once a curse on his property became a blessing. An orchard that once looked shattered and ruined now looked like a magical garden. Something wonderful can always grow and become lovely from something that was once ruined. Inspiration is a gift; taking comfort in the support that we've been offered from above is a wonderful reward for trust; and rebirth is miraculous! There are always threats to goodness, beauty, innocence, and life but we don't have to tackle these dangers alone; we don't have to shoulder any of it alone. We can always ask for help.

47

Salvatore

Today I had to call the doctor about this darned knee. It doesn't seem to be getting any better. It hurts like a dickens when I walk and I've been trying to keep it propped up on the coffee table when I'm sitting in the living room because I can't bend it very well. The doctor wants to see me in his office this week so I'm going to take a cab because I don't want to bother Joe about something so small. I also don't want to listen to his rant about moving into *one of those nice places that has doctors right there on campus.* I know Joe means well, but I am just not ready to give up my home and my lifestyle. Things might not be perfect; I may not have the best circumstances, but when has that ever been the case? When Annalisa and I were first married, we lived in a boarding house for heaven's sake. That was not ideal. We barely had two nickels to rub together. We didn't even have a car to get to work or go to the market; we had to take the bus or walk! When the kids came along we got by, paycheck to paycheck. After the kids left we were finally able to put a little money aside and that's what is helping me now. So, I'm *old* – that's the only issue that bothers everyone and I don't see why I have to move out of my home just because those kids of mine think I'm too old to live alone. They seem to think a small condo is the best idea but I don't think it's a good idea at all; I think it's a stupid idea and I'm not going to be pressured into it no matter what they say. I like my life the way it is; it's never been easy before, why should it be easier now?

Mrs. Gray, a couple doors down, has offered to pick up some groceries for me and when I asked her what Korean people ate she said she had no idea but she would take a look when she went into the city and come back with a typical dish. When I'd asked her about it she'd raised her eyebrows but she didn't question my request; that's what I like about Mrs. Gray – she's very helpful but she minds her own business. She came back from the grocery store with my groceries and a styrofoam container filled with fish stew and vegetables. You could smell it a mile away. She said that the man at the food bar recommended it. I thanked her, and I was happy that I would be able to surprise Simon when he came by today; perhaps to repay his kindness for that delicious Italian sandwich he brought me.

When Simon arrived I told him to sit down and close his eyes. He looked at me warily and then closed them. I put the fish stew in front of him and told him to open his eyes. "It's not a sandwich but I thought you might like it." When he opened the styrofoam container and saw the stew he grinned from ear to ear. He ate it slowly and thoughtfully like he was remembering a different time in his life. He offered me a bite but I declined. He insisted so I took a bite. It tasted like it smelled but I pretended to enjoy it since he seemed to like it a lot. After he finished I asked him if he would mind walking with me to the garden. Last week he'd helped me find an old crutch out of the basement. I remembered it was down there from when Gino had broken his leg playing football in high school. There had been a pair of crutches but one of them broke when the boys decided to use them as stilts. Crazy kids; surprising they hadn't broken more legs. Simon grabbed the crutch for me and I managed to put my weight on it instead of putting all of my weight on my bad knee. The kid looked at me like I was crazy.

"What?" I asked. "I can do this."

"Okay, Sal, but if you fall down again and get hurt I won't be responsible."

"Who said you'd be responsible?" I snapped in my grumpy old man voice. "I'm fine. I just want to see what's going on out in the yard. Sometimes there are a few apples left on the tree even at this time of the year. There isn't any ice out there on the sidewalk is there?"

"No. There's no ice, but can't I just look for you? I can tell you if there are apples and then you can come and get them if you want to. Why make the trip all the way out there if there aren't any?"

"It's not the apples I want; it's the trip out there. I'd like to get some air. Is that all right with you?" We made it only as far as the back porch before I grew too tired to continue.

Simon shrugged his shoulders. I didn't want to make the kid feel bad. I know he's just concerned. He's the one that helped me out of the shed after all.

"Look," I said, "I may be a bit past my prime but I still like to make my own decisions while I still have enough seeds left in the old squash. Understand?" Simon looked at me with the most confused look I'd ever seen. I tapped on my head. "My squash, my melon… It's my brain. I don't like people telling me what I can and can't do, what I should do, or what I shouldn't do all the time. Understand?"

Simon replied, "If I don't understand much of anything else, Sal, I understand that." Of course he does. Kids get tired of being told everything all the time.

"Let me ask you something. If you were me, an eighty-five year-old man, with a bum knee, shaky hands, and eyesight that isn't what it used to be, what would you do?"

Simon thought for a moment and then said, "I don't think there is anything you *can* do. It's who you are. What else can you do?"

Such clarity of thinking. I liked this kid from day one. Then he added, "You're the best you that you can be right now, Sal."

"Do you think I could be better if I lived in a place with other people my own age?"

He laughed. I think that's the first time I saw him laugh since I met him.

He answered, "I don't think you like people your own age. Why would you want to live with them?" He had a point.

"Do you like people your own age, son?" I asked him.

He shrugged his shoulders and didn't answer the question. I sensed that that was the wrong question to ask. He didn't seem upset but he said he had to get going and he helped me back inside the house. I do wonder why he likes to spend so much time here. He needs to be around other kids, doesn't he? Shouldn't he be playing soccer after school or chasing a girl, or something? We may have some things in common but our situations are different; he has to grow up and part of that means learning how to get along with other people your own age. I've already done that and I don't have to get along with people my own age anymore. They're not around long enough to make it worthwhile. We all know what lies ahead for people my age.

48

Simon

That was pretty awesome what Sal did today. He can't even get out of his house to check on his yard but he asked some lady to get me some fish stew from the store. For five minutes I felt like I was back at home, eating a rare treat of fish stew with Dasan. Usually, we ate the fish stew on Christmas Eve. It was like a special tradition we had, not just Dasan and I, but the few people we knew that also believed in Jesus. We weren't allowed to talk about Jesus, or go to church, or wear anything that symbolized him, so we ate fish stew on Christmas Eve because we learned from the priests that Jesus had multiplied a few fish for thousands of people. The priests that slipped into our village discreetly were very careful about preaching Jesus' message. They told us that the secret blessing of Jesus' life is that something as big as God's kingdom can come from something as tiny as a mustard seed. A few measly fish can become thousands of fish. A little yeast can become a lot of bread. A short life here can become a life forever with God. Anything that is small and poor can become large and great, just like Jesus himself. But, for us, it was against the law to follow these teachings; our government wanted to make sure we knew we were small and we were supposed to stay that way. According to those in power, we were supposed to all be exactly the same and under their big thumb, no room for growth or diversity. That's what Dasan always told me. The leaders didn't want us to believe that we could get anything better while we were alive, or even after we die. *They even want to think they can control our eternal destiny*, he'd said. Maybe Dasan was too vocal about what he believed. Maybe that's why they took him away.

I'm pretty sure Sal believes in Jesus, too; he has a cross in each room of his house. He wears a cross on a chain around his neck and he even has a picture of Jesus by the front door with his hands reaching out and rays of light coming from his heart. He said his wife Annalisa put it there. She was sick before she died, he said, but she was a big believer in Jesus' mercy. Sister Maria Nicola talks about mercy all the time. She has us finding examples of it every time we read a new story in our textbook. It's like her big thing – *look for mercy in the story. Look for mercy in your life. If you look for mercy, you can find it. If you can't find it, then show it so someone else can find it.* She says that over and over and over again. Today, in class, we were talking about Advent again and about what the anticipation was all about. She read us the story about Mary and Joseph going to Bethlehem and there was no room for them at the inn. She read about Jesus being born in a stable and the angels were singing, and the shepherds heard the angels and went to visit him. Then, the Magi came to bring Jesus gifts and King Herod wanted to kill the Baby Jesus so he killed a ton of babies in Bethlehem. Sister asked us to find examples of mercy in these stories. Some people said that the innkeeper showed mercy and let them stay in the stable instead of letting Jesus be born in the middle of the street, and others said that the angels showed mercy by singing about Jesus and making the baby happy. Other examples included the shepherds' visit as an act of kindness and the wise men bringing gifts and then showing mercy by going a different way back home instead of telling Herod where he could find Jesus. I didn't raise my hand; I didn't think that all those babies getting killed was very fair. It was almost like Sister read my mind. She told us that Herod's actions were monstrous back then but that there are a lot of "Herods" out there in the world even now; there are many people who do bad things against children. *That's why it's important to keep mercy alive*, she said. *If the wise men hadn't followed the message in the dream instead of what the king ordered them to do, Herod's men would have killed the Baby Jesus before he could have completed his mission of mercy to save all of us. The best way to fight the Herods in this world is with mercy – never forget that. Without any mercy, the world is full of Herods only and the world becomes cold and bitter. Follow the path of mercy – if you look for mercy, you can find it. If you can't find it, then show it so someone else can find it.*

Sister wants us to do a short presentation the week before Christmas break on Christmas stories from around the world and, of course, we're supposed to point out where we find mercy in the story. I think Sister gives us too much homework; I wish she would show *us* some mercy once in a while. For tomorrow she wants us to write a paragraph to tell her about our idea for our presentation. Before I could even think about what to do, there was a knock at my bedroom door. According to my old-fashioned clock, it's only a quarter till five. Mom and Dad don't usually get home from work until six.

"Simon, can I come in?" It was Dad. He's never home before Mom.

"Yeah," I said.

Dad came in looking happy about something; I wasn't sure what was going on. I was sitting at my desk tapping my pencil on my notebook when Dad sat down on my bed.

"Doing homework?" he asked.

"Yeah," I answered.

"Sorry. Do you have a lot of homework? I thought maybe we could go out and do something together today before Mom gets home, kind of a surprise for her."

I shrugged my shoulders. "I don't have a lot; just some, and I haven't figured out what to write yet. What are we doing?"

Dad beamed. "Get your coat. Let's go. I'll tell you on the way."

A few minutes later we were on the highway headed toward Fairfield County. Dad had put an axe in the back seat of his SUV. "Where are we going?" I asked.

The smile on Dad's face was growing by the minute. "Simon, we're going to go to a tree farm! We are going to chop down our own Christmas tree this year! What do you think about that?"

I shrugged my shoulders. "It's cold outside. What about the white tree in the box downstairs? Aren't we going to put that one up?"

Dad looked at me and laughed but I'm not sure why. "Mom can find a place for her white tree and pink feathers if she wants to. I thought this year you and I could do something special, something only us guys can do. We're going to use that axe back there and chop down a tree, strap it to the top of the SUV, and put up our own tree and decorate it with something other than pink feathers. What do you think?"

I shrugged my shoulders again. "Do we know how to do that?"

"We can learn together," he said. "Does that sound good to you?"

"Okay."

I know Dad meant well but chopping down a tree isn't easy at all; I know this because just trying to chop a branch off of Sal's tree made me sore for a week. Dad works at a desk so he doesn't get much exercise and I'm only seventy pounds; I think a tree weighs more than I do. At the tree farm we looked for a good sized tree, not too big but not too small, either. We found one that we thought we could handle. Between the two of us we hacked away at that tree, but after an hour, we hadn't even cut halfway into the trunk. Dad was sweating a lot; he'd taken off his coat and hat. He seemed out of breath. I took the axe and swung it as hard as I could but I could never seem to hit the same spot twice so I was actually making little dents in random places. Dad patted me on the shoulder and said *good job*, but seriously... we weren't getting anywhere. We'd chopped it enough to release some pine scent but that was about it. Finally, the big guy from the tree farm came over to help us. He took three swipes at the trunk where Dad had made some deeper slashes and the tree came down in one minute. It would have taken us all night to chop this tree down. (I'll have to remember this example for sharing time when Sister asks us about where we've seen mercy this week.)

It didn't take long after that for the tree guy to help Dad strap the tree to the top of the car. When we got back into the car, Dad threw his head back and laughed, letting out a lot of sighs in between laughter and groans.

"We did it, Simon! We chopped down our first Christmas tree. Okay, we had some help, but maybe next year we can go to the gym first. What do you say?"

"Yeah," I said. It was kind of lame, but maybe by next year he'll forget about doing this again. I don't remember me and Dad ever doing anything, just the two of us. "Did you tell Mom where we were going?" I asked.

"I wanted to surprise her but I think she suspects something. I told her not to expect us home for a while. What would you say if you and I go get something to eat from Hamburger Hal's on the way home? Mom probably wouldn't like that, either, but it's a guy thing. Are you up for a burger?"

I shrugged my shoulders. I wasn't really hungry at all because of the fish stew I'd eaten earlier at Sal's but it seemed important to Dad that I go along with his "it's a guy thing" plans for our evening. My arms were hurting, so was my back and I could tell that Dad was sore, too. But, at least we could say we did *guy things* together. I felt too tired to do my homework tonight; I really don't care anymore anyway. I have no idea what to write about and when it comes right down to it, I'm not really enthused about the Christmas season at all this year. What a bunch of hype. I'm too old to care about toys and I'm too young to care about much of anything else. Everyone is getting into the *Christmas spirit* and I don't know what that is anymore. I don't even care. If I could picture myself in a different life right now, I think I would enjoy being in nothingness – no holidays, no school, no parents wanting to bond by doing guy stuff, no expectations of feeling happy because it's Christmastime – nothing. If Sister asked me that question today, that's what I would tell her – I want to experience nothing; that's about as far removed from where I am as I can imagine.

49

Stella

By the time I arrived at Emma's house, hung my coat in the mud room and removed my shoes (something I'm trained to do in my own home but doesn't seem to be a norm around here) I found that Emma was sitting in the kitchen with her head on the table. She looked slumped over like she'd been there for a while.

"What's wrong, Em? Are you okay? When did you get here?"

"Stella, I can't do this anymore. Can we please stop? I can't live in your moccasins one more minute. Your life is suffocating me. Please, let me out of this project; let me have my own life back, I'm begging you. I want to come home to my own house, and eat my own junk food, and sleep in my own room and in my own bed and yell at my own siblings and despise my own parents. I don't want to hear all the noise in your house anymore; everyone talks at the same time at the dinner table. How does anyone hear anything that's being said? I don't have room to move around; I can't hear myself think because there is always something going on somewhere in the house and the garage may be quiet but it's freezing in there this time of year! I don't know how you live with parents that ask so many questions, and sisters that talk... all... the... time. They never shut up, and brothers that are constantly having some kind of a brawl. I can't make heads or tails of your schoolwork; it's way ahead of me. I feel lost and confused. I swear your life is what I imagine it would be like to live in a mental hospital right before the meds get passed around. Please, Stell, if you're my friend, let me out of this. I promise, out of sheer pity for you, I will let you have your way on anything you ask for from now on. I miss my own stupid routines. I miss my friends at school. I miss seeing Jack, at least just to get a glimpse of him every day...

"Emma, what on earth do you see in that guy anyway? I don't think he's a nice guy. He's so full of himself."

"Hey. Don't say anything about Jack. I'm glad you don't like him so I don't have any competition from my best friend, at least, but don't say anything mean about him. I like him a lot."

"Okay, sorry, I won't say another word about Jack, but Em we only have a couple more days of this. It's almost over and I have to finish a group project I started in your history class. I can't bail out on them now and it's too far into it for you to help the group. All you have to do is read the chapter on the Delaware tribe and answer the questions at the end of the chapter. Our group each has a part to discuss about how the Delaware came to live here by the Muskingum River, while others went to northwestern Ohio and how they became a powerful tribe after they came here. It's really interesting. You know how much I love history and even though the rest of my group isn't as thrilled about this project as I am I like that I've had a chance to step up and be the team lead on this. That kind of thing doesn't happen in my life. If you think your life has been a breeze for me this week, think again. I feel like I'm floating around in a fog most of the time. If you think my moccasins are suffocating you, I feel like a little pebble in your moccasins; there is so much room to grow, and do stuff I have never done before in my life. Please, Em, just a couple more days. We don't have to continue until Sunday morning but at least give me until Friday."

"Do I even know you?" Emma asked. "You have got to be kidding me. You want to stick with this ridiculous life-swap for the rest of the week because of a group history project? There is something wrong with you. I've never seen this dorky side of you before."

"Yes, you have."

"Okay, maybe I have but your dorkiness was never wearing *my shoes*!" Emma groaned and threw her head back down on the table. I could tell she'd had enough. As challenging as my friend's life has been for me, I was intrigued enough to stick it out. Giving up too soon just felt wrong, like what was the point of doing this in the first place if all we get out of it is that we can appreciate our own lives a little better once we get back to them. I think we figured that out on day one. There has to be more to learn from this but I had to throw Emma a bone because she's my best friend and I don't like to see her suffer.

"You know, there is one more reason why I think we should stick with this."

"What? So you can solve extra equations on the board in math class?"

"No. I think Jack has noticed that you're not there. You know how people take certain things for granted when they see them every single day? Well, maybe after you've been gone for a whole week he'll pay more attention to you." That got her attention. She lifted her head.

"You think so?"

"Yes, I do," I said. "Think about it. If you went back tomorrow he'd probably act like you'd never really been gone. It's only been a couple of days but if you're out the whole week, you might be more interesting. Not that you're not interesting! It's just that you said that before he didn't even notice you but now he might. That's all I'm saying."

"Fine, you have a point. But Stell, please give me some helpful hints to deal with the constant craziness at your house. I can't even get away from it to go to school since your home is your school! It's non-stop."

"I have an idea. I haven't had time to do this as much as I need to but my Mom and Grandma have been after me to try and keep up with it. The library has this program where you help kids younger than you with their homework. It's like a tutoring thing. Em, you're a great reader and some first graders need help. It's simple really. You just sit there and help them read a book. Sometimes the kids don't even show up and you get to relax and chill in the library for a while. It's an escape for a couple of hours and again, it's only for a couple more days. You can get a break."

Emma sighed but she saw that it was a worthwhile plan. She needed a break and she'd found a way to have one. We were in it for the long haul now but it wouldn't be much longer. I admitted to her that I found her life very difficult for me, as well. It was just so different. When I get up in the morning in my own life I don't have the worry of trying to fit in to the world around me. I already fit into my family – it's kind of a package deal. I told Emma that I find it very exhausting trying to fit in with her school friends every day; I always feel like an outsider, probably because I am one.

"Huh," Emma said, "It's like that every day, Stell. After a while you get used to it; it's a struggle to fit in every day because the ground rules change all the time. Everyone's constantly trying to mark their territory and designate their own spot. The only person who occupies an unchallenged spot is someone like Jack. That's why I find him so interesting. I wonder how he got there and how he manages to keep that spot."

"What do you know about him personally?"

"His Dad is one of the head coaches for football at OT Univ. Supposedly, he was once in the NFL but had an injury that cut his career short but he's a pretty successful coach. And get this: his Mom was once a contender for Miss America. Jack has an older brother at Tech that's a great football player and everyone says Jack will probably follow in the family footsteps. How cool is that?"

"Does Jack even play football? He seems kind of lazy."

"*Stella!* He's not lazy. Maybe he just doesn't have to work as hard as other people do."

"I guess. He just doesn't seem very motivated to do much except hold court."

"Enough. We're not talking about Jack anymore. I think he's doing just fine."

"If you say so, Em. I know you like him a lot so I won't say another word about him. Just be careful you don't admire him for what you think he is instead of what he really is, okay? Everyone else seems to be doing that. You don't have to. That's all I'll say. Oh, by the way, Ms. Glass, your art teacher says she wants you to make a collage that illustrates your week away from your life. She said you can use whatever media you want, real photos, abstract shots, whatever. She's looking forward to seeing what you come up with. I thought that was an interesting assignment. I'm not sure what I'm going to do for my collage yet, I'm kind of stumped. So, think about yours and what you can do."

"I don't have to think about it. Mine's easy. I think I'll clip pictures of Picasso prints and glue them upside-down and every which way. That should represent my week."

I used to enjoy Emma's humor, even when she made fun of my life, she was making fun of it from the outside, now she has a bird's eye view. I never realized before how much I could feel hurt that my best friend hates my life so much. It's my life and it makes me who I am.

50

Befana

It isn't every day when you meet someone who has actually saved a person's life. And it is even rarer when that life-saver is not human. I'm remembering a family that lived during a very dark time in history when a terrible disease spread across most of what we knew of the modern world. People were breaking out with deadly fevers and terrible tumors which were very contagious. No one had ever seen anything like it before. Entire villages and cities were wiped out because of this dreadful disease. Many people came to believe that the illness was being spread by rats carrying germs from ships that had sailed from far-off parts of the world. Imagine what that must have been like for those frightened people when they discovered the tumors on their bodies or on the bodies of their children! There was no cure; if you had a tumor you'd most likely die within a week. One day you were living your life, minding your own business, the next day you were marked for death. Unthinkable!

It was early spring when the village of Bertolio was hit by the plague. It began in the home of the Rizzio family and quickly spread to neighboring families that shared the same well. Before long every family in the village had at least one member who had become ill, even the Saverius family. Tito Saverius was the mayor of Bertolio and he and his wife lived in a modest home near the town square with their seven children. He'd watched helplessly as many of the families in his village became ill and died. When Tito found a tumor on his thigh he knew that he could not protect his family from this disease if he remained in the house with them so he gathered up a small sack of food and left the village for an abandoned barn on the outskirts of town. He asked that anyone in the village afflicted with the illness join him so that their loved ones might survive. Sooner or later either everyone in the village joined Tito in the barn and perished or they fell ill in their homes and met with the same fate. The only surviving resident of Bertolio was Tito's youngest son, Domenic, who was only four years-old at the time. Left alone in the house, young Domenic ate what little food remained but out of fear of becoming ill like the rest of his family he did not leave the confines of his home in search of more food. He was too young to come up with a survival plan. One evening when Domenic was hungry and tired he heard a scratching sound at the door. He stood on a chair and peeked out of the window where he saw a dog carrying some sort of sack in his mouth pawing at the wooden door. Domenic opened the door and let the dog into the house. The dog sat near Domenic and placed the sack on Domenic's lap. The child was thrilled to see a four-legged companion and he opened the sack to find a large loaf of bread. Domenic did not know where the dog or the bread came from but he did not care; he broke off small chunks of bread for himself and hand-fed some them to the dog. Day after day, the dog would leave the house and return with a loaf bread and the two shared the meal for a month until helpers from a neighboring village came along and found Domenic and took him to a safe house opened by the King to help the surviving victims. The dog continued to travel from village to village carrying a loaf of bread to abandoned children who were hungry. No one knows for sure from where this dog had come, and no one ever discovered what became of him. Legend has it that this wonderful dog once belonged to a special knight who had rescued the King's firstborn son from the hands of his enemies. This child, when he grew older, became a king who eventually saved his nation from this devastating plague by seeking out the best physicians in the land; he also never forgot the importance of his canine rescuer. His love for dogs was renowned and he was remembered by all as *King Chien* because he created the first dog rescue society and built a haven within the palace walls for unwanted, lost, or stray dogs. These days, a nicely fashioned marble statue of a dog is mounted on the grave of *King Chien*.

51

Sister Maria Nicola

Screams and shouts could be heard coming from the hallway during my last period English class. There was some kind of commotion that resonated throughout the building. Someone was shouting that the school was going to be sued and that they'd have someone's head on a platter before the end of the day. Of course all the students were out of their seats in a flash and trying to crowd around the classroom door to get a better idea of what was going on. I can't say I wasn't curious as well but I knew that it would be impossible to settle the class down and get back to work unless the disturbance stopped. It didn't sound like it was going to quiet down any time soon. Someone was shouting that the police were on their way. I clapped my hands together loudly and told the students to get back to their seats. Of course they resisted at first but eventually when I physically crept in between the little crowd and the door I managed to convince them that if they returned to their seats now I would cancel all homework assignments for tomorrow. They sat down in a hurry. In the last half hour of the day, I read to them from *The Hobbit* while the noises eventually calmed down:

> "Where did you go to, if I may ask?" said Thorin to Gandalf as they rode along.
> "To look ahead," said he.
> "And what brought you back in the nick of time?"
> "Looking behind," said he.

"Now, quickly, answer this question. Raise your hands. When you look ahead to your futures what do you see?"

Christmas break, no school, game time, snow days... came the answers.

"When you look behind at your past, what do you see?" I asked.

Suddenly, it grew quiet, they were too busy thinking and not as responsive. I'm sure something was popping into their heads but they had to think about what they wanted to say out loud. Sharing a memory from your past requires a level of trust, unlike the future which isn't certain anyway. It was only Kelly and Jeanie that had the courage to share a memory from the past. Kelly said that she saw her grandmother when she looked back because her grandmother only lived in the past, not in the present or future. Jeanie said that she saw the carefree days of playing as a child and having no school or homework to worry about.

Thankfully, the end-of-day bell rang and the students bolted out the door faster than usual. The ruckus had died down and I followed my charges into the hallway where I saw the parent volunteers (those saints that help with library and computers, recess and study halls) moving the students down the hallways and out the main door as quickly as possible. Mrs. Jade asked the teachers who were filing out into the halls to go directly to the library for an emergency faculty meeting. Everything would be explained there. The students were moved promptly out of the building and the faculty was organized just as efficiently into the library.

Sister Maria Reyna was standing by the check out desk in front of a stack of reference books the students had been using to do their Wednesday research exercises. Mrs. Winterberry was standing next to Sister and gesturing as she spoke, pointing to the back of the library and at each of the tables. It was difficult to surmise the nature of the conversation by the look on Sister's face or the gestures that Mrs. Winterberry was making that seemed to be directed at every corner of the room. Finally, after Sister was satisfied that we were all present, she closed the door. It was faculty only; all parent volunteers were thanked for their help and informed that Sister would meet with them personally one day next week.

Alice Rybold, the science teacher, spoke up immediately. "What's going on, Sister? What happened today?"

The stillness in the library was a formidable presence and for once Sister Maria Reyna was not. Normally, when teachers congregate there is a steady din that grows with intensity but today we were a gaggle of muted nuns and lay teachers. Sister usually initiated our meeting with a strident announcement that grabbed our attention and stifled our chatter but today she began to speak in a low voice as if her speech was intended for her ears alone. Her demeanor spoke volumes; she was reticent about saying anything at all. Someone, perhaps Mrs. Winterberry, told her she must.

Eighty year-old Sister Becket rang out, "I can't hear you!" from the table by the door. Sister Becket says that at every meeting, even when Sister Maria Reyna is in standard form, but today she spoke for all of us.

Sister Maria Reyna cleared her throat and began again. "We had a situation today in the library. Earlier this afternoon, during seventh period, a student... uh, Lawrence Crosby... Suddenly, there was an acknowledging murmur amongst the assembled group – everyone was familiar with Lawrence... He began by causing a disturbance in his research group. Mrs. Winterberry had just distributed the assignment for the session and instructed the class when Lawrence yelled out that he was sick and tired of doing these stupid research assignments. Mrs. Winterberry asked Lawrence to be silent, reminding him that this is a library where we use quiet voices. The class began the assignment and the students went in search of research materials. Lawrence sat in his seat and refused to move. Mrs. Winterberry asked him to begin his assignment or he wouldn't have time to complete it by the end of the period. Lawrence responded by slamming his fist on the table and telling Mrs. Winterberry that she could go to hell. He wasn't going to do anymore stupid research assignments, he told her. Mrs. Winterberry told Lawrence to calm down and go to my office. Lawrence refused. He said he was sick and tired of this school, of the teachers, of the work that we ask them to do, and he was sick and tired of all the ranting about God. Mrs. Winterberry told Lawrence that perhaps he'd be happier in a different school, but for now he was still in our school and he needed to comply with our instructions and rules. She asked him once again to go to my office to have a chat with me. I commend Mrs. Winterberry for her unfailing patience with all our students, but particularly with a student as challenging as Lawrence. It was at that point that Lawrence arose from his seat, threw down the chair in a tantrum and began to charge through the library, pulling books off the racks, ripping pages out of some of the books and smashing other books against the wall. He circled the entire library during his tantrum and at this point Mrs. Winterberry was concerned for the safety of the other students. She asked all students to come to the front of the library while she phoned my office and summoned me to the scene. Immediately, I called Lawrence's parents and told them to come to the school. When I arrived at the front of the library, Lawrence was coming through the door into the hallway. I held him by his arms to prevent him from going any further without supervision. He struggled to get free. He said that he hated this school because we were all liars, that there is no God and that we made up the commandments just to control people. I told him to calm down and we would talk about this in my office. He struggled even more and his shirt ripped as he pulled away from my arms." Sister Maria Reyna paused. She seemed visibly uncomfortable, but she continued. "Lawrence stomped on my foot in order to get free and he ran down the hallway toward the main doors just as his mother was coming into the building. When she saw Lawrence in his heightened state of mania and his torn shirt, she became incensed. I managed to guide her into my office; I described the situation and the consequences for her child's actions – that he may not return to school until he has seen an appropriate physician - but the more I said, even with Mrs. Winterberry as a witness, the more his mother became distressed and lashed out. She asked how we dared assume that Lawrence needed a physician and began to threaten the school with a lawsuit and to press charges for child abuse. I ask for your prayers and support in this matter because I sincerely believe the family situation has reached some sort of breaking point. Please discuss this with no one outside our present group, particularly with the parents. I will be speaking with the superintendent of schools as soon as we are dismissed. I have much to do. I will not be taking any questions today until I have had a chance to speak with the superintendent. This informal meeting is adjourned."

As we arose to leave, there was a barely perceptible murmur among the faculty as we headed for the door. Just as I passed in front of the check out desk where Sister was still standing, she motioned to me to wait a moment. She turned and dismissed Mrs. Winterberry, asking for a moment of privacy. Once the library was cleared, Sister turned to me with a severe look of condescension in her eyes and waited a moment or two before she began to speak. I could feel myself shaking beneath my habit; she always had that effect on me.

"Sister Maria Nicola, I have much on my plate today because of the circumstances of which you have just been informed, however, until that moment when the crisis of Lawrence Crosby occurred, I was occupied with the business of what to do about *you*. Certain matters have come to my attention and I feel that your position here at St. Asterius has reached the point of new direction. Obviously, I have other pressing matters to attend to at the moment, but expect to have a private meeting with Father Raymond and myself by the end of the week. If possible I would like to schedule the meeting for tomorrow; it's very important."

I opened my mouth to speak, but nothing came out. I wanted to ask her if there was something wrong, something of which I am unaware, but she didn't give me a chance. She turned quickly away from me and strode off determinately in the direction of her office and left me in a cold wake of impending doom. I remained behind in the library for a few minutes. The Advent calendar sat neatly next to the manger scene (sans Baby Jesus) and I stared at the nativity suppressing any thoughts that might conflict with the tranquility of the expectant parents in the small wooden stable. The characters in the drama of Christ's birth had plenty of reasons for anxiety: parents who could find nowhere safe and sterile to give birth to our Lord, no loved ones nearby to help them, the eventual violence and acts of ancient terrorism that Herod would unleash upon the quiet town of Bethlehem. Yet these individuals look perpetually calm and free of apprehension. They remain the epitome of placing complete trust in God. They knew what it is taking me a lifetime to learn, God is enough – he is always enough. I cannot allow Sister's threatening tone to cause me fretfulness and doubts. Breathing deeply, I left the library at school and headed directly for the public library. It remains my Wednesday routine.

52

Salvatore

All things considered I guess it's a good thing that Joe gave me the little contraption called a cell phone. Simon showed me how to use it. The kid took a lot of time and patience today to show me all the things this little plastic gadget can do. I can look things up on the internet or take pictures, or record my own voice. Who knows what the phones of the future will be able to do; maybe we'll even be able to take our own x-rays when we fall so we can decide whether or not to go to the hospital. Two minutes after he showed me, I couldn't remember how to do much more than just make a phone call; what else do I need to know? I didn't really need to know all that other stuff. It came in handy today. The first thing I did when I got up this morning was to check the weather. The little window in the phone showed me a picture of cloudy skies (what else is new?) but no chance of rain or snow. I wanted to do something nice to surprise Simon when he comes by this afternoon. I patted my butt to make sure I had the cell phone in my pocket.

As carefully as I could manage I went down into the basement to find some Christmas decorations. It took me over an hour to lift one box from step to step while alternating the use of the crutch with lifting the box. That's okay, I didn't mind the effort. I managed to get the box all the way upstairs and into the living room. The only box I cared about was the one with the nativity set we always put on top of the fireplace and the 18 inch pre-lit, pre-decorated Christmas tree that goes on the table in front of the window, the one Annalisa and I purchased together the year she died. She didn't want a lot of fuss, she said, she just wanted the simplicity of the first Christmas and she wanted our family all here together for once. Well, she had the simplicity she'd asked for but not all of the family came by – just Joe and Joanie and Liv, their youngest daughter. Everyone else couldn't make it, but they promised to come by later, which turned out to be at my sweetheart's funeral.

Annalisa was made of gold; she had the biggest heart of anyone I've ever known. She only asked one thing of me at the end, *Promise me*, she'd said, *no matter what happens, Sal, don't ever grow into a bitter old man. Life can do that to you but you don't have to let it. Stay strong and hopeful; have faith, love our family no matter what they do; don't let them make you bitter. I didn't marry a bitter old man. I married a sweet, devoted, loving man. Stay that way.* Of all the things she asked me to do over the fifty-five years we were married, that was the hardest. It was easier to stay strong when I was staying strong for her; it wasn't difficult to remain hopeful when I had her at my side – we gave each other hope. I could hang on to faith and love because she had enough for both of us. The only way I've found to avoid feeling bitter is to not have expectations. If you stick with simple gratitude, you'll be fine, I tell myself each day, but it's not easy.

I peeked outside my window. Still no rain or snow. Good. I decided to grab one more decoration from the basement. I wanted the inflatable snow globe that had the nativity inside the bubble. It wasn't heavy to carry and it had a button on the bottom that made it self-inflate. Simon might get a kick out of seeing it on the lawn when he comes by today. I went down the stairs carefully again and almost made it back up to the top by carrying the deflated snow globe under my left arm with the crutch and using my right hand to hang on to the rail, but the crutch got caught on the step and I didn't keep my balance; I fell back down the stairs and landed pretty hard at the bottom. The pain shooting from my bum knee was nothing compared to the throbbing sensation in my back. Doggone it. It was under similar circumstances that I had met my friend Simon in the first place. I tried to get up but it was no use. I reached inside my pants for the phone. Who the heck should I call? Joe is at work, so is his wife. I couldn't bother them. I was pretty sure Simon was still in school. I decided to find Mrs. Gray's number in my phone and after several rings she finally picked up the phone.

"I need a little help," I told her.

"I'm sorry, Sal, I've already been to the market this morning. I should have called you to see if you needed anything."

"No. I don't need any food. I just need a hand getting upstairs. I'm in the basement."

"Sal. Are you okay? Has something happened? What are you doing downstairs in the basement? Are you hurt?"

"I just wanted to bring a couple of Christmas things upstairs. Can you come over? I think the back door is unlocked. Just come right in. I'm downstairs."

"I'll be right over," she said and hung up.

Mrs. Gray came over very quickly but when she saw me lying at the bottom of the stairs on the concrete floor she gasped. "Sal, are you okay?"

"Yes," I told her again. "I just need help getting back upstairs. Here, if you don't mind, grab this snow globe first and take it up there so you don't have to do both at the same time." Unquestioningly, she took the snow globe upstairs and left it in the kitchen. Then she came back down the stairs to help me.

"Sal, I'm not sure about this. I think we should call 911. I can't lift you. You might be really hurt."

"No!" I said, perhaps a bit too forcefully. "I'm okay. You don't have to lift me. Don't call 911. I don't want them to put me in a home. I just need your hand; I can lift myself. Just give me your hand, please. I will do the rest."

Poor Mrs. Gray, she held out her hand dutifully and I grabbed on to it, but I could not follow through on my promise. I could not lift myself and I could not budge an inch. My back would not cooperate. Jets of pain shot through my body every time I tried. Patiently, Mrs. Gray tried to hold my hand and my arm; finally she sat down on the bottom step and asked me what she should do now.

I lay on my back looking up at the ceiling and fought the feeling of despair that threatened to keep me down. I had now brought not one, but two, accomplices into my stubbornness to resist help. Simon had had the same look of helplessness when he first found me. Mrs. Gray could not help me up these stairs and we both knew it. She was no spring chicken herself.

"Do you want me to call someone else?" she asked. "I mean, if you don't want 911, maybe someone stronger can help you up the stairs." She spoke very quietly, afraid to say the wrong thing, I guessed. "Maybe one of your kids?"

I shook my head. "No, not my kids. Please, no, I don't want to bother them. They'll see this as proof that I need to be locked up in some safe place for old people. I don't want to go there. This is my...." Mrs. Gray politely turned her head when my voice cracked.

"I think we need to get you to a doctor at least. Your back is hurting. He can give you something for the pain, right? How about if we just call the EMT's to get you to a doctor? I promise I won't call anyone else. Is that okay?"

I nodded my head. What else could I do? I've resisted this moment for a long time. I squeezed my eyes shut and said a silent prayer. *I don't want to go to a nursing home, Lord. When it is time for me to die, I want to do it in a place where I have lived. I want to go from my home to yours. Please.*

53

Befana

When I see someone in trouble, my hackles go up and I know that when it is serious that's when I'm going to need help from above. Things can get very dicey and go from bad to worse in no time at all. When a child is born between two other siblings, it is difficult for him to find his place. The poor little middle child quite often slips under the watchful eye of his parents while they strive to teach the older child how to do everything correctly and coddle the younger child so that he remains cocooned and sheltered from certain dangers. That is the theory, anyway. In the Brownville family Ricky, the oldest, seemed to garner his parent's indulgent attention because he had what his mother called "the face of an angel;" Pete, the youngest, was exceptionally bright – he had an unusually strong take-charge personality so more was expected of him. That left Andy in the middle with the same issues that most middle children have – finding his role in the family. As for his looks, he took after his father's side of the family with the face of a tired, aging terrier dog – not the face of an *angel*. And Andy's personality lacked any motivation at all, even to get out of bed in the morning. Andy seemed to wander through life and usually only had his parents' attention when he did something he shouldn't have done or failed to do something he should have.

It was the morning before his tenth Christmas that Andy's behavior scared the corns right off my old, tired feet. I couldn't keep up with him that day. He was up before his brothers and, to me, this was the first warning sign that he was up to something because on most days his mother would have to drag him out of bed just to come down and eat his breakfast. Andy took a few pieces of bread from the pantry, a chunk of his favorite cheese from the ice box and a bottle of milk and put on his dark green winter jacket that was two sizes too large, but his grandfather had given it to him so it was *special*. He filled his knapsack, turned to look at the Christmas tree in the entryway, and then walked out the front door, heading down Belaria road towards the factory district where the town's cotton works made bandages for the army. Andy walked for a mile or two, nibbling on his bread and cheese and drinking his milk until he passed through the cotton district. When I looked at this small boy, I thought there was something different about him on that day. While he usually seemed very uninterested in the world around him, that day he seemed like he knew exactly where he was going and why he was going there, and along the way he was studying every detail about the journey. I think he was trying to remember his way home. Once he passed the cotton factories, he ventured into the glass works region. The air was heavy that morning and the clouds hung in the sky like weighed down bed sheets filled with rocks. Andy didn't seem to notice the cold but kept walking steadily, and occasionally turning to see if anyone was around or watching him. He was keeping a keen eye out for anything out of the ordinary or any troublemakers. He had no intention of dealing with any problems. He had his mission in mind and he wanted no trouble for it. I just wish I knew what it was.

When Andy came to the doors of the glass works he found that they were bolted shut; the workers had begun their holiday early and had no intention of coming in to open the factory that day. Andy slipped his pocket knife into the lock to try to jiggle the latch but it wouldn't move. Next he tried to wedge the knife between the door jamb and the door but he still couldn't maneuver the lock. How did the guys on the television make this look so easy, he wondered? Any time Andy watched the good guy/bad guy shows on the small metal television in the corner of his family's sitting room, he made sure he paid careful attention to how the crooks broke into old buildings. They always wanted to get their hands on money, or on property they could sell for money. Once in awhile they wanted to hold somebody hostage in there but that's not what Andy wanted to do. There was very little I could do to stop him; he was determined to get into the glass factory and I could tell he was not going to leave until he'd done so.

He began to grumble out loud. Andy didn't have the money to buy anything for his mother for Christmas but one day in Mr. Ellingsworth's shop he'd seen a glass ornament with the etchings of the holy family in the center and he knew his mother would love this ornament and he wanted to give it to her for Christmas the next day. His mother loved Christmas more than any other day of the year and she always said that Baby Jesus' mother loved this day the most, too. She said that Jesus' family was the most special family the world had ever known; there had never been another family quite like it. Andy had asked Mr. Ellingsworth where these wonderful glass ornaments came from. The shopkeeper told Andy that the factory outside of town made them each year and shipped them to other places, too. I realized then that Andy wanted to get his hands on a glass ornament and nothing was going to stop him. He was resolute about giving his mother something special for Christmas. He wasn't thinking about what would happen if the constable caught him breaking into the factory. He gave no thought at all to how his mother would feel if he ended up in jail for Christmas. Nor did he consider her feelings if he were to be hurt in some way because of his mischief, let alone how she would feel about receiving a stolen gift. Andy loved his mother and he was tired of feeling like nothing about him stood out. If only he could give his mother a gift that would set him apart from his brothers, he would feel better. He would be noticed and it wouldn't matter if he didn't look as handsome as his older brother and that he wasn't as clever as his younger brother. He would be the son that gave his mother a glass ornament with the holy family in the middle.

After several minutes of watching him trying to jimmy the lock on the factory door, I tried to nudge Andy to give up but he decided to circle the building to see if another door was easier to open. I needed some help to distract this child from doing something he might regret. I raised my weary eyes to heaven and asked for some kind of diversion but Andy was too concentrated on his mission to notice that it had started to rain, freezing rain no less!! As he reached the back of the building, and much to his disappointment, he found that the back door to the factory was about six feet off the ground to allow the lorries to unload the sand directly into the upper level of the building so the sand would remain dry. There didn't seem to be a way for Andy to try to climb up there and so he picked up a rock and threw it at the building out of frustration, then he walked to the corner of the property to see if he could climb into a slightly open window. If there was no open window he thought he would go ahead and break one of them with a rock. He was not leaving there without a gift for his mother.

As he reached the corner of the old brick glass works, he came nearer to the refuse bin. It was a rusty metal bin that usually held small wooden crates filled with straw. On a regular basis the factory custodian would set fire to the crates and straw but because of the holidays he had not gotten around to burning the trash. From the bin Andy heard a small wailing sound like that of a cat meowing in distress. Andy was not the curious sort but on this morning the small shrieks grabbed his attention. He thought that if maybe he could dump the contents of the bin, he might be able to turn it over and use it to climb up to a window or the upper door.

When Andy reached the bin and looked inside he saw that the bunch of straw covering one of the crates seemed to contain the cat or whatever else was moving in there. The animal must have gotten trapped in there, he thought. He reached into the bin and removed the straw and jumped back! It wasn't a cat or an animal; it was a baby. Andy looked around to see if anyone had put the baby down for a moment to carry out some kind of a chore but he didn't see anyone around anywhere! The baby was crying in a weak pitch and shivering. The freezing rain had started to pelt the baby's face now that Andy had removed the straw. Andy looked around again to see if someone had forgotten their baby in the bin. Still, he saw no one. The baby's arms feebly began to flail at the rain and Andy thought that whoever forgot their baby in the bin should have covered it better. The poor baby was getting wet and would catch a bad chill. He reached in and picked up the baby with his hands and lifted it out of the bin. Again he turned around to see if he could find the baby's mother and again he saw no one in sight. For a few minutes Andy just stood there holding the baby at arm's length and looking all around him. The freezing rain was beginning to change over to snow. Andy knew that this meant that the temperatures were getting colder. He didn't know who this baby belonged to but he also knew he couldn't just leave the baby in the bin for the mother to come back because the poor little thing would freeze to death. Andy forgot all about his desire to break into the factory and steal an ornament for his mother so he wrapped his blue shawl around the baby and started to walk home. When the baby fussed, Andy reached into his knapsack and found that he had a bit of milk left in his jar. He offered it to the baby but the baby's tongue waggled and made the milk spill down its chin. Andy realized the baby didn't know how to drink from a jar so he decided to hurry home as fast as he could.

When he reached his house he found that his brothers had already left the house with their father to chop down a small tree for the sitting room. They were going to string dried apples later on and decorate the tree. As he entered the kitchen he could hear his mother in the next room humming to the tune of *O Holy Night*. His mother couldn't sing, she said. She had the singing voice of a wounded elephant. Andy didn't know what a wounded elephant sounded like but he thought his mother's humming was the most beautiful sound in the world. She would always hum to the boys at night before going to sleep and Andy would have the nicest dreams about biscuits and honey when Mamma would hum *A Gentle Rain is Falling on My Love.*

Andy found his mother in the bedroom she shared with Papa. She was changing the sheets and putting a few pine branches along the bedpost for decoration. The room was filled with the scent of pine and fruit peels. The baby squirmed and fussed inside of Andy's shawl. His Mamma turned around and barely glanced at Andy.

"What are you doing standing there?" she asked. "Where have you been? Papa and your brothers left without you to go to Yancy's Farm to get a tree. You've missed out, Andy. We didn't know where you'd run off to."

"Mamma," Andy said. "Somebody forgot their baby in a bin." His words did not exactly make sense to his mother at that moment. She was thinking of the mixed fruit pie she would be baking and the sweet breads that she would make for Christmas Eve.

"Andy, what on earth are you talking about?" she asked.

"Mamma, listen to me," Andy replied, "someone forgot this baby in a bin near the glass works and I brought it home because it was starting to snow. I thought the baby would catch a chill out there like you're always telling us when the weather gets bad."

Now Andy had his mother's attention. She turned around and looked at her middle son and gasped. She saw that he was holding a small infant in his arms and he had wrapped it in his blue shawl that she'd made for him last Christmas. Slowly, she walked towards Andy in disbelief. Andy held the baby out to his mother and she gently took the infant from his arms.

"I looked," Andy said, "but I couldn't find its Mamma. There was no one around anywhere. I went all around the factory buildings but I didn't see anybody."

"What were you doing by those old buildings Andy? You know they are dangerous. How many times have I told you to stay away from there?"

Andy hung his head down, then looked up at his mother. "Who do you think it belongs to? Honest, I didn't see anybody around. The baby was covered with some straw in the bin. How could they forget their baby in a trash bin, Mamma?"

Andy's mother looked at her son tenderly and stroked his cheek. "Babies left in bins are not forgotten, sweet boy. They are left there for someone else to find. You are the one to find this child. Fetch the lap blanket from my chair in the corner, this little one must be freezing."

When Andy returned to the bed where his mother had laid the child, she told him to go into the kitchen and bring the sheep's gut she had ready for the haggis and a cup of milk. They would have to try to get the baby to drink a bit by pouring the milk into the lining and letting the wee one suck the milk through a little hole. When Andy returned with the sack filled with milk, he found his mother on the bed holding the baby in her arms and crying. He was instantly worried that the baby was sick and Mamma was sad. He had brought something home that made his mother unhappy on Christmas. He shuffled into the room with the milk in his shaking hands. He sat next to his mother on the bed and as she held the baby close to her heart with one arm she put her other arm around Andy and began to hum *Silent Night*. Andy melted into his mother's embrace and felt sad that he could not have brought her the glass ornament with the picture of the holy family etched in the middle.

Suddenly, Andy's mother stopped humming and looked at her son. "Did you see her?" she asked.

Andy shook his head. "See who?" he answered. "I told you Mamma, I couldn't find the baby's Mamma anywhere."

"No, Andy, I don't mean the mother. Did you see that this is a baby girl?" His mother smiled largely. She's going to be okay because you found her in time. She was just cold and hungry. I think maybe her mother probably couldn't take care of her and she left her there for you to find and bring her home. Andy, my dear little boy, I have always wanted a baby girl, too. You have brought me one of the greatest gifts in the world. Nothing could have made me happier this Christmas than to have you find this precious baby." Andy swallowed hard. He didn't know what to say or what to think. His mother seemed so happy.

"Listen to me, son. Babies are such blessings in life and they can create such magic, but they are also a lot of work so I'm going to need your help to take care of her. Can I count on you to help me?" Andy nodded his head. "She will be our little gift from God, yours and mine. You have a special place in this child's life, just like you have a special place in mine. I'm going to let you name her. What would you like to name this baby?" Andy had no idea.

Suddenly, he had a thought, "I found her on Christmas Eve, Mamma. Can we call her Eve?" His mother smiled again and hugged her son. "Eve is the perfect name, Andy. She is our first and only girl – she is Eve."

I don't care what anybody says, things like that don't happen by accident. Andy forgot all about breaking into buildings and stealing glass ornaments. He didn't have time for mischief and he didn't have the luxury of being lazy anymore, he had a little sister to look after. Having a new child in the house that night felt like the very first Christmas. Baby Eve lit up the Brownville world with her smiles, just like the little Baby Jesus must have done in a cold stable long ago.

54

Simon

I keep staring at this little statue that Sal gave me hoping for some help, or inspiration, or something, to do my homework but my motivation to work on this project just isn't there. Christmas was once a time when people celebrated that the birth of Jesus meant something. I think it used to mean something to people personally and maybe it meant something to them as a group of believers, but I'm not so sure it means much to anyone anymore except that it's a time of year to pay attention to something you may or may not understand, or for that matter – believe. For me, when I lived with Dasan, Christmas was secretive; it was a day when we used to go about work like we always did but in secret we would find a way to help a child that was hungry or homeless. If a Christian was captured and jailed we would go to the jail and take them something extra to eat that day, more than we usually did. That was our way of celebrating Christmas. The few secret Christians in our village used to bring something of what we'd produced that day to a prisoner, a homeless person or a poor child. It was our way of saying *Jesus, if you were here in our village today we would not shut our doors to you, we would welcome you into our homes and feed you*. I remember the last Christmas I spent with Dasan; our neighbor, Kai, traveled on foot from street to street bringing some cooked rice to the very poor people on the streets when suddenly a policeman stopped him and asked him what he was doing. Kai was wearing a cross under his threadbare shirt and the police saw it. They grabbed the rice from Kai's hands and tossed it to the dogs in the street then they hauled Kai off to jail. Later that day, Dasan took me to see Miss Ling – she had made small loaves of sugared bread but she was too afraid to leave the house to distribute them so she had bundled them up individually and she and Dasan tucked them into the binding I wore under my shirt. Since I was a small child myself I would arouse no suspicion if I went along the streets to give out a small loaf of sugar bread to the poor children. This was the Christmas tradition I remember. It wasn't about receiving; it was strictly about giving.

Sister wants us to present a story about Christmas that demonstrates some kind of mercy. I've read the usual Christmas stories, and it seems like all of them try to send a message about believing in Santa, or elves, or flying animals. I've gone over those stories and I can't find what Sister wants me to find. There aren't a lot of Christmas stories from my part of Korea and what little I could share about being secretive might be ridiculed. The *Befana* statue I've been carrying around in the pocket of my shirt might give me some ideas. Somehow I just feel like *Befana* understands things that even I don't understand, but I don't think there is anything she can do to help me. Sal told me that this statue brings something special to each child she visits. Her story kind of sounds similar to the memories I have of my early years with Dasan. I've been staring at this statue all afternoon but I can't think of one thing she's brought me that's special and I can't think of what to write about. She just has this grin that looks like she's clever or something; but she isn't helping me one bit with my homework. I may have to wing it.

I hope that I won't have to present anything tomorrow. Maybe Sister will let me off the hook if I just keep my head down and refuse to speak. Sometimes it works, sometimes it doesn't. I think Sister Maria Nicola has a lot of things on her mind lately anyway. Usually she's on top of us like a fly in fish stew but since that problem with the Lawrence kid, all the teachers seem a little stricter. If Sister calls on me tomorrow, I'll just tell her I haven't done my homework; I'll take an F and I don't really care. It's all just a waste of time anyway. I think that's what's better about a life of nothing; it doesn't have to mean anything.

55

Sister Maria Nicola

"There is someone I know who works for "A Way Out Program" and she thinks she can help us," I told Sandy the afternoon that Sister Maria Reyna told me that I'd reached a point of new direction.

"I don't need no help," Sandy told me for the umpteenth time. "I don't need your help; I don't need their help and I don't need no way out of nothing. I'm fine. Got it?" Her pipe was nearly empty. I took some luncheon meat and cheese out of my backpack and held them up to her.

"Surely, you want some of this! I didn't have time to get some bread but we can still eat the insides of a sandwich, can't we? I never thought the bread was the best part of a sandwich anyway. It's just used to hold the good stuff together." But Sandy wasn't having it. She was out of reach today. I was so worried that she'd go too far this time. Sometimes, reminding someone of what they dearly want in life, like Sandy's desire to have her daughter back, can increase the levels of despair instead of helping them to set goals to achieve their desires.

"Sandy, please take a walk with me. Let's get some air, okay? I want to show you something." I felt like I was leading one of the blind-folded children at a birthday party in the direction of a piñata, guiding a stick into their hands and telling them to swat at something they cannot see for if they hit it hard enough they are sure to get a jackpot of candy and prizes. But while they are swinging the stick they can see nothing, certainly not the object of their desires. Sandy was being led away from our meeting place but she was too high to know where she was being led, or for what purpose. I walked her down Main St. and we turned right at C St. As soon as we turned the corner Sandy became sick into a nearby trash can. People avoided eye contact with us and diverted their path around us by a wide berth. Finally we arrived at the small blond-brick building with the glass block windows. The doors were locked but I knocked on the glass door with my foot. After a moment, Ralph, the counselor with whom I'd spoken last week came to the door. He opened the door widely and looked around, then he helped me to guide Sandy inside the door and seated her on the sofa in his office. The building smelled of bleach and something akin to rotting melon rinds.

"How long has she been like this?" Ralph asked me.

"I don't know," I answered. "I found her like this when I arrived a few minutes ago. I walked her over here. I don't think she's doing very well."

"Let's get her onto the cot for a minute. I wish you'd brought her to us sooner. She's a real mess."

"I tried. She wasn't receptive at all. I also tried to get her to eat something but she wouldn't eat. Is Phyllis here?"

"Yeah, she's here, but she's with Annette."

"Annette is back?"

"I've told you, sometimes they have to come back several times before we can give them the help they really need. Don't give up. If it weren't for you I doubt we'd reach this many. Wait here with her, I'll get Phyllis."

Sandy was slumped over on the sofa where she sat. I lifted her legs onto the sofa so she could stretch out. I turned her head to the side in case she became sick again. As I smoothed her matted hair back away from her face, she opened her eyes slightly and looked at me. She spoke in a low, hoarse voice. "You're not who you pretend to be, are you? Like he said, you're not really one of us?"

"Sshh. Don't worry about anything right now, Sandy, I want you to start feeling better; I care about you and I want you to recover from this sickness, this addiction that has such a hold on you. I want you to get your daughter back. You told me that's what you want too. These people – all of us – can help you. I am like you in so many ways, I feel lost and scared, but I want to help. I won't stop trying to help you until you have what you want, until you have your life back. Your child needs you, Sandy."

"I don't… I can't… I don't think I have the energy…"

"That's just it, Sandy, you don't have to do it all on your own. That's the point. We're here to help you. Together we have enough energy."

"You brought us food every week."

"Your body wanted more drugs, honey, but what you needed was food. Your heart and soul wants love, and that's why I'm here; that's why we're all here because we care. This is the way back to your daughter, back to your life, not the drugs."

"You seem to think you know everything I need."

"I don't know everything but I keep in close touch with someone who does. Jesus never lets me down, Sandy. I have given my life to Him and He helps me every day. Now, you get some rest. My friends here are going to help you. Is that okay? They have some medicine to help your body detoxify and they have some food and lots of TLC. I will come back to see you. I promise."

Sandy nodded weakly. She closed her eyes and slept fitfully. I remained with her until Ralph came back with Phyllis. I left them with the food I'd brought this week. Annette was doing better, they said. She had a long road ahead of her but she was going to be okay. On the bus ride home, I had a little chat with God. I didn't want to have to choose between one direction and another and I suspected Sister Maria Reyna would be demanding that I make that choice. I suppose a person can't travel in two different directions for very long, but how could I choose between caring for people who desperately need help and teaching such beloved children? Children are not as okay these days as some people would have us believe. They are growing up in complicated home situations with confusing moral standards, fluctuating ethics, and rising instability. So many children have emotional issues, learning problems, and special requirements. They need the kind of care they can count on, that doesn't change, and that makes them feel secure. The problem is not about making a child feel *happy*, it's about making them feel like the ground beneath them is not going to shift each day when they wake up because the worldly voices set such high standards for individual happiness. As they grow older, more of them are turning to addictions to find a way to cope with this world they have been plunged into too soon. As adults they end up in this heartrending circle of hell and they need help because they're not all right. As I stared out the window at all the festive lights downtown I felt my heart grow very heavy. I am not so sure I'm helping anyone anymore.

56

Stella

#Moccasinswap Journal: Day 5
My hands are still shaking. It's at times like these that I need to talk to Mom, or Grandma, or Dad. One of them is always willing to listen. Here at Emma's house, there is no one. Her parents aren't home yet; they are either at work or taking one of her siblings to one of their activities and when they are here, they're tired and sitting somewhere together sipping wine. I don't know how they get by in this family! Who does Emma turn to when she needs someone to talk to; I just don't get it! She doesn't always talk to me; I guess she just figures things out for herself and that's what I'm going to have to do today. I certainly can't talk to her about today's problem. She told me she doesn't want to hear anything negative about her friends. I feel like my head is spinning and I want to scream. I've never seen anything like what I saw today in my whole life – nothing! Even my squirrely brothers know where the line is and when not to cross it. I feel at loose ends because I have no one to confide in right now and I desperately want to hear someone tell me that things are going to be okay.

It all started this morning in home room. I went in as I usually do after hanging up my jacket in Emma's locker and grabbing my morning books. When I entered the room I sensed that something wasn't right. Usually, everyone is making a ruckus of some sort, talking pretty loud, or laughing about the weirdest things, but this morning it was really quiet in home room. The teacher wasn't even in there yet. I sat down and suddenly I felt that all eyes were on me.

Jack strode over toward my seat and asked me if it was my last day today and I said that it was. I opened my history book because I really didn't want to have a conversation with him. He slammed my book shut and asked me wouldn't I rather stay here at school with normal kids than to be a freak and be homeschooled. I didn't respond. Then he bent down and got in my face and said "You think you're better than the rest of us, don't you?" I still didn't answer. At that point the bell rang and Mrs. Horner came in to take attendance. Everyone was laughing out loud when she told them to pipe down. I honestly hadn't thought about how these kids perceived me. I've been spending all week studying them, trying to figure out what makes them tick and seeing if I could fit into their rhythms and ways of doing things but I never stopped to think about how they saw me, what it would take for them to fit into my world (not that they'd want to – something I've learned from Emma this week.) Do they honestly think I believe I'm better than them somehow? Just because my parents have raised me differently and our family doesn't follow the norms, or I study my lessons at home instead of an institution doesn't mean I have ever thought for a moment that I'm better. I always thought I was the square peg – there was never any doubt in my mind about that. So, where would Jack, the best-loved student in school, get the notion that I think I'm better? I have to be honest with myself at least. Besides my family and school situation what separates me from these kids?

All day long I mulled over these questions. I was glad that this week was over but the most perplexing aspect of this little experiment occurred today after school. As I walked home from the school I noticed that there was a crowd of kids down by the old bridge. That passage always looks rickety to me and I always worry about someone falling into the river. I hoped that that was not the case today, but the crowd was not stationary; it was moving steadily. I decided to follow them just to see what was going on. I kept my distance, however, because I didn't want any more confrontations with the almighty Jack. As I crossed the bridge, I could see that there was someone walking in front of the crowd. He was walking rather quickly but he didn't seem to be making any headway in getting away from the crowd. The group of kids moved in on him and began to surround him. Most of them were laughing; only one of them was talking. It was Jack. He was speaking rather loudly and poking the kid in front of him. I noticed that the kid in front was not a Granger student; he had on a uniform under his coat. His jacket was unzipped and now Jack was pulling at the jacket. I got close enough to hear the comments.

"Can I have your snazzy jacket, Asian boy?" Jack was asking the kid as he grabbed it away from him and threw it into the river. "Uh-oh, little Catholic punk, what are you going to do now? Are you going to dive into the freezing river and get your coat? Are your beliefs going to save you? Are you going to turn the other cheek? Here let me help you," and he hit the kid across the face. The kid fell down on the pavement and didn't get up. The other kids stood by and either laughed or simply did nothing at all; they just watched, almost as if they were taking lessons. Jack continued with his rant. "Come on, punk, get up. Let's see you turn that other cheek. Let's see if you're saved." I couldn't believe what I was seeing and hearing. I've never been so horrified in all my life. I walked closer to the group. As I did, Jack kicked the poor kid on the ground and I noticed that a small object that had fallen out of the kid's pocket. Jack bent down to pick it up.

"Oh, my god! The Asian boy carries a doll in his pocket! Oh, muah, muah, muah!" Jack pretended to kiss the little statue. The group laughed and started passing the statue around to take turns with it. I guess I'd reached one of those moments that Mom calls "seeing red." I couldn't take it anymore. I marched up to them and lost my temper.

"What do you think you're doing?" I demanded. "Leave him alone!"

"Shut up and mind your own business, freakshow. Get lost before we teach you a lesson, too. And I'm pretty sure you don't get this kind of lesson in your home school." he said, and everyone laughed. He looked like he was seeing red, too.

"I will not. You think you're all-that, don't you? I don't know what made you this way, whatever it was, you should know it's not right and the rest of you should know it, too. What's the matter with you people? You have no right to treat anyone this way. I can't believe you stand around and enjoy watching someone being hurt. There is no excuse in the world for treating anyone like this. Are not one of you capable of standing up and doing the right thing, standing up and defending somebody that's done nothing wrong?" I stood there shaking but I couldn't back down if I'd wanted to.

Jack came toward me and with two hands he pushed me but I didn't budge. I raised my hands to ward off any other attack. All of a sudden I saw that Jack was making a fist and it was aimed at me. "What's wrong *with you? You want to defend that little pansy over there? You deserve the same treatment…" he was saying as I grabbed his wrist and twisted his arm back. With his arm in a twisted position I pushed him back away from me. The kids weren't sure what was going on at that point. Out of the corner of my eye I saw the young Asian boy stand up and run away.*

I looked squarely at all of them and yelled, "I've spent all week watching you guys paying some kind of weird homage to this… this… bully! I really don't get it. Do you feel good about yourselves because Jack isn't doing this to you? Is that where you get your sense of worth? This bully says all the right things to you to get your admiration, but he's not someone to admire and you all know it. Don't you see what he's done? He's made himself so likeable to you, so popular with all his lies so that he can flex his muscle, do whatever he wants even if it's wrong, and you all follow him like you don't have a thought of your own. He's taught you to put other people down – what, just because of their beliefs? That's sick and you're all sick because you've all acquired this mob mentality; you don't even stop to think for yourself anymore if what he's doing is right or wrong. You just trail after him like sheep. Does it really take an outsider to see what's wrong with this picture? I can't believe some of you are so willing to ignore your own consciences for the sake of belonging to the popular group. Go home. Start your Christmas break and when you come back to school after the holidays, grow a spine!"I started to back away but then I said one more thing directly to Jack: "And you, don't you ever come near me again, or let me catch you harassing anyone. I have quite a few brothers that can teach you a lesson." I turned and walked away. I was shaking from head to toe, not so much from the cold afternoon, but from sheer adrenaline pumping through my body. As I headed across the bridge, I saw the little statue on the ground. I picked it up and put it in my pocket.

I don't know what to do about Emma. She is one of Jack's most devoted admirers. There is no way she could know him this long and not see what kind of bully he is. What does this say about my best friend? I don't even want to think about that right now. I don't know who that kid was that was being bullied but I hope he's okay. It just boggles my mind that not one of those idiots could see the situation for what it was, that they all went along with it – and I wonder how long it has been going on? God, I don't even want to think about it; I'm still so mad. I wish I had someone to talk to. I can't stay in Emma's house another minute, but I can't go home yet; I'm the one that made Emma stick it out for the rest of the week. I don't think I can even face her right now. I decided to go to the library and hide behind a stack of books. I needed to get away from here.

57

Salvatore

I don't think very many people like hospitals and truth be told, I've always hated them, not because of the nice people that work here, because God help us, I don't know what the world would be like if there weren't people willing to do this kind of work taking care of sick, elderly and feeble-minded people . I'm neither sick, nor feeble-minded, but it's time I admit that I'm just not as young as I used to be. Being elderly is not a sickness; it's a temporary condition – it does have a permanent cure. I'm not as old as some others; that is what I keep telling myself. I want to go home and that's what I keep telling the nice people that come in here to take my temperature, bring me gelatin and pudding, and wheel me down for more X-rays, even though they can't find anything broken. The doctor they've assigned to me says I can go home when he's sure they've checked everything and that I can get around on my own. They seem to be more concerned about my back than about my knee. I keep telling them over and over again that my knee is the problem; that is what caused me to fall; give me a shot in the knee and let me go home. So far, I've been lucky that they haven't insisted on calling anyone (like my next of kin). Mrs. Gray, bless her heart has come to the hospital to see me and is keeping her promise to not call anyone. She also said that she would drive me home when they release me. I owe her a cake or something. That is what Annalisa used to do anytime someone did us a favor; she baked them a cake. I don't know if I can bake a cake but I'll figure something out.

What I'm worried about is whether Simon has stopped by the house or not. I told Mrs. Gray to keep an eye out for him but she said she hasn't seen him for a couple of days. Darn it, I wish I could let him know I'm okay. The kid doesn't seem to be doing so well these days and I'm a little worried. When I gave him that fish stew you'd have thought he hadn't eaten anything in years by the way he reacted to it. I know he gets enough to eat, he looks healthy enough – physically – but I swear on these creaky old bones there is something else going on and I don't know what it is. I don't even know where he lives. I don't know his family. Darn it all, I need to get home. I have a life I'd like to get back to. I want that doctor to release me right now.

They can't hold me hostage for heaven's sake. If the X-rays don't show any problems, I'm going to call Mrs. Gray and ask her to pick me up and if she can't, I'll call a darn cab. I can't stay here anymore; I think that kid needs me!

58

Simon

Perfect. Mom texted me to remind me that she and Dad are going to his office party tonight after work; they wouldn't be too late. She said my favorite dinner is in the fridge. They still think my favorite dinner is chicken tenders because that was all they were able to get me to eat when they first brought me home from the foster care house. I don't blame them for that; I really don't blame them for anything. They have been good to me in every way. I don't communicate with them as much as they'd like. That is not their fault, either. I don't think I could have asked for better parents. They provide me with everything a kid could want; they have enrolled me in a better school when I had problems in the last one; they've even taken me to Disneyworld. It's not their fault for the situation I am in. I care about them very much but I can't keep going on like this. I don't want them to have to find me another school again, I don't think it's fair for them to keep trying to find new ways to make me smile; I am not a good son. I respect them and I try very hard to obey them, but I cannot expect them to keep bending over backwards to make me happy when I fail at being happy no matter what they do.

Mom had jumped up and down that night when Dad and I came home with a tree we had supposedly chopped down ourselves. She was so happy she let us make ice cream sundaes for dessert. It takes very little to make Mom happy. She couldn't have any children of her own so having me around, even if I am useless, makes her happy. Dad seemed very proud that he was able to do guy things with a son, but I'm not a worthy son. Dad is a good man and he deserves a better son than I can ever be. I am a disappointment to my American parents and I know I am disappointing my kind and well-meaning teacher, Sister Maria Nicola. She knows I can do better at school and I cannot rise to her expectations.

Today's experience after school was another reminder that perhaps I should stop hoping for something called friends. The last two days I've been to Sal's house he hasn't been home. Maybe his kids finally put him in a home or maybe something worse has happened to him. I even checked the shed in the back yard, just in case, but he's just not there. I called his cell phone but he hasn't picked up. Those Granger kids followed me again but I didn't have Sal's house to duck into for safety. They took their best shot today; if it wasn't for that girl I'd never seen before, I'm pretty sure they would have kept going until I did something I'd be ashamed of, as if I'm not ashamed already. It took a girl to help me out of that mess. A girl. I have no way of defending myself; I have not learned to stand up to such confrontations; and I don't think they're entirely wrong about me. The ringleader seems to understand my weaknesses and he makes them bigger than they are. If I didn't have any weaknesses he wouldn't be able to do that. I'm tired. I can't keep trying to avoid people that will hurt me like that – it's impossible.

I didn't know what else to do for my project in class today. I hadn't prepared anything at all. I was hoping that Sister wouldn't call on me, but she did. I winged it. I'd taken the little *Befana* statue out of my pocket and explained the Christmas custom in just a couple of short sentences. I explained that she is an Italian legend and that she travels around the world to visit children and that her journey leads her to seek Jesus. She had the courage to follow him but sometimes following Jesus is dangerous. The class seemed bored but Sister seemed very happy. She asked me how this Christmas story demonstrates mercy. I took a guess. I said that she treats all children the same, whether they are rich or poor, or happy or sad. She gives to everyone. John Harris, the kid in my class who is friends with that Jack kid from Granger must have told Jack about the *Befana* "doll" I was carrying. Until that moment outside the school when I saw all of them waiting for me, I felt like she could protect me. She can't; no one can. I really didn't care about all the names they called me but I wasn't going to let them take her. She was a gift from Sal. I didn't handle that scene very well. Crying is the greatest weakness of all.

I'm sorry for my parents, that I have let them down as a son. They waited so long to have a child and then they adopted someone like me. I'm sorry for Sister that I can't be the student she'd like me to be. I'm sorry Sal, wherever you are right now, that I can't say good-bye in a proper way that someone should say good-bye to a friend. You've been my only friend. I'm also sorry to that girl, whoever she was, that she risked her own safety to preserve mine. I'm also sorry, Dasan, wherever you are (I think you must be dead by now) that I can't be the good boy you wanted me to be. Maybe you and I will be reunited soon.

I know there is a gun in Dad's gun case, but he keeps it locked up. I know that Mom has a bottle of sleeping pills but when I checked yesterday there weren't very many in there. I know that there are other ways to deal with things but I feel like I am letting everyone down whether I stick around or whether I go. It's just easier if I go. I pulled a razor blade out of my top desk drawer. I know that the practice slashes I've made on my arms haven't done much to help me feel any better; it's going to take some major slashes to end my worries permanently.

Now, I keep telling myself as I stand in front of the mirror in the bathroom that everything is going to be okay. Even though I don't have the *Befana* statue anymore maybe the special gift she was meant to bring me is courage. The anonymous girl after school that stood up to that beast said that none of the kids that stood by and watched had any courage. She is the only person I know my own age who seemed to have any courage at all. But, she shined a pretty bright light on my weakness as well. Not only did she accuse the group of kids of being cowards, she made it clear that to have courage means to stand up to bullies, which I have not done. I am just as much a coward as they are, right? It doesn't matter. I've made my decision and I now believe it takes more courage to do what I need to do than to put myself in the same situation over and over again after school because that is not courage, that's just stupid. The first slash did not hurt as much as I thought it would. I can already sense the relief that will come to me soon, and then there will be nothing.

59

Sister Maria Nicola

From the entryway of the convent, just past the statue of St. Jude, I could see Sister Maria Reyna in her office; she was standing by her desk with her arms folded, tapping her foot on the dark blue carpeting peppered with small white crosses in impatient anticipation of our meeting. When I entered her office, I found Father Raymond seated in the faux leather wingback chair directly across from her by the window with his head bowed down and his hands clasped in front of him on his lap. When I closed the door behind me Father Raymond looked up, but not at me; he was focused on Sister Maria Reyna, while she stared straight in my direction. The house was quiet except for the grandfather clock making its usual clanking sounds as it ticks away the minutes of our day. I suspected that the other Sisters were all upstairs in their rooms grading papers as is their usual custom at this hour.

"Sit down, Sister," my superior told me. "This meeting today is very important." For a minute or two she was silent as I sat down and prepared myself for what was coming. Father Raymond was looking down at his hands once again. He looked like he was praying; he remained silent.

"Do you know why we have asked you to be here?" she asked. I was not sure how to respond.

"Have I done something wrong, Sister?" It's the only thing I could think of to ask. I didn't want to be the one to open up the wrong can of worms. Instead of answering immediately, Sister's eyes narrowed while they bore into my soul and then she made a sound like she was chuckling; it was the sound of an indictment like she already knew the answers to the questions she had yet to ask.

"Have you done something wrong?" she repeated my question. "Let us examine the facts and determine the answer to your question." I felt like I was a student in her classroom and not a colleague. She was looking down at me with the same debasing stare that she directs at our students. "It has been brought to my attention that you have been conducting yourself in a manner which is not appropriate for a member of our religious community. Is that not the case?"

"I do not believe I have behaved in a way that is contrary to my station in life," I answered.

"You don't believe you have done anything contrary to your station in life?" she repeated. "I see." She paused and let the question hang there like the pendulum in Poe's pit just before it began to swing. "Then allow me ask you some questions. Have you been going to the local library, changing out of your nun's habit and then boarding a bus headed for the city? Then, upon your return to the library, have you changed back into your habit and returned to the convent? This happens on a weekly basis, does it not?"

My chest felt tight; I wanted to take a deep breath but it was impossible to do when it felt like someone was sitting on my chest. I could not even lower my eyes. I continued to stare at her waiting for the next question or whatever accusation she was about to make. I did not feel the humility she expected from me at this moment. So, she continued, "The clothes you don for your escapade are rather appalling street clothes, are they not? Is it your considered opinion that the habit of our order is an outfit that can be changed depending on your plans for the evening?"

At this point Father Raymond raised his head and looked first at Sister, then at me. Sister pounded her fist on the desk behind her. Though to me the temperature in the room felt icy I could see beads of sweat forming on her forehead. "Your insolence in this matter, Sister Maria Nicola, is intolerable. It has been said that you look like a homeless wanton rogue, not a respectable Sister, not a notable teacher of the children in our community and in our care. You are bringing suspicion and disgrace on our mission here at St. Asterius. I dare not ask the object of your escapades or whatever you believe is important enough to discredit our order. I have counseled you on a number of occasions about your lack of classroom management and teaching style. Your students do not seem to respect your position and if it is common knowledge in this town that you lead some sort of secular life outside this convent, how can you command the respect of your students, their parents, your colleagues here at the convent, or *anyone*? As a teacher, you seem to fall below our expectations, as a member of a religious order you have taken your own path, not one of unity in our mission. You were aware, were you not, Sister, when you joined our religious order that you are to abide by our tenets?" She had not raised her voice a single decibel; it remained low, cold, and calculated.

"I have recommended to Father Raymond that your case be placed under review with the Bishop and I have composed a letter to our Mother Superior in Pittsburgh explaining the circumstances of your behavior and your work ethics. It is my recommendation that you be removed from this school at once and that your affiliation with our order be terminated. You may read the letter and sign the bottom indicating that you have perused the letter and understand the terms." She turned around and reached for the letter on her desk. I did not reach out to accept the letter but allowed it to be suspended in her hands between us.

"It began with the well-being of one of our students last year. Carla Little. Do you remember her?" I began to speak. Sister Maria Reyna pursed her lips.

"Whatever you have to say changes nothing," she retorted.

"Let her speak," Father Raymond finally spoke up, but Sister seemed reluctant to comply. She turned her head toward him stiffly as if she'd forgotten he was in the room and she'd suddenly heard an undistinguishable noise. I seized the moment of vulnerability and spoke quickly.

"It has never been my wish to contradict the mission of our order, Sister. I have always felt a calling to reach out to children and teach them, but also to reach out to those children at high-risk in our communities who are living with such despair that they take the path of a very slow and agonizing death. These people suffer greatly; they are tormented beyond our understanding; and they cannot see a way out. Whether it is my students, or their loved ones, I try to meet these people where they are and sometimes that involves doing things a little differently." I noticed that Father Raymond was now watching me closely.

"Sister, I have done as you said. I have gone to the library on Wednesday after class and changed into ragged street clothes. I have taken the bus downtown. This undertaking began last year when Carla Little confided in me that she was desperately worried about her mother. If you recall, Shauna Little was a single parent and the grandparents were financially supporting Carla's ability to attend our school. Shauna Little was in trouble, Sister. I came to you at that time and asked you if I could please support Carla by trying to aid her mother to seek help for her addictions. You told me to stay out of this situation. Because of my own experiences I felt that I could not stand by and do nothing. I accept full responsibility for disobeying you, Sister, but my conscience compelled me to help, if possible. If you recall, Shauna died of an overdose, and Carla went to live with her grandparents in Pennsylvania. Sister, on a weekly basis I do travel into the city and within my backpack I carry food to give to those who are homeless and suffering from deadly addictions. I try to lead them to a different path, to seek help, and to recognize their need for treatment. I do not believe that if I went downtown in my nun's habit that I would be allowed into the circles I visit. There is a tremendous sense of mistrust among people with addictions and whether we have contributed to that inability to trust by our past behaviors or we have disappointed them somewhere along the way, I don't know. My decision to do this without your permission was wrong. I will admit that, Sister, and ask your forgiveness. I should have come to you once again, but I felt you would disapprove because I know part of your duty is to protect us. I regret my insubordination but I ask you please to reconsider your pronouncement. I have actually been able to help some young women and one young man to seek treatment at a clinic in the city where I have become familiar with some of the staff."

Father Raymond shook his head gently and looked down at his hands again. Sister Maria Reyna seemed to swell with increasing impatience. Finally, she unfolded her arms and pointed her finger in my direction. "It is not for you to decide your involvement in the lives of our students and their families. It is not your place to slink out of the convent secretly to embark on your own mission. Your vocation extends as far as teaching these students within the scope of your assignment and that is all. You're not a trained substance abuse counselor! Not only did you put your own life in jeopardy but you can't seem to comprehend the danger in which you placed our entire community if you make a mistake and cause more harm than good."

I don't know where my impudence came from at that moment but I felt that if I could not make her understand she would follow through with her judgment and so I had nothing to lose by standing up for myself. I remained calm and even. I knew I was wrong in many respects. Perhaps she was right and I'd chosen the wrong vocation, but I did not want to be punished for enlarging the vocation in my heart. I wanted to widen the scope of helping children beyond teaching them to read.

"Sister," I began, "I understand what you are saying about my behavior and I am not trying to shift the focus away from my own disobedience. When I entered into this vocation it was with the idea that I could live my life in a way that extends love and assistance to those in my care; it was not limited to teaching literature and grading essays; I wanted to make a difference in the lives of these children. They are up against a tidal wave of dysfunction in their families and in the world in which they live. Nothing out there is stable. The impetus of our society wishes to abbreviate innocence and in due course, childhood itself. If my vocation is limited to reading and writing assignments alone, how does that distinguish me from teachers in secular classrooms? Aren't I meant to do more than that? If that means I must get involved in the lives of my students and try to make the world around them a little better, one person, one problem, one crisis at a time, then perhaps I can save just one child from tragedy."

"There is no place in our religious community for dreamers, for superheroes, or for rogue idealists. You are way out of your league, Sister."

"Is there any place in this religious community for mercy, *Sister*? I've seen the way you treat these children and the members of our religious community. You bring down a mighty axe on anyone that doesn't follow your rigid lines and there is no discussion, no compromise, and no resolution which fosters growth and caring. You are harsh, without compassion, forgiveness, kindness, or sympathy. Why is that, Sister?"

"I am not the one whose behavior is in question here, Sister. Don't forget that."

"*Aren't you*? Haven't members of our church and the world around us questioned the behavior of our sisters and our priests? Haven't we been placed on trial for our crimes, our abusive behavior, our negligence, our hypocrisy? At what cost? Most people have even forgotten that there still remain good, caring, and faithful members of the church. The general population has turned its back on God because of the antagonistic behavior demonstrated by the self-righteous and they have lumped us all into one category. I do not believe for one moment that we can regain the trust from our brothers and sisters out there by behaving with bitterness towards those who have lost faith; I do not believe we can turn away from those in need just because their needs do not fall within the scope of our assignment. And I do not believe we can teach anything about love if it is not accompanied by mercy. I understand that there are other religious orders whose mission it is to go out into the poorest, most destitute parts of the world and at the same time they teach children to read, they cultivate relationships and extend their compassion in a variety of ways. But there is more than one kind of poverty – there is physical poverty and there is spiritual poverty and it is not limited to geographic locations. Our communities right here, all around us, need our compassion as well. Is it roguish behavior to do more than what one is asked to do? Is it so wrong to tend to the wounds of the people right here in our own neighborhoods? I do ask your forgiveness for not doing this in a way that complied with your leadership but I hope you will take what I have said into consideration. I have obeyed my conscience, Sister, even if that meant disobeying you and for that I realize I must be held accountable." I looked at Father Raymond as well. He was standing now. He was looking directly at me but I could not read his expression. Sister handed me the letter I was meant to sign and her appearance had not changed. She was right; I had violated my vow of obedience and for that there are consequences which I must accept. I finally exhaled. I bent over her desk and signed the letter and quietly left the office.

60

Stella

#Moccasinswap Journal: Last day of experiment
People can make excuses for anything. I think they can even rationalize evil. Somehow they find a way to believe only what they need to believe instead of the truth. It's kind of scary. Even good, well-meaning people can be blinded by their own fears or their own desires. I think they can even be taught to be prejudice against what is good. They can be lead to believe that what is bad is not bad, and what is good is not good. This week has been a real eye-opener for me. Emma thinks my life is unbearable. She has found it too small and too boring. She likes her life the way it is and she likes Jack.

I called Emma and told her I needed her to take a walk with me. Emma looked relieved to see me. I told her to follow me down to the river. On the way down there she kept repeating the same things she'd been saying all week about the need for space in my life. She said that she learned a lot by taking my place and that now she understood what I needed to make my life better. I needed to get out of homeschooling and go to a real school. She felt very strongly that I didn't understand the real world and how to function in it. I let her talk but I did not respond until we reached the river. It was cold today and I knew that if I were going to say what I had to say I had to do it quickly; Emma wouldn't have the patience to listen for very long out in the cold.

I asked Emma what she likes about Jack. She said that he was cool and that he liked things that were cool. He was very good at helping others to understand how to come together, too. Being cool, fitting in, not being different is important when it comes to the real world, she told me.

I asked her if she thought that in some way this trend was a juvenile-survival-of-the-fittest? She looked at me like she didn't know what I was talking about so I asked her if she thought that weeding out the weak kids was important. She either seemed confused at the questions I kept asking her or she pretended to be confused so she wouldn't have to answer me. So, finally I laid it out straight: did she think that bullying is okay as long as the cool person is the bully and the lesson is to teach others how to be cool and steer away from being different, or worse to reveal weakness so that they can think they are the strong ones? She stood in front of me and suddenly looked angry. She said I was being ridiculous and that I didn't know what I was talking about. She asked me if I was accusing Jack of being a bully.

I asked her if she participated in the group when Jack picked on other kids. She didn't answer. I asked her if she thought that singling out a kid that's "different" and harassing him to the point of tears was cool. She turned away from me and told me we were not going to have this discussion. I said I witnessed it for myself but she didn't want to hear it. I let her walk away from me. I called out to her that I'd reported the incident from this afternoon to her principal at her school. She turned around in a rage. She told me I had no right to do that – it wasn't my school, those kids are not my friends, and none of that was my business. I reminded her that I was in her shoes for a week. I did have the right to do that. I told her it's my right as a person. I also told her that I had no desire to be friends with people like that and that it is my business, even if I happened to be a complete stranger, to stand up for what's right. I asked her what was wrong with her? Didn't it bother her that kids could treat each other like that? Is the need to fit into a group more important than caring about a single person? She was furious with me. She told me that I was too sheltered and that I didn't understand anything then she turned around and left. Apparently, she went straight to her house, not mine. The experiment was over.

I didn't leave right away. I sat on the log by the river for a while. I was trying to remember the purpose of our little experiment to begin with. Was I supposed to step into her shoes so I could learn to be more like her? Was she supposed to step into mine so that she could see the "error of her ways?" No, I didn't think so. I think it was meant to help us understand each other better, but now I felt like I didn't understand my best friend at all and she certainly made it clear that she didn't understand me. How could I be friends with someone for so many years and not really know them? How could someone I trusted and confided in be so confused about what's right? I feel like maybe two things have come out of our experiment – I may have lost my optimism and Emma's sense of humor looks flawed to me now. I'm not sure I can laugh with her anymore, knowing that she can laugh at others who are being treated unfairly. Maybe she can't trust me anymore, either, because I didn't back down from what I believe is right. I don't know what this will mean for my friendship with Emma. I know she is angry with me, and I feel disappointed in her.

Suddenly, I felt a huge weight drop down on my spirit like a boulder. I knew I had tipped the balance of my friend's life. Things are going to be different for her when she gets back to school after the holidays. There will be backlash; I'm sure of it. I think that some of the kids standing by today weren't comfortable with what was going on but they were too scared to say anything. I'd spent over an hour in Granger School's principal's office today explaining the horror of what I'd witnessed. The counselor and principal seemed genuinely concerned and took everything I told them very seriously. They promised to follow up on this and they thanked me. I didn't feel good about what I'd had to do, though. I mean, I felt good about standing up for that poor kid, but I felt like a lone rat and Jack doesn't impress me as someone who won't insist on having his pound of flesh, as my Grandma likes to say. He has a following and they have his back. I would do it all over again if I were in the same situation but I'm also feeling kind of depressed that it had to go this way; for the kid, for me, for Emma, for any other kid out there that has to experience that kind of cruelty.

I've seen the kid before but I've never met him. He goes to our church with his parents. I think my parents said he's adopted from Korea, and that they are a nice family. I don't know his name, though, and I've never seen him out and about with friends. When I saw the kid's face when he stood up he gave me a look I've never seen before. I can't even describe it. I hope he's okay. He had a bloody nose when he turned and walked away from the group.

I'm still feeling so angry about this whole situation; at Emma, at those kids, at whatever there is in this world that makes kids, grownups, or whoever, think that they can just hurt each other and get away with *it. I wouldn't want to see this sort of unkindness towards anyone, even if I didn't like someone. Ooo, it just makes me so mad.*

61

Befana

When old *Padrona* sent me away I didn't know where to go. For the first few weeks I scrounged around the hillside looking for berries growing among the bushes in the densest thickets. I found some dandelion leaves and ate them even though I'd always hated their bitter taste. I built a little refuge out of some rocks to protect me from wild animals while I slept at night. When it rained I covered my little haven with some leaves thinking it would help but the wind blew them away and I was soaked to the bones in no time. Living in the hills didn't frighten me because there weren't too many people out there who could hurt me. It was actually the fear of the unknown that ended up getting the best of me. I didn't know where all the possible dangers could come from. Maybe it wasn't only people that could hurt me, perhaps there were things I didn't even know about that would come along and do me harm. I didn't even have the imagination to think of what the dangers could be so I could prepare myself. Then one day a new fear crept into my bones: the idea that this was how my life would always be, that I could never have anything more than this day-to-day animal-like existence. The fear that I would grow older eating berries and dandelion leaves, cover myself with rocks at night and never have anything to laugh about, to dream about, or to strive for made me feel sick and miserable. I trudged down one of the steep hills trying to be careful among the rocks but some of the rocks were loose and when I stepped on them they broke loose, tumbled down the hillside, and so did I.

I must have hit my head pretty hard on some of the rocks on the way down because when I woke up I noticed that my head was bleeding and my foot was swollen. I tried to get up but my foot was in so much pain I couldn't move. There was a stream nearby so I scooted on my bottom over to the stream to get a drink of water and wash the blood from my head. I hadn't eaten anything all day and my stomach hurt. I looked up at the sky and saw that the dark clouds were moving together and that lightening was trying to break them apart. The downpour hit before I could even blink my eyes. I was helpless, sitting at the bottom of a hill in the pouring rain with an empty tummy, a swollen foot, and an aching head. I don't remember if I started to cry or if I merely shook my fist at the sky and used some swear words I'd heard *Padrona* use when she was mad. Sometimes I recall this memory one way and other times I remember it in other ways, but whatever I did at that moment I know that something inside of me begged for something: mercy, help, or death.

I didn't know about the caring God: at the time that tender, loving, saving Christ had not yet come into the world. But when my young heart cried out, I know now that it was he who heard me. It had to have been him; there was no one else around. I had hit the rock-bottom of my short life and I thought my life might as well end right there and then. Obviously, it didn't. I don't know why but I sank back into the mud on the bank of that stream and I started to laugh at the ridiculousness of my situation. This kind of thing could only happen to me, I thought. I laid there for a long time letting the rain wash over me. So much rain fell that the stream rose and my sore foot was submerged in the cold water. The chill of the water made the swelling go down and the rain seemed to wash away the pain on my head. Then, a blustery wind came along and pushed the clouds away. The sun came out, dried me off, and gave me the sense that I had been very wrong about things: if the weather could change that fast then so could my life. Nothing stays the same for long. The tempest had chased away my fears that my life would always stay the same; if the rains could come along so quickly followed by the most wonderful sunshine, then everything else could change, too. I felt rather silly for thinking that I would have to live like an animal forever.

It's not only at the top of a mountain, or by a seashore when there is a dazzling sunset, a hillside covered in poppies and sunflowers, or a waterfall draping a cliff in a dense forest that you can experience the splendor of the caring God; you can also (and quite meaningfully) find him at the bottom of a hillside in a pile of rocks during a bad thunderstorm, or when you're broken and hurting very badly, or when you're lost, lonely, and afraid – yes, here you can feel the arms of the caring God, too. Yes, that's right! Even an *Old Befana* can learn new things. He wasn't born in a palace with servants attending him while he lay on a fluffed up feathered crib; he was born in a manger attended by the warm breath of animals, with his newborn flesh being pricked by the roughness of straw. That's our caring God – he knows the extremes of joy and those of pain; make no mistake about that. If you're not in the mood to enjoy a nice sunset because your life feels like it's over, don't worry you're never alone. He understands how we feel, and now I understand that sometimes we can see him more clearly through eyes filled with tears.

62

Sister Maria Nicola

The old chapel, dimly lit by flickering votive candles at the altar always soothes me, no matter what is going on in my life; this is my little haven. The little statuettes of angels looking up at the crucifix always reminds me that I am never really alone and angels are always nearby, no matter what cross I must carry in life. The crèche off to the right side of the chapel is still waiting for the Christ child to be placed in the manger. His mother and Joseph wait patiently over the empty wooden cradle with a serene knowledge that their child will bring God's mercy into the world.

As I sat there in the chapel pondering the meeting I had with Sister Maria Reyna a sense of calm washed over me. Regardless of the outcome, I'm at peace with my actions. I know I have made mistakes; my accountability is not without due cause. *You have made some difficult choices, but you can't save everyone, Sister*, was all Father Raymond said to me as I left the office. Well, Father, you're right about that; I can't even save myself. I've known that for a long time. If I've learned anything along the way it's that I can only do what I feel God is asking me to do, the rest is up to him. If he wants me to step down, retreat, or take a different direction my obedience is to him. If I've erred I am deeply sorry. He knows my heart. He understands that if he places someone who needs help in my path, I will at least try to do all I can. But success is not mine to enjoy, the glory belongs to him alone. Each day is a new challenge to trust in him and he has not failed me yet.

After Father Raymond had fulfilled his role to witness the meeting and the signing of the document, he also left the room. Sister followed me out into the hallway and said, "Something tells me that you are not truly regretful of your actions, Sister. I believe you're sorry you've been caught, but I think you'd do the same thing all over again if you could. Am I correct?"

"I suppose you are correct, Sister, but I am sorry if I have disappointed you. That was never my intention." We were now speaking more calmly with one another. Her mission was accomplished; she'd forced me to sign away my vocation and she was at peace.

"I'm long past disappointment, Elizabeth." She was already calling me by my given name. I hadn't even been defrocked yet. "People no longer disappoint me; I no longer have high expectations. I just deal with things as they come along and there is always something to deal with because people are going to do what they are going to do."

"But the children, Sister, the children need us to help them; their parents need our help, too, even if they don't know it. We need to make sure that children are safe because you're right – people are going to do what people are going to do. Sometimes people's motives outweigh what is truly best for a child and they will always find a way to justify their actions. I've always tried to put the needs of children first." I didn't think she was listening anymore.

"You're an idealist. You strike me as someone who has never seen the horrors in life. You have a Disney-sort of spirituality. There is always magic somewhere and it all works out in the end, is that it?"

"Sister, forgive me for speaking up like this, but you're wrong, I am anything but an unrealistic idealist. I have seen far greater horrors than you can imagine but God spared me from the worst possible outcomes. There is no magic, but there are miracles. I firmly believe that. I have seen the darkest side of humanity and I've seen the healing that comes with God's abiding mercy. It is very real. I want children to see and experience mercy, not just learn the definition of a word."

"*When God chooses* to show his mercy, you mean. He doesn't always come to our rescue like Superman. Sometimes he allows suffering to go too far."

"If God parted the Red Sea every single day, what effort would be necessary on our part? He works through us; we're not spectators in a divine play. Suffering only goes as far as it needs to and if it goes "too far" that is how far it needed to go for God's holy purpose and for our own benefit. Okay, so maybe I do sound like an idealist, but Sister, if we don't allow his mercy to work through us, what are we doing? The only reason I am able to move forward in my search for him is because I believe the sea was parted only once, the rest is up to us; we have to cross to the other side."

"You've had your head in too many stories and fairy tales, Sister. It's time to grow up."

I took a deep breath. It was time for truth and not fairy tales. "Many years ago my father nearly beat my mother to death. It wasn't long after he left that she ended her life with sleeping pills. My sister tried to do the same by the time she was fifteen. I have stared evil in the face more times than I care to think about. Of course I have suffered, beyond what you may be able to understand but I'm not sitting here today talking about faith and trust because I've never known suffering in my life. I am able to talk about it because I have been down that path and I opened my eyes to see that Christ was carrying his cross alongside me."

"So you're not the Pollyanna I think you are, huh? Good for you. You found your way out of misery. I'm glad to hear it. Not everyone has. Remember that."

"Sister, with all due respect, there are two sides to mercy – one side is offered and the other side, which is just as important, is acceptance. Remember Hugo's *Les Misèrables*, the bishop offered Valjean mercy, a chance to leave behind a life of suffering and start anew, but Valjean had to accept the mercy he was offered and reform his life, his way of thinking. I do believe that at one point or another, we all encounter God's mercy. The question is, do we receive it, accept it, and let it transform us? His mercy doesn't always solve our problems but it always helps us through them. We can't help the homeless and addicted by offering them food alone. Friendship is a mercy. We can help them in a more meaningful way if we aren't afraid of forming a relationship."

"Ask Father Raymond if you can deliver a sermon at Mass this Sunday in his place. It is not as easy as you make it sound. You may go, Sister." As I turned to leave I noticed how life-weary Sister Maria Reyna looked. I wished I could do something for her. She looked so broken beyond repair. The kind of brokenness that only God can heal – if we let him.

In the chapel I began to pray for Sister Maria Reyna. God knows what she truly needs and maybe my little "sermon" was the last thing she needed. Maybe when God's mercy came along her arms were too broken to accept it and she grew bitter. I cannot judge her; I don't know what happened in her life to make her so bitter and mean. I know there is much anger and resentment in her spirit which may cloud her ability to see God's mercy but she is just as much his child as I am; he doesn't give up on any of us. I prayed that her heart would soften so she could feel his love. If I begin to resent her because I have good reasons to do so, then I will become like her, someone who has every reason to be resentful.

I also prayed for my sister, Gen. Life in prison was not going to be easy for her. Perhaps it was time for me to focus on her needs a bit more; I've been writing to her every week but she's only written once. She is very depressed and said that she wishes she had been successful when she had tried to end her life. *God, please help her to see your merciful love.* Then I prayed for God to help my fellow sisters here in the convent; I know that I have probably made things more difficult for them by having caused a scandal. I hope they can forgive me. I prayed for my students and for their families. Things are never easy, but with God all things are possible. I especially said a prayer for Simon Rossi. That poor child; I reached out as much as I could; I asked God to please help him now. Christmas is in two days; it's a good time to ask for a miracle. I leaned forward and knelt down in the pew and fell asleep in the peaceful chapel.

63

Salvatore

I couldn't have been more than eleven or twelve years-old when my older sister, Lina, pulled me by the ear and made me return to the scene of my crime. The old lady at the end of the piazza in town had complained to my parents that I had taken all the figs from her wooden crate in the backyard. I had only taken one fig but my friends had helped themselves to the rest. *The old lady shouldn't be eating all those figs anyway,* they'd convinced me. *The figs will give her the runs.* So I took one; I already knew that too many figs can do that; why would I want to take more? Graziela walked all the way over to my parents' house to complain about the figs. She used a homemade cane to help her walk and she always carried a satchel on her back filled with some kind of fruit. We knew this because a cloud of fruit flies followed her wherever she went. I was with my father out in the fields when Graziela came to our house and moaned about my thievery, so my mother sent Lina to get me and take me to the old woman's house to make restitution. I had to scrub the bird droppings off her bench as my punishment, but a few minutes into the task I abandoned my post. I happened to notice that her crate of figs was still empty and there were some figs high on the tree toward the back of the yard that were probably out of her reach. I decided to climb into the tree to get her some figs; it was my thinking that restoring what had been taken would be more appropriate than scrubbing bird *caca*. When she came out of the house and saw me up in the tree picking figs, she assumed I was up there to steal more. She grabbed her broom and hit me with it until I jumped down. I dropped the figs into her crate and ran from her yard as she tried to hit me. When I arrived home I tried to explain to my mother what had happened but she didn't believe me, either. Sometimes, when you lose someone's trust it's very difficult to get it back.

Over the years, I can't say that I have been any more trustworthy of people's motives than I was on that day in Graziela's yard. I am not a crook or a fraud; it's just that sometimes my good intentions go off track and my judgment isn't always on the mark. I mean well, but I mess up. Apparently, this situation with falling down the stairs, going to get checked at the ER, and not calling my son, Joe, has made me as untrustworthy as a politician who swears to tell the truth. Joe was listed as my emergency contact on my medical records, but by the time they'd reached him at work, I was already sent home with a bottle of painkillers and a stack of medical orders to see my doctor about my knee and my back. Nothing was broken but I was a little black and blue.

"Dad, what were you thinking?" Joe asked me when he finally calmed down.

"I was thinking that Christmas is in a couple of days and I wanted to put up some decorations. Is that a crime?"

"Don't get smart with me Dad. You shouldn't have been trying to do that on your own. You could have asked me. Why didn't you call me? I could have come over to help. You didn't even call me when you fell." Joe shook his head. He looked hurt. I didn't feel like having this discussion again about not wanting to be a burden, and having no desire to live in a more comfortable place, so I remained silent.

"I'm picking up Allegra at the airport tomorrow. She said she doesn't mind staying at my house if it's too much for you to have her here with you."

"What the heck happens to you kids when you move out on your own? Do you forget that this was ever your home, where you were born, where you grew up? If she wants to stay here, she is welcome to stay here. If you want to come by to see me just to have a nice visit, you are welcome, too. I know you are busy and you have your own family, but I sure as heck don't enjoy feeling like an obligation or worse, like something fragile to tip-toe around. Doggone it. I appreciate that you stopped by to let me know I should have done things differently when I got hurt but I'm okay now. I need some rest; it's been a long day. Go on now; I'm tired," I told Joe.

After Joe left, I wondered if Simon had stopped by while I wasn't here. Poor kid; he told me this was the last day of school before Christmas break and he was going to tell me all about his presentation at school; he was going to use the *Old Befana* story that I told him and the statue I gave him. He had thanked me for giving him this idea for his homework since he didn't have any other ideas. Simon is a good kid. I don't know why he enjoys hanging around an old geezer like me but I have to admit, I enjoy his company. He is the only one that doesn't make me feel bad for being old. His friendship is a kindness that I didn't expect, like a gift that came out of nowhere. Luckily, I asked him for his phone number last month. I told him I wouldn't call him unless I got trapped in the old shed again. He'd laughed and given me his number. I thought I should call him now and let him know what happened and find out how things went at school. I pulled out my contraption and dialed his number. I like that I have a friend to call, a friend that has two feet firmly planted in this world and not taking a step into the next. It's a good, solid feeling. It's what an old man needs.

64

Befana

What comes out of our good or bad decisions is not always visible right away, that's what really old people like me find out over time. Sometimes it takes a while to see how things really turn out. Sometimes it even takes a different time in history to see the big picture. From what I've seen over the years there can be unexpected outcomes to our best plans and our best ideas can be outsmarted over time. Take, for example, that mistrustful and arrogant King Herod who was obsessed with power and decided to kill innocent babies to protect his throne from a prophecy; it probably seemed like a good solution to him to get any and all threats out of the way when he heard from the wise men that a baby king would be born in Judea. Certainly the Romans, those power-hungry vultures themselves, saw nothing wrong with Herod's deeds. People can justify pretty much anything they want to do, whether it's a bad decision, a policy with good intentions, or an unspeakable crime. I've seen people smooth out the edges of some outrageous choices they've made, even when the welfare of children was at stake. Don't let people's opinion fool you; a lovely picture can even be painted out of guano.

I'm pretty sure no one knows the story of Ruebi, the six month-old boy whose mother saw what was happening to her neighbors in the streets of Bethlehem and took desperate measures to protect her child. There was a small cellar under her hut where Allia kept dried herbs during the winter. Before the soldiers reached her hut Allia removed the blocks from the floor, gave her child some herbs to make him sleep soundly, and buried him in the small cellar. Once she covered over the hiding place with the blocks she ran from the house carrying a melon wrapped in a blanket, pretending to escape from the soldiers. She could not outrun the king's finest soldiers, however, and when Artemis the chief of Herod's army caught up with Allia, he pulled the blanket from her arms and swung his sword to kill her child. Instead he had split the melon in two. Realizing that he'd been tricked he put the sword to Allia's neck and threatened to kill her if she did not reveal the hiding place of her child. Allia refused to tell him. She said that she would rather die than tell him anything and that he would never lay hands on her son. Artemis killed the woman on the spot then ordered his troops to search all the homes again for any hidden child. The soldiers made a clean sweep of all the huts in the village but did not find Reubi sound asleep in the herb cellar under his mother's kitchen floor. But what was to become of a helpless six month-old buried in a cellar when no one was aware of his predicament? The infant slept all night long and well into the next morning when all of Herod's soldiers had gone back to the palace and the sound of men and women wailing over their slain children filled the streets of Bethlehem. It was a horrible time. The women grieved severely and the men carried heavy burdens of shame, guilt, and resentment for their inability to protect their families. The events of the night before would always be remembered as an act of terror in the little town of Bethlehem because of one man's greed. Even though Herod felt he owed no one an explanation, apology, or excuse, his evil plans were not fully realized, for he did not succeed in killing the Christ child and another small infant of no consequence.

It wasn't until some thirty years or so later that the grown Jesus travelled around the region where he'd often travelled with his parents as a child. Along the way, he taught people about his loving Father, our caring God, and to show them just how compassionate and merciful he was, he nurtured and healed the people that came to him. One day he encountered another man about his own age who was blind from the time he was a baby. Whether it was some of the pernicious herbs in a cellar that caused this man's eyesight to be ruined, or if he had been born that way it was never known. A dog in the village where the man had been born had excavated him as an infant hidden in a cellar, and with his teeth clutching the swaddling blanket, carried him to the home of a grieving mother whose own infant had been slaughtered by the king's soldiers. She had taken in the child and raised him as her own, praising God for sparing this baby's life.

When the man once known as Reubi was brought to Jesus, he asked to be cured of his blindness. He wanted to be able to see the things he heard, the children who laughed, the women who sang, and the men who preached of better things to come. He wanted to catch sight of the marvels that evoked such wonderful aromas in the world: foods cooking over fire, flowers and herbs that gave a rich scent to the breeze, and the animals that stirred up unusual smells. He'd heard of the man named Jesus who could help people see who had never seen before and he wanted to beg for his mercy. Some of his friends helped him to find this kind-hearted Son of God. Jesus met Reubi and took pity on him, made mud from the ground and placed it over the man's eyes. Though Reubi did not understand what was happening at that moment, all at once his eyes opened and he could see, and the first thing he had ever laid eyes on in his life was the face of God.

65

Stella

Before going home and facing my family, responding to questions about my week in Emma's life, and trying to fit back into my own, I decided I needed some time to think and the best place I have found to do that when it is too cold outside is the town library. My usual seat by the window was taken and the only spot I could find was in a common area near the biography section. I just needed some time to calm down and sort out my thoughts before going home. I'm glad I have a place I can call home where I feel safe and my family, even if they are as loud and intrusive as Emma suggested, is the core of who I am. We may fight and bicker and get on each other's nerves, but there is always a line we don't cross because it's made of love and respect. I know we're considered odd because we don't go with the flow and we may even be considered outdated because we don't jump on every new craze like some people do but we are not an unhappy family. We work together – most of the time. I've heard Dad say that not everything that is old-fashioned is bad and not everything that is modern is good, that's why we need to weigh our decisions carefully. A lot of times we make decisions as a family, and that always includes Grandma. Everybody gets a voice and by the time we hash things out, we've at least heard other thoughts and ideas instead of just our own. Not everyone in our family agrees and thinks alike. Far from it; but it's healthy to hear how others think; that's the way to learn about understanding, Mom says, not by congregating with everyone who thinks like you do. But, she warns us, some ideas are bad ideas and you need to hold them up to the lessons from history. There really isn't anything new in the world. Somewhere along the line, everything has been tried out before. My parents and my Grandma are smart and I trust them. I know that bullying isn't anything new; our generation did not invent it, and I know that kids and even adults have been quite hurt by the cruelty of bullies. The active bully is the one throwing the punches; the passive bully is the one who knows about it and does nothing. I'm so upset to discover that Emma isn't who I thought she was. I have seen a new side to her, a side that reveals that she can go along with something that is bad just because she likes the person that's doing it. I don't know how to be her friend anymore and I don't know if it's right for me to loosen my ties with her because of it. I saw her face when I confronted her about this poor kid that was being bullied; she knew about it and she'd stood by, and to some degree defended it by always protecting Jack.

I was trying to fight away some tears when Sister Maria Nicola came to sit in a seat near me. I don't know if she realizes it but everyone knows that she goes into the bathroom to change out of her nun's habit and gets on the bus wearing street clothes. We all wonder what she does when she leaves here. It was odd to see her here today; she's usually at the library on Wednesdays. Today she didn't seem to be ducking into the bathroom. She looked as bummed-out as I felt. I couldn't help staring at her and finally she looked over at me and smiled. I tried to smile back at her but I was still struggling to stay calm.

"You okay, Stella?" she asked me.

"Yes," I answered, not convincingly. She moved a seat closer.

"I've had a nasty day, how about you?"

"I didn't know nuns had nasty days." I swallowed my own hurt, confusion, and irritation. Now, I was curious about her nasty day.

She laughed. "Of course we do. Our expectations of good days are higher so when we get hit with a nasty one, it can feel like a real sucker-punch." She looked at me seriously and said, "You've had a bad day too, I gather. The library is a good place to chill-out when the world outside seems scary."

It was like she was reading my mind. I've always felt that way about the library. A person's home or neighborhood is usually the only world they know, but a library is like a universe and you can step out of your own world and into any part of the world or space just by opening a book.

I didn't say anything. I felt like if I talked I would start to cry. She was never anything like I imagined a nun would be. I always thought nuns were mean and strict and you had to be afraid of them. Well, she did duck into bathrooms and change clothes after all, so she wasn't very scary. She decided to do the talking.

"My day was kind of nasty because I tried to help somebody and when I did I discovered that my methods had gotten me into trouble, for one thing, and it's also possible that I may lose something I love very much, all because I tried to do a good deed. 'Ever had that happen to you?" she asked.

I nodded my head. "Were you at least successful at helping the person?" I asked her.

"Yes," she said, "and that's supposed to make it worth it, right? Yet, for some reason I don't feel as good about it right now as I should. Does that make any sense?"

"More than you know," I told her. I managed to swallow down the walnut-size lump in my throat. "I've had the same kind of day. It's kind of funny, actually." She sat there with a kind look on her face and didn't pressure me to talk, so I began to confide in her.

I started by telling her about how my experiment with Emma turned out differently than I thought it would. She was intrigued, she said. She'd been wondering how we were getting along. She thought that every student should experience the opportunity to truly live in someone else's shoes. It was too bad it wasn't practical – or safe – for that matter. Then, I told her about Emma's crush on Jack and how I found out he was a terrible bully. She was upset to hear that I'd witnessed such meanness but she expressed her respect for me because I stepped into the situation.

"That takes a lot of courage, young lady," she said. "You did the right thing; you could have done what a lot of people do, walked away and just minded your own business."

At this point I couldn't hold my tears back any longer, they started to fall silently while I told Sister the rest. She put her hand lightly on my shoulder.

"My greatest fear right now is that I've jeopardized my friend Emma by opening up a can of worms she may not know how to deal with when she gets back to school, and the part I'm confused about is that I don't know how to be friends with her anymore, knowing that she was aware of this situation, and not only did nothing about it, but she actually adores the person who is doing the bullying. I don't understand her and I don't know if I can like her anymore."

For a moment or two Sister was silent. She was either waiting for me to continue or she was thinking of her own situation. Finally, she nodded for a bit before she spoke, "When I tried to help some friends I had to do it on the sly, and I found myself in very dangerous places and with some very dodgy people. By doing this on my own I also jeopardized the community in which I live. My superior was beyond angry with me after she discovered my deceit. We seem to have lost respect for each other over time and I don't know how to continue to work with her now, but she may have solved that problem for me by trying to get rid of me. I do understand what you're going through a little bit. Obviously, I can't understand it fully. I don't know what your friend meant to you, how much you loved her, or how you'll feel in the next few weeks or months." Sister sighed and shook her head.

"You're not alone, Stella. We're never alone in what we go through in life. We may feel alone many times but that's because God is so gentle, sometimes it's hard to feel his presence. Even though you have stepped into your best friend's shoes you came in somewhere down the path. You haven't been walking in her shoes as long as she has so you may not know why she has acted the way she has. Your friend Emma is going to have to work through this, too. You essentially put the right thing to do above your friendship with her and now you're struggling with your feelings about her ambivalence or apathy. It's not easy. Of course we must exercise good judgment when it comes to friendship. We don't want to encourage a friendship that can lead us to do wrong or go against our conscience, but we should consider the possibility that we can help lead a friend away from wrong. Your friend, Emma, may have never found herself in dire or scary circumstances and so she may never have been deeply affected by an act of mercy. Everyone receives some kind of mercy in their lifetime; it's a gift, but like any other gift, a person can think they're entitled to it or they take it for granted, or maybe they don't know how to use it and it's forgotten. Pardon me for bringing my own beliefs into this but Jesus extended an awful lot of mercy in his lifetime yet he didn't control what people did with it. Some people changed their lives with it and shared it, and others did not know what to do with it and did nothing. You showed mercy to that poor kid being bullied and it was a good example for everyone else. That bully, the other children, and your friend Emma may not understand it now but eventually they might. Maybe it's not their time, yet. Be patient and see what happens."

It was interesting to me that she understood what I was feeling so well and that she could put things into words that I could not. I was worrying about the outcome but I was even more worried at the moment about that poor kid. "He didn't look okay," I told Sister, "It was awful; what I saw, Sister, it was the worst thing I've ever seen. That poor kid looked so broken, like he didn't even care anymore. He had this little statue with him and it fell out of his pocket when Jack was hitting on him. He seemed so sad to see that the meanness extended to something he cared about, not just himself. I managed to retrieve it for him but he left before I could give it to him."

"Statue?" Sister asked. "What statue?"

"It's a little old woman. Here, I'll show you. I don't know, it's not a toy, though. It is like a little precious figurine, like an antique. The old woman was holding a broom." I pulled it out of my backpack. "Here it is."

"Simon! Oh, my God, it was Simon! He used this statue for his presentation today at school. It's an *Old Befana* statue, he said. Oh, no. Oh, Stella, you have no idea how worried I've been about

Simon. He is one of my students. So *that* is what has been going on with him, he's being bullied! Oh my dear Lord. I have to go to his house and see if he's okay. Precious Lord, poor Simon; he wouldn't tell me what's been bothering him. Kids are so afraid or ashamed to say anything. I have to go see him right now."

"Do you know where he lives? Can I come with you? I want to help, Sister."

"Yes, Stella. I know his house. Please come with me. He'll wonder why I'm there if you're not with me. It would be better if you come along and you can return his statue. Let's go."

And so I went with Sister Maria Nicola to Simon's house.

66

Salvatore

Snow isn't the worst thing in the world. I don't go out if I don't need to. I remember back when I had to get to work on time and I would have to get out and shovel the driveway and get the snow off my car first. Snow made it a little harder to get going in the morning but there are other problems that are far worse than some snow, like ice, or hurricanes, or tornadoes, or tsunamis; I could go on. Perspective is important. Snow is worse than rain but better than ice. Allegra hates snow with a passion. From the time she was a little girl she avoided the snow; she wouldn't go out and play in it when she was a child, and she refused to help clear the driveway to get her car out when she was older. When I look at snow I see stillness; snow is peaceful, it helps the world to recuperate and slow down. Does everything always have to be in fast gear, or can we just slow down and coast for a couple of cold months? I realize that snow doesn't always fall gently; sometimes it comes in with a blustery wind – like my daughter, Allegra.

"It's high time we talked, Dad, one adult to another."

"Hello to you, too, Allegra, and Merry Christmas."

"Merry Christmas, Dad. Sorry I haven't been around much. I know I should get here to see you more often. You know how I feel about winter weather. Summer is a busy time for me so I usually head to warm climates during the winter months when things slow down at work. I see you put up a few decorations. Joe told me about your accident. You shouldn't be doing that all by yourself, Dad. You know, if you lived in an assisted living facility, there are more decorations than you know what to do with, and there are plenty of activities..."

"Stop, Allegra. Just stop for a minute. Tell me about you. What's happening in your life? How are you since you and Steven went your separate ways? Are you okay?

"I'm fine, Dad. You don't have to worry. I've been taking care of myself for a long time. He's never been home much, anyway. I'm okay. It's felt like a natural end, a slow coming apart. It's amicable."

"Don't you want to try and naturally come together again? Things don't have to end, do they?"

Allegra didn't respond. She seemed to have other things on her mind that she wanted to discuss. She fussed around the room and pointed out some of the things that I could get rid of – downsizing, she called it. "Is there something you want, something you'd like to have?" I asked her.

"No, Mom gave me her jewelry before she passed. The rest..." She didn't finish her sentence.

"Dad, Joe and I had a long talk on the way back from the airport last night. He's really worried about you living all by yourself."

"Are you worried?" I asked my daughter.

"I want the peace of mind knowing that you're okay and taken care of," she answered.

I closed my eyes and put my head back on my chair. I knew this discussion would be unavoidable. I'm starting to feel like I'm being selfish by insisting on living alone in this old house, *my house*. I'm not sick; I'm still pretty healthy. Okay, I have a few accidents here and there but I'm not an invalid. Yet, my son is worried and my daughter needs peace of mind and I'm the cause of such worry and lack of peace because I stubbornly hold on to what I want. I'm tired of this. The day will probably come when I won't be given a choice. They'll sell the house and stick me somewhere and I won't be able to make my own decisions about it. They won't have to worry anymore and they'll have plenty of peace. I must be selfish because the only way I can see they care is if they worry. If they stop worrying, will they visit? If they are at peace, will they give me a second thought? I have resisted the idea of being tucked away like mom's old jewelry. I like the peace of mind I have of being with my memories. They are all I have left. I still enjoy walking in my garden and grabbing a tomato or two off the vines, fussing with some basil and parsley, and putting some water on my hydrangeas. I suppose this part of my life is naturally coming to an end, too; slowly my life and I are drawing apart, like my daughter's marriage. But is my parting amicable? I wasn't ready. Are we ever? I don't want to be a bitter old man.

"You know, Allegra, now that your husband has moved out, I could always come and live with you!" She didn't find the compromise as amusing as I did. She went pale.

"Dad, I'm never home. I'm always at work. I..."

"Relax. I was kidding," I told her, but the conversation died and the pizza man arrived. Allegra ordered some dinner for the two of us to share. Tomorrow, she said, for Christmas Eve, we would go to Joe's house if I felt up to it. I don't feel up to it at all. I feel very, very tired.

67

Sister Maria Nicola

If there is anything I know for sure – God is not deaf. On the way to Simon's house it began to snow and I began to pray: *Hear me, Lord, please. I'm asking for your help today. Simon is just a young boy and he's been hurt for a long time, probably longer than any of us have realized. If anyone understands the hurt that comes from inhumanity, it is you. I ask for your mercy for Simon, and to help him to accept it. If he has been feeling lonely, help us to alleviate the emptiness that comes from such isolation. If he is lost, help us to guide him back to you. If there is despair in his heart, help us to show him that life is filled with so many second chances each day and that things can change. If Simon needs more love help us to embrace him. Please, Jesus, send your angels down to help us bring joy and peace back into his life. We cannot do this without you.*

Stella and I knocked on the door several times and called out his name. As we were about to go around to the back of the house to knock on the back door a car pulled into the driveway. Mr. and Mrs. Rossi stepped out into the snowy driveway and simultaneously asked "Can I help you?" In her anxiety, Stella jumped in and said, "We need to see Simon!" I walked up to Mr. Rossi, shook his hand, and reminded him that I am Simon's teacher.

"Yes, I know, Sister," he answered, "but what's going on."

"Stella, here, one of our local homeschooled students, told me that Simon has been having some problems with a group of students from Granger and I wanted to check on him, ask him some questions, and see if there is a way for me to help. Would it be okay if we come in? I know it's getting late but we won't stay long."

"Yes, of course," said Mr. Rossi. Together we walked toward the front door. The house looked quite dark as if no one was home. I prayed once again that Simon was here and not somewhere out there in the cold, looking for a way to escape his problems.

"What kind of problems has he been having with the Granger kids," his mother asked.

It was Stella who answered, "I've been going to Granger for just this week because my friend and I swapped lives for just a week, and I while I was there I noticed that some of the kids were being very mean to Simon. I told Sister about it when I saw her at the library and she thought we should come by and see if Simon is okay."

"When you say, *mean*, are you speaking of some type harassment?" Mrs. Rossi asked.

"Yes, ma'am. They were harassing Simon and trying to hurt him. He lost his statue that he used for a class project today and I wanted to return it to him." Stella answered. Mrs. Rossi said she had never seen this statue before when Stella showed it to her and wondered where Simon had gotten it. Her eyebrows were creased with concern.

When the door opened and we entered the dark and silent home it was Mr. Rossi who began to call out. "Simon?" his voice was high-pitched with apprehension. "Simon, are you upstairs?"

Mrs. Rossi switched on all the lights as we followed them up the stairs to Simon's bedroom. His door was open and his room was dark. No Simon. Mrs. Rossi noticed the bathroom light under the door and knocked. "Simon, honey, are you in there?" she asked and knocked again. Simon did not answer. Mr. Rossi knocked but then decided to open the door. It was not locked. As his parents entered the bathroom, it was the blood they saw first; the blood on the sink and some blood on the floor. I believe their first instinct was to believe that he'd been wounded when he'd encountered the kids after school but then they saw the razor lying in the sink.

In breathless horror, his mother cried out, "Simon! My God, Simon! Stella, was he hurt when you saw him?" Simon's mother asked.

Stella shook her head. "Just a nosebleed. He wasn't cut. I don't know what happened after he left. I was yelling at the kids. I'm sorry."

Mrs. Rossi frantically looked around the bathroom, behind the shower curtain and in the linen closet. Simon was not here. Stella and I continued to follow Simon's parents as they searched through the house looking for their son. He was nowhere in the house. Where could he have gone? Mrs. Rossi wondered if they should call the police. Mr. Rossi said we should think first if there is somewhere where Simon might have gone, perhaps to a friend's house.

Mrs. Rossi yelled, "What friends?"

Simon's parents looked at each other in a desperate way. They did not know of any friends that Simon might have.

I recalled my mother's repeated attempts to end her life. For months she never lost the look of despair; a shadow of emptiness that clung to her skin, resonated in her hollow voice, and caused the reflection in her eyes to fade away - it lingered in her face when she died. It looked like Simon had considered suicide as a solution to the problems he'd been having with other children. Why, dear Lord, are we seeing so many *children* turning away from hope? Where was Simon now? Had he gone somewhere else to end his life? Had he changed his mind?

As we stood in the foyer of the Rossi home, we quietly considered the options. If Simon had run away, where would he have gone? If he had hurt himself and was lying somewhere in need of medical attention, how could we find him? We didn't even know where to begin. Calling the police seemed like the only option at this point. Mr. Rossi brought out his cell phone to dial 911. At that moment we heard a voice coming from the door to the kitchen. Simon slowly and softly began to speak. "I'm sorry," he said. He repeated it several times like he was talking to himself and no one else was present. His mother ran over to him and pulled him into a firm embrace. "

"Are you all right, Simon? Where have you been? We've been so worried."

Mr. Rossi put his arms around his wife and child. "Simon, please tell us what's going on."

As she smoothed his hair, his mother began to cry softly, whispering "We love you, Simon."

Finally, Simon looked up at his parents. "I'm sorry, I had to go someplace," was all he seemed to say. There seemed to be more to Simon's sadness than his encounter with bullies. They'd merely picked up on it and abused him for it. Whatever he'd been feeling it had been a part of him for quite some time.

Stella had been holding on to my hand but she let go and took a hesitant step forward. "Simon, I'm Stella." He looked up at her and seemed confused by her presence, but he did recognize her. "Simon, I don't think you have anything to be sorry for. You shouldn't have to face that kind of stuff on your own; no one should. You are not the one that needs to apologize. I'm sorry you came across those kinds of people. Not everyone is like them. The rest of us need to stick together, okay?" Stella pulled the statue of *Old Befana* out of her pocket and extended it to Simon. For a moment he merely looked at it like he was seeing it for the first time. Then he spoke, "My friend Sal gave it to me. She's a Christmas legend about someone looking for Jesus." He took it from Stella's hand and stared at it while we all looked on.

Now, his parents seemed curious about the small statue and about this friend named Sal. We had never figured out who he was. At that point I moved forward as well. Simon's parents were still on either side of him and holding him closely. We all wanted to know what we could do to help him, but I don't think Simon has been able to put his sadness into words, at least not words in our language. Maybe this is a point to consider for later when we figure out a way to help him.

I finally spoke, "We care about you, Simon. You are a remarkable young man. Your sensitivity is not a weakness; it is a strength." Simon looked up at me and for a moment I believed he was starting to listen so I continued, "You know, I enjoyed your story about this little statue very much. I noticed that the students in our class were listening, too, because it wasn't the same old story they've always heard. It was different because, as you said, it wasn't a story about a one-time event; her desire to seek Jesus never ends. Her pursuit is as timeless as his arrival into our hearts. You grasped the meaning of *advent*. Most students wouldn't have been so open to *Old Befana's* story about looking for Jesus, much less about sharing it in the way that you did. It took your insights to bring this profound experience into our lives. Her story is very important, Simon. If she doesn't bring us closer to Christ, or encourage us to seek him, then she is just a little statue and nothing more. If we understand the story, she can lead us to our only source of strength and hope which is Christ. You are a sincere and caring young man, Simon. I hope you never doubt your worth because it is not determined by the ignorant, it is determined by God."

I knew that this little family had a lot to talk about and I sensed that they really needed privacy right now. I told them that tomorrow, Stella and I would come back for a short visit, if that was all right. "We'll go now so that you can be with your parents. You need to spend time with them tonight. As Stella and I left the house we heard Simon tell his parents once again that he was sorry. He said he didn't mean to take so long to be their son. He just didn't know how.

68

Salvatore

What an evening! In the time it took for me to find where Simon had stored his phone number in this stinkin' contraption I had the feeling that I needed to call him more than he might need to hear from me. He was probably playing a video game or out somewhere with his family. I tapped on the glass where it said contacts and moved down to the place where it said Simon. Making a phone call is not what it used to be. When Annalisa and I first bought a telephone, we had to look up a number in the phone book and then dial each number one at a time, wait for the rotary dial to revolve back to start and dial the next number. It wasn't difficult but it took some time. Now, you find a person's name on your phone and you tap on the glass and the phone knows the numbers to dial. *Mamma Mia*, it seems to me that the easier or faster a task becomes, the more detached we become from the way it works. We're getting so far away from knowing how to do something from the beginning, whether it's dialing a number, growing some vegetables, or cooking them. Everything is already ready at your fingertips.

I could hear the line at the other end ringing. Do they still call it a line? It's all wireless. I don't even know how to talk about making a phone call! Simon's phone rang five times and then some machine voice answered and asked me if I wanted to leave a leave a call back number or a message. I didn't know how to do either. I hung up. No, there was nothing to hang up; I pushed the end button. Maybe I dialed the wrong number. No, I had tapped on Simon's name; he put the number in there, it had to be right. I did it again. It rang four times and then Simon answered. He didn't sound good. Something was wrong.

I started talking. "Simon, is that you?" He didn't answer right away so I called out his name again. "Simon? It's me, Sal."

"I'll be right there," he said, and the line went dead. The kid sounded funny, almost like he was at the bottom of a well. Maybe that's how people sound on these contraptions. I didn't ask him to come over here, why would he say *I'll be right there*? Something wasn't right; I could feel it in my bones. His voice was low, like he didn't have any energy. I started to worry. I thought maybe I should try to call him again, but he'd said that he was coming right over. If he wasn't here soon, I'd call again. Just then there was a knock at the door.

"Simon, is that you? Come in." The door opened and Simon came in gazing around like he was looking for something. Then he saw me sitting on the recliner.

"Are you okay?" he asked.

"Yeah, kiddo, I'm okay. Are you? You don't look okay." I noticed the dried blood under his nose.

"You called me."

"I did, but..."

"You said you'd only call me if you were trapped in the shed again. You weren't here for two days. I thought something happened to you. When you called I thought you were hurt," he said, "so I came right over." His voice was shaking. He seemed very scared. I think he's been as worried about me as I've been about him.

"Sit down, son. Let's talk." Instead of sitting on the sofa like he usually does, he sat down on the floor in front of the recliner as close to me as he could get. I reached over and patted his shoulder. "I'm okay," I told him. "I fell down the steps and thanks to you showing me how to use the phone I called Mrs. Gray. She helped me get to the hospital. I didn't break anything, thank the good Lord, but they kept me hostage until they were sure I was okay to go home. I'm sorry. When I got to the hospital I realized I didn't have my little contraption. The EMT's didn't bring it along for me. I didn't have your number to call you; it was stored in my phone. I'm sorry, kiddo. I'm all right. I'm just sore and I have to go to the doctor after Christmas to follow up. What about you? What's going on?" He hadn't taken his coat off; he didn't seem like he would stay long but then he didn't make any moves to get up, either. "How did your presentation go at school?"

He shrugged his shoulders. "I don't know," he said. "Are you sure you're okay? I thought they took you to the home, that I wouldn't get a chance to say good-bye or anything."

I chuckled. "They're not going to take me away that easy," I told him. "Listen, Simon, you were worried you wouldn't get a chance to say good-bye, I was worried I wouldn't get a chance to say thank you. This past month or so I've been watching the clock in the afternoon each day until I knew it was time for you to stop by. It's meant a lot to me, kiddo. You and I have become buddies, haven't we?" He nodded his head. "Buddies have to stick together. I've been meaning to tell you that you should bring your parents over one of these days. I'd really like to meet them."

He nodded his head, again. "Yeah, they want to meet you, too." He sat there quietly for a minute or two and then he asked me, "Sal, have you ever felt like you're at the end of your rope?"

I chuckled again. "Heck, yeah, kiddo. Sheesh, I've been at the end of my rope more times than I can think of. Everybody reaches the end of their rope at some time or other. It happens."

"What do you do?" he asked me.

"You get a new rope! If you reached the end of the one you have, you don't need that one anymore. Let go of it. Whoever said you only get one rope in life? See that nativity set over there? I brought it up from the basement. It's pretty old; I'd brought it over with me from Italy a long time ago. When that scene took place for real, Simon, the world itself had reached the end of its rope. It couldn't keep going on the way it had been. Jesus being born gave the world a new rope, something new and wonderful to hang on to. It's called hope. Don't forget that, okay? That's why we celebrate this holiday every year. That's why it's called the season of hope."

Simon covered his face with his hands. There was some blood on his hands, too. I don't know what happened. He didn't seem to want to talk about it. Boys get into scrapes, I know that. All three of my boys came home bloodied up from time to time. But, Simon wasn't like any of my boys. It took my boys a lot of scrapes to become men. Simon was already more mature than they were at his age. He didn't need scrapes with other boys to grow up. He'd been scraped by life. I patted his shoulder again. He looked up at me, he looked a little calmer.

"I think it's time for me to go to my home," he said. "You're okay?" I nodded my head.

"I'm okay. You go home to your family, kiddo. And have a Merry Christmas."

"I'll be back. You have a Merry Christmas, too."

69

Stella

A not-so-final journal entry:
If nothing else, I think one of the things I've enjoyed the most about this past week is this newfound love of journaling. Mom had a good idea when she asked me to write about my experiences this week but why stop here? I like the idea of thinking out my day on paper. It allows me a freedom I didn't have before. I can go to the library, or Grandma said I can use her room when I want a few minutes of peace to write in my journal.

When I came home from Simon's house and Sister went back to the convent, I had this feeling that everything was going to be okay. I told Mom, Dad and Grandma all about my week, about what it was like for me personally in a public school and how I had a new appreciation for what my parents do for me every day. I don't think homeschooling is for everyone. Some parents don't have the opportunity to do this and some kids would probably hate it. It works for our family and I wouldn't trade it for anything.

My family was able to give me some extra perspective on the bullying incident and how to approach Emma. My siblings had a million different thoughts about it. Ditch Emma. Teach Emma how to fight. Tell her to ditch Jack. Ask Emma to come back; she's a lot quieter than you and she minds her own business. My younger sister said she wanted to go and live with Emma and my brothers suggested that Emma and I learn karate. My parents said they were proud of me and my Grandma said I would do well as a teacher, a police officer, a lawyer, or a judge. I had to laugh. I don't envision myself in any of those jobs, but who knows. I want to give Emma some time off from the craziness she's had this past week. She needs her quiet time with her family for a while. I don't know how things will go with her but I know it will be okay, one way or the other.

When Sister and I went back to Simon's house this morning, he seemed a little better. He was still very quiet but maybe that's just his personality, however, it doesn't give anyone the right to abuse him for it. Sister Maria Nicola and his parents were both eager to learn where he had gotten that statue of the little old woman named Befana. Simon didn't seem to want to answer at first. Sometimes a person needs to keep something to himself. A kid doesn't always feel like sharing everything; I understand this, some things make good secret treasures. It was like the story Grandma told me about when she was very young and how she felt the first time Grandpa kissed her at the state fair. What she told me was a secret between us, she said, and I didn't want to tell anyone that Grandma said that after he kissed her, she liked it so much she initiated all the kisses that followed.

Finally, Simon told us that the Befana statue was a gift from his friend, Sal, an old man he saved when a tree fell on his shed. His parents jumped on that immediately. They wondered why he hadn't told them about the incident but they let Simon tell the story in his own way. Simon quietly told us that Sal is an old Italian man he met one day on the way home from school. He was trying to get away from the Granger kids and he ducked into Sal's backyard when he noticed that a big tree had fallen. The old man was trapped in his shed and Simon had helped him out. To say thank you, Sal had given him the Old Befana statue – a symbol of Christmas devotion in Italy. Apparently, he was a nice old man and has been Simon's friend ever since. He told his mother how much Sal had appreciated that deli sandwich and had repaid the kindness with some Korean fish stew. He said he had been worried about Sal because for the past few days he hadn't answered the door. Simon didn't know what to do without his friend, Sal. He'd gone straight home after the incident with the bullies. But, Sal had called Simon on his cell phone to check on him. It had been Simon who had shown Sal how to use that "stinkin' contraption." We were all so curious about this old man named Sal. We asked Simon if we could meet him. He'd said, yes, he thought Sal would enjoy meeting us. We all decided to put our coats and boots on and pay a visit to Sal, the old Italian guy. As a group, we walked the two blocks together.

When we arrived a middle-aged woman answered the door. She seemed either shocked or irritated that Sal should have a group of strangers presenting themselves at the door on Christmas Eve and asking to visit with him. The woman was named Allegra (though it seemed like an awful misnomer because it means happy in Italian) and she was Sal's daughter. Sal wasn't able to get up from his recliner because he had hurt his back this week. He invited us to come in and we sat down in the comfy living room that was decorated with a beautiful hand-painted nativity set from Italy and a small pre-lit Christmas tree. Allegra sat off to the side and eyed us carefully. Simon's mother had gone out and bought a large Panettone to bring with us (it's a cake-like bread with dried fruit that Italians eat at Christmastime). I don't know if the poor old man always has watery eyes but he did during our visit. Sister Maria Nicola introduced herself after Simon presented his parents to Sal. She told him she was Simon's teacher at school. I told him my name was Stella and his hands went up to his cheeks in amazement. "That means 'star' in Italian," he told me. I knew that already but as it turned out it was also his mother's name, and it seemed to make him so happy. I told him I hoped it was okay that I came along. He winked at me and told me that I could come by the house with Simon any time. Sister told Sal that she was enthralled with Simon's school presentation about the story of the Magi and Befana's search for the Baby Jesus. Sal said that Befana has a special way of being where she needs to be; that's what happens when you keep your heart open for Christ.

Simon's parents said they'd wished he'd introduced them sooner. Then, Simon gave Sal a small gift wrapped in tissue paper. Sal opened up the gift and held it up. It was a rope. "You might need a new rope someday," Simon told him. The old man looked at Simon and they both laughed. Sal clapped his hands gently and winked at Simon. He was grinning from ear to ear. Obviously, it was a personal joke between them. Our little group seemed to bond instantly; it felt like meeting a long-lost family, not strangers at all. We sat for nearly two hours sharing stories and looking at pictures in Sal's photo albums which sat on his coffee table. Even Allegra seemed to join in and laugh with us. She said she was glad her father had friends. Sal went on to say that was so proud of all his children and his late wife. I think my Grandma would love Sal, not in a weird way, but just to have someone her own age to talk to. Before we left we wished Sal a Merry Christmas and told him that we'd be back.

It's been good for me to get out into the real world a little bit more than I had before this week. I've met new people, had some new pleasant (and unpleasant experiences) and I feel like my world has gotten a little bigger. Sister had to get back to the convent for the Angelus prayers and Simon's parents walked hand-in-hand in front of us. Simon and I trailed behind and talked a little. I did most of the talking. I think Simon is more comfortable with that and I don't mind. I feel like I have a new friend. I hope Emma will learn to like him, too.

70

Befana

Well, bless my broomstick, I get tickled right down to my worn out old boots every time I'm able to witness a Christmas miracle. People often minimize just how many miracles there truly are in the world. Just because you can explain something, doesn't mean it isn't amazing and if you can't explain a miracle then the amazement is just that much greater!

Christmas itself is a miracle if you think about it. Part of what makes it so special is that people can still relive the wonder, the anticipation and the delight of that first night, no matter how many thousands of years go by. I've seen it and felt it myself – all the emotions the birthday of Jesus stirs up: excitement, nervousness, joy - just as if God's entry into the world had occurred at this very moment. It is an occasion that two thousand years of time has not diminished; it is something that we can live out again and again.

People can get discouraged as they go through life, and not just once, mind you. It can happen often, and each time discouragement overwhelms us it can bore in more deeply. Loss can leave people feeling discouraged. Worries can cause a person to lose hope. These kinds of thing can happen because of rejection or oppression in their living situation. People can also become discouraged when they see all that they have strived for go to ruin: whether it is their livelihood, the well-being of their loved ones, or their work.

I found out as a young person that loss is a part of life; we lose people we care about, we lose things that once meant the world to us, and along the way we can even lose a part of ourselves. The miracle of life is replenishment – what comes along to fill the space left by loss. With the help of that great big, lovable, sweet-as-honey, caring God we can be renewed every day and the hurts from loss and rejection can be healed with the most unexpected surprises. He opens new doors for us every day. It's up to us to walk through the door, go on the adventure and follow wherever he leads. Some of us do it carrying a broom and a satchel full of cookies.

71

Hyo

The last time I saw him was when he came to our village in Sanpo. When he first arrived we all stared at his shoes for they were oddly open-toed, but they were not sandals. His shoes looked like they'd once been ordinary boat shoes but someone had cut out the front of them and now they looked like half a shoe on each foot. He walked with some difficulty, whether because of his ill-fitting footwear, or because he had grown very weary from his trek across the fields. The small Cessna Bobcat that landed on the other side of the Sanpo rice fields had circled three times above the fog before it found a clearing to land. There were only about five of us waiting for him in the old market building. Hwan, Joon, Ki, Seok, and I had sent each other notes written in English that said "We need fresher fish in the market place." Today was not a market day otherwise the place would be jammed with *halmeoni*, those pushy old ladies that used their elbows like weapons to force each other out of the way so they could grab the best fish and snap peas.

Our ruse about needing fresher fish in the market place was meant to be so banal that we would not attract the wrong kind of attention. So far, no one has noticed anything out of the ordinary. The five of us meet here every now and then, not on any routine schedule, with a small sampling of fish from the local waters to determine which body of water supplies the best fish. Sometimes Ki brings us some bread to share, and while we examine the specimens of fish, we quietly chant verses we have memorized from the gospels, most especially the gospels about Jesus feeding five thousand people with just five fish and two loaves of bread. If we were to be caught giving any kind of credence, thanks, or praise to God, through Jesus Christ, we could go to jail and be fined. If we were to openly preach about Jesus we could face torture and death. There are no laws against persecution because the majority of people in our country are nonbelievers. When the majority of people say there is no God and the pressure to keep one's beliefs to oneself increases, the desire to know him increases as well. The desire itself cannot be outlawed. Occasionally, a priest will come to our village to boost our faith with his deep reflections about how all these teachings from the gospel are real and present in our lives today. When a priest does visit us he comes along discreetly, dressed in our own street clothes and carrying nothing with him but a change of clothes.

Hwan was the first of us to spot him through the dense fog as he shuffled into the village wearing khaki pants, a white t-shirt covered by a plaid work shirt and on his head, an American baseball cap. He carried only his green backpack and an umbrella. Seok and I walked out to greet him; we did not know whether to bow, shake hands, or display some other type of appropriate greeting so we did nothing but smile. Seok offered to take his backpack and I put my hand on his back to guide him into the market place.

"What few memories I have of this place are vague, but the market place has not changed from the way I remember it," he said.

"My name is Hyo," I told him. "I am the one who wrote to you."

"Hello, Hyo, it is very nice to finally meet you." He didn't look the way I imagined he would. He seemed very serious and restrained, though his correspondence was uplifting and enthusiastic. He had a deep crease between his eyebrows and below his left eye there was a shiny small scar from an old injury. As he extended his hand to each of us, we introduced ourselves and shook it. The priest smiled timidly with each introduction and then we sat on the market tables and shared our bread and fish with him. He said he was very hungry; he had not eaten since his layover in Beijing, but before we ate, he spoke quietly, blessing the bread and breaking it for us to share.

We ate in silence. Hwan continued to stare at the priest, hoping for some words that would help us to make sense of all this covert devotion. When the priest finally spoke, he told us not to worry about anything, *ever*. He told us to remember always that God is in control and that if we are forced into a situation that is difficult or even painful, we must bear with our circumstances patiently and to never give up. He quoted Jesus by saying, "Do not be afraid; henceforth you will be catching men." He told us that by our living example we could bring others to Jesus. As we sit here we see that we are the very proof of this – no amount of anti-religion laws can extinguish a love for God."

That was the last time I looked into his eyes. After a swift embrace, the priest handed me his backpack and said a quiet blessing and we parted. I only turned around once to see him sitting in the market place; he stared with an air of nostalgia at the empty market tables for a moment and then he disappeared into the streets of Sanpo. My friends said goodbye to me and scattered in different directions. Only Seok walked with me to the far end of the fields where the small plane waited. My friend's face was bright with anticipation.

"I will send for you as soon as I can," I told Seok. He nodded with a hint of tears in his eyes. I turned and boarded the plane. When I looked out the window, Seok had already disappeared into the mist. The priest had secured my travel papers to go to America and enter the seminary while he remained here with my friends. Once the pilot turned to me and said we were out of North Korea, I began to weep and prayed the Lord's Prayer *out loud*. I looked down at the fog and whispered into the distance, *thank you for this opportunity. Thank you, Father Simon.*

The middle-aged nun waiting for me at the Port Columbus Airport on that cloudy afternoon was waving a handkerchief and standing on her tip-toes. Her black and white nun's habit was adorned with a large crucifix hanging from a chain around her neck for everyone to see.

"Hyo, yes?" she greeted me.

"Yes, Madame, I am Hyo. Thank you. I am grateful for you to pick me up."

She smiled broadly. "It is my pleasure, Hyo. I am Sister Maria Nicola. You will join me at the mission for a few days. Then I will drive you to the Josephinum College next week. You remind me so much of Simon when he was younger! How is he? Did he arrive in Sanpo all right?"

"Yes, Sister. He is well and at peace." Her face was beaming with pride.

"He was my student, you know, when he was younger," she began as we walked through the airport and boarded the shuttle for the Parking Lot B. "I am so very pleased with him. He is such an inspiration." She spoke continuously on our drive from the airport to the mission. She told me about the small scandal she had caused in a rural town nearby many years ago. Rather than going along with her superior's proposal to have her deposed, however, the good priest of the parish, Father Raymond, had strongly recommended to her superiors that she be transferred to an inner city school where she could both teach and minister to the needs of the poor. Sister radiated with joy as she told me all about her vocation and she firmly believed that if God had called me to the priesthood I would never find greater joy in anything else. I do believe her for I have never seen anyone smile as she does.

She said that Father Simon had worked with her very closely to help the homeless and dejected. He even opened a house for the aging homeless population; he had a very soft spot for elderly people, she told me. Once, when he was younger he had befriended an elderly man in his neighborhood. They had remained close for years, like grandfather and grandson, until the old man passed away with Simon at his side. That had been a major turning point for Simon, she continued to tell me. He knew from that time on that he wanted to help people who were lonely, abused, rejected, and frightened.

I knew from my correspondence with Fr. Simon that he had had great difficulty adjusting to life on the other side of the world when he was a boy. He had assured me that if he could endure negativity and cruelty that God's grace would see me through no matter what circumstances I faced. I must embrace courage as a gift, he'd written. With the grace of courage, one can take even the most tragic experiences in life and turn them into a wonderful gift. Miracles happen every day.

On the evening that I arrived at Sister's mission, I sat in a circle with a group of people that live at the transitional housing mission. The therapist that led the group was a young woman named Stella. She had the most compassionate face I have ever seen. She encouraged each resident to speak and to support one another by sharing their experiences. One by one, these people – both men and women - told their stories of how they had once been physically abused, neglected, molested, or abandoned; they spoke in great detail of their brokenness and misery. Then they went on to tell about how they had used their addictions to alcohol and drugs to dull the pain from their past, and how for many years they had delved into a private hell that seemed to have no way out. It was when they each spoke of their conversion to God, transforming their dependency on substances to dependency on God's love, that I was deeply touched by the healing power that they described.

When the meeting was over, Sister escorted me to my room and bade me goodnight. I sat on the bed and opened the backpack Fr. Simon had given me. Inside he had provided me with a suit of appropriate clothes to wear when I arrive at the college on Monday. At the bottom of the backpack there was a small gift wrapped in tissue paper. As I unwrapped the yellow paper I saw a small figurine of an old woman. She seemed to be handpainted but most of the paint had worn off because of age. She carried a broomstick that reminded me of the kind the *halmeoni* back in Sanpo used to brush the cobwebs from the doorways and windows and sweep their front steps. I could not understand why Fr. Simon would give me such a strange gift. In a small note attached to the figurine Fr. Simon wrote, "*She sees and hears the cries of mothers and fathers for their children; she brings Christ's love to every child as she journeys toward heaven. She is Old Befana and she is here to help every child of God. Let her lead you to him.*

Author's Note

Readers will have to forgive the liberties I have taken with the old Italian legend of *La Befana*. The kernel of her story, a woman who travels through time and space in search of Jesus, opened up an infinite avenue of story possibilities for me. It occurred to me that anyone who sets out on a determined journey to follow Christ does not pass by each person with indifference. From the earliest days of Christianity, following Jesus Christ meant following his example of getting involved with people. Traveling through Judea, Galilee, Capernaum, or wherever Christ travelled, he was not an apathetic observer – he touched lives. In her own way this is what *Old Befana* attempts to do as well – to touch the lives of the people she meets on her journey. Her story not only inspires the imaginative dreamer, but it also challenges the heart of humanity to take love to another level and to take it to where it is needed most.

Today, in North Korea, a simple clause in the constitution allows for freedom of religion, but atheism has dominated this small country and replaced many Buddhist and Christian communities. For the past thirteen years North Korea has been ranked number one as the country where persecution of religion is most extreme. North Korea, however, is not the only place which has seen extreme religious persecution; the trend is growing throughout many parts of the world. We are reminded each day how precious it is to celebrate the ability to live freely in accordance with our relationship with God.

I must thank Father Paul Quang Nguyen for his kindness and spiritual direction, and for allowing me to help him with his writing. His stories of Vietnam truly touched my heart and planted the seeds for this story.

On a personal note, I must always be mindful to thank those members of my family who remind me to cherish every moment we have together. Whether because of circumstances of birth, decisions to secure a livelihood, or situations beyond our control that have placed us in distant locations, I must always put forth the effort to stay connected to loved ones and travel wherever and whenever possible.

I have been fortunate in my life to have discovered a treasury of friendships that inspire and strengthen me. Friends are the surprise blessings in life. We need them on our journey to encourage us, especially when we begin to lose our way.

Always, boundless gratitude goes to my husband, without whom I could not do all that I do. Most of the time I thank him for his support, but I must acknowledge that in this past year with my *Befana* series he has actually rolled up his sleeves and jumped in to help me in practical ways! My children are my life and my hope for the future – they have given me more joy than I could have ever imagined! And now, as I await the birth of my first grandchild, my heart, already filled with the joy of friends and family, will surely burst!

My greatest thanks goes to God, the sweet-as-honey, caring God that gives us more unconditional love than we generally know what to do with. The best thing we can do with the surplus is share it!

Donna Kendall
2015